# Praise for Bianca D'Arc's
## *Dragon Storm*

"The twisting and turning plot will keep you on the edge of your seat and, in true D'Arc fashion, wishing for more by the stories conclusion. There is so much more here than a tumble between dimensions. Each world is so complex, and so thoroughly developed, you can't help but be transported and immersed."

~ *Whipped Cream Reviews*

"Love Ms. D'Arc's dragons? If so, this book will make you love them even more. As a fan of romance books with dragons, I was thrilled when I read the first book in this series and I have continued to be amazed as the books keep coming. ...This book is full of sexy shapeshifters, loads of sex, and massive doses of magic. This is one book and series I would recommend to anyone who enjoys books about shapeshifters, especially dragons."

~ *The Romance Studio*

"Dragon Storm by Bianca D'Arc is a wonderful book and I look forward to the next book in the series. Even though this story is involved in a multi story arc, I believe that the story could be enjoyed on its own. Each book is based around the royal family of Draconia, and yet each story is uniquely its own. I recommend the entire series as one of my favorite worlds to visit and re-visit."

~ *Two Lips Reviews*

# Look for these titles by
## *Bianca D'Arc*

### *Now Available:*

*Dragon Knights Series*
Maiden Flight (Book 1)
Border Lair (Book 2)
Ladies of the Lair—Dragon
Knights 1 & 2 (print)
The Ice Dragon (Book 3)
Prince of Spies (Book 4)
Wings of Change (Book 4.5)
FireDrake (Book 5)
Dragon Storm (Book 6)

*Tales of the Were Series*
Lords of the Were (Book 1)
Inferno (Book 2)

*Resonance Mates Series*
Hara's Legacy (Book 1)
Davin's Quest (Book 2)
Jaci's Experiment (Book 3)
Grady's Awakening (Book 4)

*Brotherhood of Blood Series*
One and Only (Book 1)
Rare Vintage (Book 2)
Phantom Desires (Book 3)

Forever Valentine
Sweeter than Wine

*Print Anthologies*
I Dream of Dragons Vol 1
Caught By Cupid

# Dragon Storm

*Bianca D'Arc*

A Samhain Publishing, Ltd. publication.

Samhain Publishing, Ltd.
577 Mulberry Street, Suite 1520
Macon, GA 31201
www.samhainpublishing.com

Dragon Storm
Copyright © 2010 by Bianca D'Arc
Print ISBN: 978-1-60504-812-3
Digital ISBN: 978-1-60504-829-1

Editing by Bethany Morgan
Cover by Kanaxa

First Samhain Publishing, Ltd. electronic publication: November 2009
First Samhain Publishing, Ltd. print publication: September 2010

# Dedication

To the awesome readers who allow me to continue writing the books of my heart. Dragons started this whole roller coaster a few years back, and they remain some of my favorite books to write. So I suppose I should also dedicate this book to the dragons! Rawr!

I'd like to thank my family for their love and support. Thanks also to Bethany, editor extraordinaire, for not laughing too hard at some of my typos. And finally, thanks to the fans who kept asking for another dragon book. As long as they keep asking, I'll keep writing!

# Chapter One

It was early morning when a near-breathless messenger arrived from one of the southern cities. He rushed into the throne room, falling to one knee before King Roland.

"My liege." The man breathed hard, as if he'd run all the way from Tipolir to Castleton. "News from the south. A flight of gryphons with mounted warriors heads this way at a slow pace. They can't be more than a few hours behind me."

"From whom did this news pass?" Roland demanded, already on his feet.

"The news started with a messenger from Tipolir, thence to Bayern, Hallowet, Sewell and on. I saw them myself, my liege. They overtook me on the road and shadowed me for a time but let me pass unmolested."

"How many would you say?" Nico helped the man to his feet, handing him a glass of water since the poor fellow looked well-worn from the hard ride.

"A dozen that I saw. The reports stated twice that many, but I only saw six gryphons—each with a mounted rider, though the riders blended so well with the gryphons' golden plumage they were hard to make out. My liege, I never thought to see the like."

"Thank you for making haste to give us this news." Roland signaled to his brother, Nico. The man known as the Prince of

Spies led the messenger from the room, passing him a few gold coins for his trouble. Nico never skimped on paying for good service. It was one of the things that made him such an able spymaster.

Roland turned to his knights, Drake and Mace, who stood nearby. Drake, former troubadour and spy, known as Drake of the Five Lands, had dealt with gryphons before. His new fighting partner, Mace, had also seen gryphons when the two had flown to Gryphon Isle to save Prince Wil from kidnappers.

"I think it's safe to bet these could be some of Gryffid's folk," Drake said thoughtfully.

"My brother Wil is flying to the south," Roland informed his advisors. "I've asked him to wait, but I doubt that will hold him." Roland stalked toward the door. "If your partners are near, mount up and fly with me. I'm going out to meet them."

Drake, Mace and several others of the king's advisors were hot on his heels. The knights raced for the ledges where their dragons waited, ready to fly. Roland, Nico and a few of the other princes shifted form and took to wing as black dragons—as only those of royal blood could do—and the large contingent headed south to meet the wizard's emissaries.


The flight of gryphons was easy enough to spot. They were not trying to conceal their path.

There were six gryphons in all, each more magnificent than the next. Two were smaller than the others. Perhaps they were juveniles, Connor thought as the two groups met up with each other in mid-air.

The dragons circled and followed the gryphons downward to land on a rocky mountainside. A small flat area allowed them room to gather and parlay. The black dragons took point, as was their right, and the others followed their lead.

Prince Wil landed first, joining the gryphons and showing little fear of them. The others followed but remained wary. Roland came first after Wil, Nico behind him. As the two eldest, their roles were clear. Connor hung back with his twin, Darius, and his other brothers, to watch and guard. He was within easy hearing distance and was curious to see what would transpire.

"Shanya?" Connor watched intently as Wil shifted form from black dragon to human and strode forward to meet the girl. She looked about Wil's age, eighteen or nineteen at most, but one could never be certain with these magical fair folk.

"It is good to see you, Wil." The girl stepped forward to meet him, her hands outstretched in welcome and a gentle smile on her pretty face.

The young prince gave her a hug and a peck on the cheek in greeting. "Why have you come? I've only been gone a few days."

"It may feel that way to you, but time still works differently on the island. To us, it is as if you have been gone a month or more. We're not sure why time sped up, when it has always passed more slowly on Gryphon Isle. Gryffid assures us it is only temporary. He is setting things to rights, compensating so that time will run normally between here and there."

The black dragons were arranged around the pair in a semicircle. The other half of the circle was made up of gryphons and their fair folk riders. Behind the black dragons, another semicircle of knights and more colorful dragons stood ready, watching for any hint of danger. A few pairs kept to the air, on patrol for any danger from above.

Roland and Nico shifted form and came up behind Wil and the girl.

"Who's your friend, Wil?" Roland asked, his tone friendly and curious. He was playing it cool, which is something Connor wasn't sure he could've done in the same situation. There was a reason Roland was king. He was more even-tempered than the rest of them—especially since he'd gotten married.

"Rol, this is Shanya. She's the youngest daughter of the Captains of the Guard of Gryphon Isle."

Shanya bowed low to the king of Draconia. "I come with gifts for two of your brothers."

Roland seemed intrigued as he and Nico shared an appraising glance. "Which two and why?"

The girl's forehead wrinkled. "One of the sets of twins. It is they I saw in my vision. Two identical black dragons. Two identical princes. I came to deliver the amulets in person because I couldn't tell which set of twins without seeing them."

Wil stepped in. "Shanya has the gift of prophecy."

"Sorry," she smiled at Wil. "King Roland, I apologize. I foresaw two of your brothers undertake a perilous journey. The Wizard Gryffid sent me here with gifts that will help protect them on their quest."

"What gifts?" Roland looked skeptical.

Shanya stepped toward the gryphons and gestured. Two of the adolescent creatures stepped forward to stand before the king. Each wore an intricate plate of armor suspended by a delicate chain that ran around their necks and under their forelegs. Shanya turned to each gryphon and removed the chains, catching the ornate ornaments in her hands. As they fell off the magical beasts, they transformed from large breastplates and harness into glittering necklaces. She held one in each hand.

"These will protect the dragon's heart in flight and help find the man's heart. That's what Gryffid said when he gave them to me. The first part is obvious. The armor will help protect the dragon's breast. The second part..." she trailed off. Stepping

12

forward, she faced the king squarely. "There is a woman. Your brothers will journey to her realm and must convince her to come back here with them. She is vital to your struggle. That is all I know at this time."

Roland's raised eyebrow would have tested the mettle of a proven warrior. The girl didn't flinch. She was made of stronger stuff than that, and Connor had to admire her strength of spirit.

"Will you ask your brothers to change so that I may see their faces," she dared ask. "I will recognize the men I saw in my vision so I know to whom these gifts belong."

*"What do you think?"* Roland sent the question silently to the black dragons gathered on the rocky outcrop.

*"It could be a trap,"* Nico observed.

*"It could also be exactly what it appears. I've known Shanya for years, and she definitely has the gift of foresight. She has saved lives with her abilities, and I've never known her to do anything dishonest or deceitful. Just look at her,"* Wil invited. *"She wouldn't harm a fly."*

*"Looks can often be deceiving, young Wil,"* Nico countered. *"You said yourself she is the daughter of warriors. Who knows of what she is capable?"*

*"Her parents have never tried to train her beyond basic self-defense. It's more than obvious to anyone who knows her that she may be born of warrior stock, but the inclination toward soldiering passed her by completely. She is a gentle soul, meant for magic and nurturing, if anything. She spends most of her days with the healers or reading in Gryffid's library."*

*"What say the twins?"* Roland asked. *"Since it is their fates we may be deciding here."*

*"I'm inclined to trust Wil's judgment on this,"* Darius said confidently. Of course, of the two of them, he was always the

brashest. *"Wil knows her. And regardless that he was gone so long and has returned to us a man grown, he's still our brother and his opinion deserves due consideration."*

Connor could easily see Wil's gratitude for the vote of confidence but did not remark upon it. It was still hard to get used to having him back and so much older.

*"All right."* It sounded like Roland had made a decision. *"How about if one of each set of twins shifts, plus the remaining brothers. If she really did see one of you in a vision, she ought to be able to recognize you without your mirror image standing right beside you."*

Nico grinned at his older brother. *"You've gotten more devious since you married. I like it."*


Connor sought out his twin on the private communication path they alone shared. *"Who shifts and who stays scaly?"*

*"Doesn't matter to me."*

*"All right, I'll do it."*

Just that easily, Connor was elected to shift to human form. He performed the change easily as his other brothers did the same. Two remained in dragon form because there were two sets of twins.

The girl looked at each human face, her forehead wrinkling again as she studied each man. Connor and Darius were the younger set of twins. They were fully adult and had been warriors for several years.

When her attention turned to Connor, her expression changed. He saw the recognition in her eyes as their gazes met and held. She walked up to him and held out one of the necklaces.

"This is for you." Her voice was low and musical. "Where is

your twin?"

*"That clinches it. She did see them."* Wil's tone was telling as he communicated privately with his brothers. He clearly wasn't happy to have his friend doubted.

Darius shifted form and moved to Connor's side. He grinned at the girl like a fool. Of the two of them, he'd always been the flirt.

"Forgive us, Lady. We wanted to be certain you really did recognize us from a vision."

"Of course." Shanya bowed her head for a moment, and Connor saw her blush. "I know all of this is strange. Even my parents aren't quite used to my abilities." She lifted the other necklace in her hands. "This is for you."

"Thank you, milady." Darius took the necklace and winked at the girl. Before Connor could object, he'd slipped the glittering chain over his head. The fool.

Connor held his own necklace in one hand, unwilling to leap in headfirst until he'd had some time to study the object. For all they knew, it could be some kind of trap—some magical talisman sent to harm them, not help. Connor was more cautious. He would study the thing before he put it on.

*"How does it feel, Dar?"* Roland asked in the privacy of the brothers' minds.

*"Okay. Sort of tingly, but not malevolent. I think it's all right."*

*"All the same, I'll keep mine in my pocket for now,"* Connor put in. *"Until we know more."*

Roland merely nodded and turned back to their guests. It looked like Shanya was the spokesman for the group, though the warriors who had accompanied her watched all.

Shanya smiled with what looked like relief and turned back to Roland.

"Thank you, sire, for allowing me to complete my task."

"Then that is all you came for?" Roland asked.

"Not all, no, sire." The pretty girl blushed. "Our mission was twofold. I completed my part, now it is time for my friends to speak." She backed away, leaving the two young gryphons facing the king.

"I am Neril and thiss iss my mate, Sscalar. We are the youngesst mated pair on Gryphon Issle." The male gryphon began to speak aloud, his beak making a hash of any word with an S in it, but he was still understandable. "Asss ssuch, our choice of nessting ssitess iss not ideal. Gryffid would like to have emisssariess in your land, and we would like a good, ssolid nesst in which to bring up our firsst clutch, which iss not far off. Therefore, we assk your permisssion to nesst in your land."

Roland seemed surprised. Connor knew there was already a pair of mated gryphons living in Draconia. It was a very recent development. He wasn't sure what Roland would think about more of the creatures wanting to make a home here. They were highly magical beasts and unlike dragons, they had few links to humankind. They were wilder and less forgiving of human trespass, even though they could communicate aloud, which dragons could not.

"In recent days, another mated pair has come from a far land to seek their nest here," Roland said formally. "Draconia is for dragons, however we also welcome any being who stands on the side of good over evil and will help us protect the dragons, humans and other inhabitants of our realm. If you can promise to do that, you are welcome."

"Asss my mate ssaid, we are a young pair, not even fully grown, but we know our own mindss," the female, Scalar said. "We mated early even among our own kind. We know what iss right and what iss wrong. We are meant to be together, and our children are meant to live among dragonss. Sshanya has foresseen it."

All eyes turned back to the fair girl who looked uncomfortable once more.

"Is this true?" Roland asked her gently.

Shanya nodded. "I see their babies flying side by side with dragons. Black dragons. They live together. They fight together. They are allies and friends." Silence greeted her words while everyone took them in. "Please, sire, it is the only way they can be happy. Truth be told, their parents are not thrilled with such a young match but Gryffid intervened. Scalar is pregnant. Her babies will come soon. Gryffid convinced the adult gryphons to leave them be, yet they will have no help and no comfort on Gryphon Isle."

"They may not have much help here either, I'm forced to say." Roland turned to address the young gryphon pair. "Our people are not used to gryphons, and we know not how to deal with them. If you stay, it will require patience on all parts. I know gryphons can be violent with humans who do not show proper respect. My people could unintentionally offend. I would not have them hurt for mere ignorance. I would expect a certain amount of forbearance on your part." He eyed the gryphons with that older-brother look Connor knew well.

"Asss you wissh, my liege." Neril bowed his head in a sign of respect. "We have had much missundersstanding and intolerance in our livess already. I would ssay we are more undersstanding and tolerant asss a ressult. We do not take offensse asss eassily asss ssome of our brethren." The young male threw a haughty look over his feathered shoulder at one of the gryphons in their escort who stood back from the others. Their coloring was similar enough that young Neril could be the older one's son.

*"I bet the dour elder male over there is Neril's papa, come to make sure his son is all right. I get the impression he disapproves of the young lovers and their rash actions,"* Connor pointed out privately among the dragons.

*"You have a good eye, Con,"* Nico answered back after a minute. *"I think you're right. Looks like both sets of parents escorted the misbehaving youngsters here."*

Connor looked at the others and realized Nico was right. At least four of the escort gryphons had similar features and coloring to the two youngsters.

"What say your sires and dams?" Roland asked aloud of the circling gryphons. "I wish no ill will between my land and Gryphon Isle. Neither do I want to see these young ones mistreated in either place. I will take them in if it will cause no political upheaval among our peoples."

An older female stood forward and nodded to Roland. "We've held Council on thiss problem sseveral timess already. The gryphonss of Gryphon Issle wissh thesse two no ill will, but neither are we happy at ssuch a young pairing. They sshould have waited for Council approval before mating. The Council iss not happy with them, but what'ss done iss done. Gryffid, also sspoke on their behalf and that holdss great weight with all gryphonss. Sso, King Roland, you would actually be ssolving a thorny problem for uss by allowing them to live here."

"Then it is settled." Roland nodded, his decision made. "Welcome to Draconia, Neril and Scalar. I would prefer you to speak with the other pair of gryphons who recently made their home here so that you all may coexist in harmony. Is that agreeable?"

"Mosst agreeable, your majessty. Thank you," Neril answered eagerly. It was clear he was happy with the result. He moved back to stand next to his mate, rubbing his beak lovingly over her neck feathers in a clear sign of happiness. A little trill sounded from her throat as well, though she did not speak.

Connor found the creatures fascinating. They were as big as most dragons but very different. It would be interesting having them around.

Shanya stood forward once more. "I only ask one more thing, your majesty."

Roland eyed her with amused suspicion. "What now, young mistress?"

"I would ask that I be allowed to stay here as well, with my friends. I can live in their cave if you wish, or if you allow, I could find lodging nearby."

"Nonsense." Nico stepped in, his smooth charm evident. "You will live with us in the castle. Your friends can fly in to visit you easily, and there is no shortage of dragons to fly you over to see them if you wish. You will act as Gryffid's emissary to our court. Isn't that what he hoped for?"

Shanya blushed even deeper. "It is, Prince Nico. You are as clever as he said you'd be. I didn't want to impose after all we've already asked of you, but I would welcome the opportunity to serve in your brother's court."

"Then it is settled. We now open diplomatic relations between our lands and people." Roland spoke to all who had assembled on the rocky outcropping. "I invite you all to join me in food and rest at the castle. You are welcome in Draconia."

The castle was in an uproar when a flight of gryphons landed on the battlements along with a large contingent of black dragons and their honor guard. Dragon talons and gryphon claws echoed in the halls as they walked together to the main audience chamber that was built to hold large numbers of dragons.

The black dragons took human form and walked beside their new friends. Others joined them as Roland's wife, Queen Lana, and his adopted dragon son, Tor, made the scene. Lana's twin, Riki, stood next to her husband, Prince Nico, and several members of the Dragon's Council entered as well.

Two more gryphons waited in the audience chamber, along with Sir Kaden and Sir Marcus, their wife, Lady Lucia, and their dragon partners, Sir Reynor and Lady Linea. The gryphons moved forward to meet the others of their kind. Between them stood Lucy, a recent immigrant to this land and new wife to two of Roland's most trusted knights.

The young set of gryphons halted before the ones who waited, and the older ones who'd acted as escort ranged themselves behind. There was a tense moment while they all sized each other up and the humans and dragons watched to see what would happen. Only Lucy stood firm in the center of the action, her lips thinned apprehensively and her husbands stationed behind her should there be trouble.

After tense moments, the young gryphon pair bowed their heads—not to the other gryphons, but to the small woman who stood between them. Connor watched in surprise that was echoed throughout the chamber, on almost all the human and dragonish faces he saw. Only Roland, Nico and Lucy's mates seemed unsurprised.

"It iss an honor to meet you, daughter of Gryffid," Neril spoke first.

"Be welcome," Lucy said formally. Connor had never really heard her speak before. He was impressed by her composure and self-confidence. She was a lady, through and through.

"I am Lucia de Alagarithia, once of the Jinn, now of Draconia, married to these two knights. This is my sister,

Nrathrella, called Ella for short, and her mate, Grallorrin, called Lorr by his friends." Each of the gryphons flanking her nodded as they were introduced.

"I am Neril, and this is my mate, Sscalar."

"Mated sso young?" Ella said softly to the younger pair. "You musst do thingss differently on Gryphon Issle."

Clacking beaks startled Connor for a moment until he realized that the older gryphons appeared to be laughing. Ella had just broken the tension with her observation, and the stress level in the room ratcheted down a considerable degree.

"Thesse two are headsstrong, I fear." The elder female who had spoken before, talked directly to Ella. "Sscalar would have him, whether the Council agreed or not."

"I ssee." Ella looked at the young pair with sparkling eyes that were not unkind. "The dragonss ssay you sseek to live here, in Draconia."

"We do, Lady." It hadn't been phrased as a question, but Scalar apparently felt the need to answer.

"Then, ssince we know King Roland hass already given hiss approval, we alsso welcome you to Draconia," Lorr said. "It iss our newly adopted land asss well. We sshall learn itss wonderss together. Asss will our hatchlingss."

Ella moved to stand next to the younger female. She was bigger than Scalar. Both females had slight bulges in their midsections that the other gryphons lacked. Both were pregnant.

Lorr flanked Neril, while the younger gryphon settled his wings in a gesture that meant satisfaction among their kind. "It will be good for our hatchlingss to have other gryphonss to fly with in addition to the dragonss."

The potential drama among the gryphons settled, Shanya

21

stepped forward to greet Lucy with a deep bow of respect. "Gryffid hoped his line had continued in these lands while he was gone. It is good to meet you. Your ancestor will be happy to know of your existence."

"We will bring word of you to him when we return to Gryphon Isle." One of the elder male fair folk who had come with the escort spoke for the first time.

Wil went over to shake the man's hand. "I'm glad you came, Eril. I wanted you to meet my brothers." Wil escorted the blond man to where the royal family stood off to one side. "Roland, this is Eril. He acted as one of my tutors while I was on Gryphon Isle."

"Then you have my sympathies," Roland joked. "Wil always hated his studies when he was younger."

Eril laughed good-naturedly. "And well I remember it, but he settled down after a time and was one of my best students. You should be proud of him. He mastered his letters and several languages while under my care. He was more articulate with languages than many of my other students."

Nico stepped forward and greeted Eril in several different languages. Connor didn't know quite as much as his spymaster brother, but he recognized enough to know that Nico was testing the man's fluency and knowledge. They came to an easy accord, and it was clear from his manner that Nico was impressed.

*"What do you think?"* Darius stood beside Connor, speaking privately on the path shared only between the two of them.

*"I'm reserving judgment."*

Darius stifled a laugh at his twin's expense. Connor didn't take offense. It was normal for them. Darius jumped in headfirst and often wound up regretting it. Just as often, Connor debated too long and also lived to regret it. Between the two of them, they usually arrived at the perfect mixture of fast and slow.

The glint of Darius's necklace caught Connor's eye. *"How's the trinket treating you?"*

*"So far, so good."*

*"Be sure to let me know if it turns against you."*

*"You'll be the first to know, I'm sure."*

*"What do you think of the girl—Shanya?"*

*"She's gorgeous, as are most fair folk,"* Darius said with objective ease. *"Older than she appears, I think."*

*"You're probably right."* Connor knew his twin was a connoisseur of women. *"She seems genuine enough."*

*"I agree."*

*"What do you think about this quest she thinks we're going on?"* Connor thought he knew what his twin would say, but he wanted to hear it.

*"I say what are we waiting for? I'm sick to death of sitting patiently at the castle while everyone else gets to do the heroics. Nico's had more than his fair share of adventures. Hell, even Rol got out of the castle and got his claws dirty. We've been stuck on boring patrols, doing nothing of import."*

Connor felt the same impatience, but he wouldn't have put it so bluntly. He understood his brother's feelings exactly.

*"Yeah, but Rol and Nico came back married. Do you really want that?"*

Darius smiled at Connor's little joke. Both men were at the age when settling for only one woman seemed a far-off thing.

*"Well, if the woman was as beautiful and daring as Lana or Riki, I might be tempted."*

*"I don't think there are any more lost dragon princesses out*

*there for us to find. We'd probably have to settle for some normal woman."*

*"Normal's not so bad. Not if she's adventurous."*

Both twins grinned at the thought. Half dragon, they were by nature exhibitionists with hearty sexual appetites. As black dragons, they didn't need to form a triad marriage like knights who partnered with regular dragons, but they'd discussed the idea many times. They were twins, and closer than most because of their unique ability to shift shape into black dragons. It was likely they'd share one wife, if they could ever find the right woman.

As it was, they were usually drawn to the same ladies of the court. The pale blonde Shanya, while beautiful, did nothing for either of them. No, they preferred earthier beauties and had found much pleasure among the Jinn wenches newly arrived in Castleton. They'd shared more than one in delightful nights of debauchery that satisfied both the dragon twins and the lucky women they pleasured.

Darius and Connor observed the rest of the meeting. It went on for some time while the gryphons exchanged information, and the newcomers were introduced to both humans and dragons. Roland called for refreshments, and chairs were brought for the two-legged among them while the dragons and gryphons settled or stood talking in small groups around the huge chamber.

All in all, it was a good start to a future alliance. Having an ancient and powerful wizard on their side should dark times come would be a very good thing indeed. Especially when the wizard commanded loyalty from every gryphon in the world. Between gryphons and dragons, air superiority would be theirs. Few could stand against either, and none would fare well with both gryphon and dragon working together.

The twins ducked out with Roland's silent approval to oversee their younger brothers as the meeting wore on. Wil had been stolen and returned five years older than when he'd left. No more mischief would trouble their younger brothers if they had anything to say about it.

They needn't have worried. The older gryphons stayed a few days to be sure their children found a suitable nest and helped them settle in, then left with little fanfare. Of the fair folk, only Shanya stayed behind, a silent presence in the castle corridors, her pale features and quiet ways making her seem almost like a ghost at times.

Shanya's steps were silent as she walked down the castle corridor. Over the days she had resided in the royal palace of Draconia, she had learned the various pathways that would lead to the battlements. She spent much time there, watching the dragons or waiting for her gryphon friends. They came to see her each day and took her by air to their new nesting site— a cozy cave in the craggy mountainside.

With their parents' help, the cave had started to become homey even before their parents departed for Gryphon Isle. The older pair of gryphons already living in Draconia had helped since then, teaching the younger pair how to set up their domain for best comfort and efficiency. The older pair already in residence had been a surprise to Shanya but a welcome one. She had worried about her friends being alone in this strange land. It was clear the Mother Goddess had other plans. Much better plans. As always.

She reached the final corridor that would lead her to one of the many landing areas for the multitude of dragons that came and went from the castle daily. This corridor had arched windows every few feet that looked out over the city far below.

The sun shone bright inside at this time of day. It was a lovely place with little bench seats placed in some of the alcoves between windows for both utility and comfort. Knights often paused here to settle their packs on their backs when they came in from patrol or a longer journey. And she'd seen others just sitting, enjoying the morning sun from time to time as she traversed the long hallway.

Shanya was about halfway down the corridor when she felt the distinct lightheadedness that usually prefaced a strong vision. She stumbled for the closest seat but was too far away to make it before the vision hit her full force. When she would have fallen to the stone floor, a pair of strong arms came around her, catching her as she swooned.

That was all she knew until the vision released her some minutes later.

Her eyes blinked twice, able to see the real world once more—no longer seeing the future possibilities. She was confused as the faces above her came into focus. She'd just seen them and now here they were. Then she realized, she'd seen their future. The very men she'd seen in her vision were here now, with her in the present.

"You will travel far in search of the one with ancient magic who will help you defend the Citadel."

It was Prince Connor who held her, she realized, as he looked to his twin in surprise. Prince Darius stood close, concern on his handsome face.

"Are you all right, mistress?" he asked politely, not commenting on her pronouncement.

She sat up, pushing against Prince Connor's hold. He let her go as she caught her breath.

"Forgive me. The vision came upon me suddenly. It was very strong. I would have fallen had you not caught me, Prince

Connor. I thank you."

"It was my pleasure to assist you, Mistress Shanya. Are you certain you're all right?"

"I will be in time. I just need to catch my breath and get my bearings. This was a strong portent of the future I have seen before. It is even more solid now. You will go far. Both of you." She looked from one to the other. "To a place unlike any I have ever seen with wondrous devices and strange people. There is very little magic, but what is there is potent. You must find it, and the one who waits. The weapons you retrieve will be vital to the defense of the Citadel, the place of power where the wizards imprisoned their enemies in ice many centuries ago. If we are to maintain the integrity of that prison, and return life to a dying breed, you will need this foreign magic. It is your task to perform. No other may follow your path."

She tried to impress the urgency of her message on them. It was clear they were skeptical of her words. They would come to see she was right in the fullness of time. She only hoped they would remember her instructions and seek the magic when they found themselves on their journey.

*"What did you think about Shanya's vision?"* Darius asked Connor privately after they left the seer on the battlements with her gryphon friends. The gryphons would take care of her, they well knew.

*"Damned if I know. She seemed very sure of herself."*

*"I agree."* Darius frowned as they headed down the flights of stairs that would take them to the family apartments.

*"I think we should wait and see. Rol doesn't have us slated to go anywhere more exciting than the Northern Lair in the next few weeks. I don't see us undertaking the kind of journey Shanya was talking about."*

"*I just keep remembering how lately the unexpected has been the norm. Between Wil's abduction and return, the gryphons' arrival and all the strange things that have been going on with the Jinn, I don't know what to expect anymore. For all we know, Rol or Nico could tell us to pack our bags tonight and head out to some foreign land.*"

"*Well, if they do, we'll at least have Shanya's words to keep in mind. Honestly, I doubt it. Nothing exciting ever happens to us. All we do is watch over the youngsters and fly patrols. Not old enough to rule over lands or spies, not young enough to need a keeper. We're the spare brothers, sent on the most mundane of tasks.*"

"*You said it. I am heartily sick of flying boring patrols over the capital region. I want to stretch my wings and go someplace more exciting.*"

"*Well, if Shanya is right, adventure may soon come knocking on our door. Be careful what you wish for, brother.*"

They joined their brothers and the new female members of the family for dinner, and nothing more was said about their encounter with Shanya.


Days later, they were flying to the Northern Lair, as scheduled, when a freak storm came upon them.

The sky burned black and green, a roiling mass of clouds and electricity. The two black dragons powered through the gusts that threatened to down them. Their task was clear, their mission imperative. They had to make it through the storm to their destination. Turning back was no longer an option. They were too far into the storm.

Lightning arced from cloud to cloud, barely missing the twin black dragons as they darted to and fro, flying as they'd never flown before. The elder of the two—by minutes only—cried out as a jolt of electricity rode up his left leg and through his entire body. His brother came to his aid immediately, only to be hit by the same bolt of lightning, traveling from the cloud, through the first black dragon, arcing into the second and back to into the angry black and green clouds.

Time ceased to exist as the two dragons were tossed into a vortex and spun. Sky became earth, and earth became sky. Over and over they tumbled, each certain the hard landing to come might be their very last. Their massive wings beat franticly, trying to regain some equilibrium, but neither of the two dragons could discern what was up and what was down as they were pulled and stretched by currents greater than even their own immense strength.

# Chapter Two

Darius came awake in the middle of a forest. One wing was badly damaged, bloodied and torn undoubtedly from his trip through the leafy canopy. Looking upward, he could see the hole he'd made on his way down. He craned his long black neck to seek a similar pattern. His brother had to be nearby somewhere, but the trees here were too dense to navigate in his bulky dragon form.

Marshalling his strength, he changed from dragon to human, willing his clothing back from wherever it went when he changed. While some of his injuries improved in the magical transition, his left arm was still a mess. Nothing broken, thank goodness. Only a long, shallow gash graced his arm from shoulder to elbow. He looked around, trying to get his bearings. Nothing looked familiar. Nothing at all.

When the storm had come upon them—so suddenly it didn't seem natural—they'd been flying northward over their own territory. They'd grown up in Draconia, learned to fly there and knew every inch of forest and field. This pine forest was familiar, yet not. This wasn't like any of the forests in his homeland. It looked different, sounded different and even smelled different.

He also scented something that immediately raised the short hairs on the back of his neck.

Magic.

The air reeked of the residual scent of massive and powerful magic.

*"I don't think we're in Draconia anymore."*

*"No kidding."*

Darius was relieved to hear the voice of his twin strong in his mind.

*"Where in the hells are you?"*

*"Step to your right and look up about twenty feet."*

He did, relieved to see the black dragon clinging to a solid-looking pine tree. Connor was in better shape than Darius, with no visible injuries. He was relieved they'd both survived that wild trip.

*"Well, we wanted adventure,"* Darius mused, looking around.

*"Looks like we got it."*

*"Any idea where we are?"*

*"There's a small cabin about a league from here with smoke rising from the chimney. Maybe we can find some help there, but it doesn't look like any dwelling I've ever seen before and I don't see any signs of other dragons."* Connor shimmied down the strong trunk using his claws to dig into the bark until he could stand—just barely—on the forest floor. The trees really were too dense to allow grown dragons to walk comfortably among them. He shifted form and appeared once again human, wearing black leather leggings, boots and a vest laced up over his solid muscles, just like his brother. Only he wasn't bleeding. *"Let me help you with that."*

Summoning just a bit of his dragon magic, Connor touched his brother's arm, helping the skin knit together. It wasn't fully healed, but it would do for now.

*"Thank you, brother. So, what is our strategy?"*

*"I believe we should head for the structure I sighted in the distance. Perhaps we can find help there—or at least someone to tell us where in the hells we are."*

Darius heard the frustration and wonder in his brother's voice. He felt it as well.

They set off through the woods, Connor leading the way to the place he'd spied from above. It didn't take long to traverse the distance, but Darius felt every step in his injured arm. It burned like fire. Not the good, cleansing sort of dragon fire. No, this felt like the fire of possible infection, and he wasn't pleased by the idea.

An infection here could spell disaster. For one thing, they had no notion of the native plants or wildlife that could be used for medicine. For another, they could very well be in hostile territory. They had no idea what they were walking into. They had to take a chance and make contact with the natives.

*"I'll go first."* Darius stopped his brother's forward motion when Connor would have stepped into the last line of trees before the clearing.

*"You're injured."*

*"Which is exactly why I should go first. If we meet with an enemy, you are whole and well able to come to my rescue. Besides—"* he played his trump card, *"—if we are lucky enough to have stumbled upon friends, I may be able to get some doctoring for my poor arm."* He held up the wounded appendage with a sorrowful look on his face that didn't fool his twin for a single moment.

Connor laughed at him, but bowed comically low and motioned for Darius to proceed.

*"I'll be watching from above. If you need help, call."*

Darius walked out of the trees, trying not to hold his wounded arm, but the truth was, it really did hurt. He would never have admitted it to anyone—even his twin. Connor, no doubt, already knew. It was the bond they shared. They always knew such things about each other, often experiencing each other's feelings. It was the main reason they chose to live and work together.

Being twins had been fun for them as children, but often one or the other of them had gone off to do something on their own. The other always knew and always felt what the other experienced. After a while, they both had stopped trying to fight fate and realized their paths in life most likely lay together. Entwined as they had been in their mother's womb. Parallel souls walking together through life.

Youthful resentment had given way to thankfulness. They had each other. They'd seen how their older brothers struggled. Roland especially seemed to have the weight of the world on his shoulders, and he'd spent much of his life alone. Only now that he had his queen, the love of his life, by his side, was that loneliness beginning to abate.

Daruis wondered if he'd ever find the same kind of deep and true love that had made Roland's and Nico's lives so full. And if he did, would Connor love the same woman? Would they be destined to share a mate as the simple knights in his land did? Or would they each find a separate woman to love—and how could that work when they were so close as to share the experience of almost everything either one did? Or would they be destined to fly forever alone, without a woman in either of their lives, with only each other as company?

Darius didn't know. He didn't often dwell on such sober thoughts, but then he'd never been swept to another land by a magical storm. Life had suddenly gotten very interesting, very fast.

Josephine Marpa was heading out to her Jeep when she saw the man emerge from the woods. Immediately on her guard, she noticed he was limping and there was dried blood on his arm. His bare, muscular arm.

He wore leather pants, boots and a sexy vest that tied up the middle over impressive pecs. His muscles bulged as he moved, the black leather hugging sinewy thighs and tight abs as if he'd been poured into it. Her gaze moved upward, and her mouth dropped open at the devilish grin on the handsome face looking back at her.

He was probably a biker—judging by all the leather—who'd been in some kind of accident. Or maybe a male model escaped from some sort of fantasy-fetish photo shoot. Only she wasn't aware of any photo shoots going on in the area.

"Can I help you?" She stood her ground while she watched him approach. He stopped about ten feet from her, making no move closer, which put her more at ease, but she wasn't going to let his amazing good looks influence her common sense. Much. She hoped.

"I'm a little lost." He favored her with a disarming smile. Sweet Mother of All, when the man smiled he was even better-looking. It ought to be illegal.

"And a little banged up." She looked at his arm, not entirely sure she wasn't hallucinating. Men like this certainly didn't walk out of her forest every day. "What happened to you?"

"I had an accident." He moved a step forward, standing closer, but in an unthreatening position. His smile turned a bit sheepish, tugging on some long-lost feminine heartstring she hadn't known she still possessed.

She sighed, more annoyed at herself than at the stranger. He seemed all right. His body language was tentative, not aggressive, and her sixth sense was telling her he was okay. She made a rash decision and moved to inspect his injury more closely.

"What happened to your bike? Too banged up to move?"

She sensed some hesitancy before he answered. It didn't feel menacing, and she trusted her special senses enough to believe he didn't mean her any harm.

"Something like that," he answered. "Look, can you tell me where I am exactly?"

One of her eyebrows went up in surprise. Maybe he'd hit his head when he crashed. "You're in the national park. About two miles from State Road 42." At the blank look on his handsome face, she went on, both eyebrows reaching upward now. "In Oregon? The Pacific Northwest? United States of America?" Instead of the laughter she expected at her little joke, only more consternation showed on his face. "Where are you from?"

His lips firmed as he considered her. It almost looked like he was debating how much to tell her. She'd seen that look before, but never so openly. Whoever he was, he wasn't a very good liar. Somehow that was reassuring rather than scary.

"Draconia." He searched her eyes for something, but she didn't know what. "I was heading to the Northern Lair."

She tilted her head, considering his outlandish words. This had to be some kind of joke. "Are you an actor, or maybe a role player, or something? Is there an SCA event going on that nobody told me about?"

"SCA? What is that?"

"The Society for Creative Anachronism. You know, the guys who dress up in old-time garb and fight with swords, pretending to be knights from medieval times? They like to pretend it's a few hundred years ago, and men still rule by the

35

sword."

"I'm a knight," he said softly, "but I do not belong to this society you speak of. I am a subject of King Roland of Draconia. To whom do you owe your allegiance?"

"Look—" she sighed and shook her head, "—the act is cute, but this is the twenty-first century and I don't have time to play games with you. Can I help you find your way out of these woods or what? You look like you could use some medical attention. I can drive you into town so you can get that arm looked at by a doctor. What do you say?"

"The wound is minor. I do not need a doctor. I could, however, use a place to wash up. Can you direct me to water?"

She hesitated about inviting him in to her cabin, but what else could she do? Her special senses continued to insist that he was a good guy. She trusted her instincts. They'd never steered her wrong in the past. But having this huge man in her tiny cabin was a daunting prospect.

"Sure." She made a snap decision. "Follow me. You can use my bathroom."

"You have my thanks."

She led the way into her cabin, pointing him to the bathroom. He was closer than he had been outdoors, and she got her first good whiff of his scent.

Sweet Mother of All.

If her nose didn't lie...

He was her mate.

The willowy beauty led him into a strangely built cabin, but he only barely noticed the structure. No, his eyes were firmly glued to the delectable curves of her ass as she walked. She was a rare beauty, her eyes slightly tilted at the corners, and her skin held a golden glow unlike any in his land. To him, she looked exotic...and beautiful.

*"Be careful, Brother."* Connor's voice flowed through his mind. *"It could be a trap."*

*"If so, I don't think I want to escape,"* Darius teased, his eyes on the woman. He knew his brother was aloft in the trees, watching what he could.

*"Just remember, the female of many species is often deadlier than the male."* Connor's dragonish chuckle followed him into the building.

She led him into the small structure and warmth assailed him. The outdoors had been brisk, with a hint of rain in the air. Inside her cabin it was snug and warm. He saw a banked fire in the fireplace along one wall. Overall the place was tidy and clean in a way that didn't exist in his homeland. Surfaces gleamed as if they were made of rock or polished metal. Simple folk in Draconia led bountiful lives, but they didn't possess items like those he saw on his path through the main room.

*"What's it like inside?"* Connor asked.

*"A cabin. Fabric covered furniture, warm fabric rugs on the floor. Many strange objects I do not recognize. Many books. An eclectic mix of possessions."* The brothers could see through each other's eyes, but it was both physically and magically draining. As a result, they tended to save that ability for when it was truly necessary. *"This is like no home I've ever seen in Draconia or any of the lands we've visited. Now leave off before she thinks me addled. I will report back when there is something to report."*

His hostess turned to him as she closed the door.

"Your home is lovely," he said, for lack of anything better to say. She already thought him odd from the comments she'd made outside. He didn't want to make it any worse.

"Thank you." She strode across the room and opened a small door set in the far wall. "The bathroom. There's liquid soap in the dispenser, and I'll get some bandages and disinfectant for your arm from the first-aid kit in kitchen. Wash up, and I'll be back in a few minutes. By the way, my name is Josie."

"I am Darius." The introduction seemed stilted, and her name was strange to his tongue, but beautiful. Just like her. He watched as she walked gracefully away into another part of the small house.

The bathroom, as she called it, was nothing like the stone bath chambers common to every Lair. No, this small room held surfaces of gleaming metal and ceramic tile with other items of some unknown substance that was highly polished but lighter than stone. He experimented a bit with the sink fixtures until he realized that cold water flowed when he turned one of the levers and hot water came out of the faucet when he turned the other. It was marvelous.

He also found what he supposed was the liquid soap she'd mentioned. It smelled strange to his nose. It lathered like soap once he exposed it to the water. It also removed the dirt and grime from his person.

Darius stripped off his leather shirt and washed thoroughly, using one of her towels to dry off. He slung the towel over his shoulder as he looked at his reflection in one of the finest mirrors he'd ever seen in a simple home. It was true silvered glass. Something most people could not afford in Draconia, though there were plenty of mirrors like this in the royal palace and the Lairs where dragons and their knights lived with their families.

Deciding his arm was already healing well, he shrugged off the strangeness of this environment and went in search of his hostess.

He found her bent over, rummaging through a small closet beneath a larger version of the sink in the bathroom. There were countertops made of something that looked like stone, but did not feel like it. For one thing, the surface was not cold like a slab of rock and did not have the same hardness to his senses when he reached out to rest one hand atop its surface.

These thoughts registered only on the surface. The majority of his attention was taken up with the delectable shape of her ass as it wiggled enticingly before him. She was small compared to him. He guessed she'd fit him perfectly in all the right places. Her body was that of a siren, sent to tempt him. He tried his best to stifle a groan as his cock twitched in appreciation of her beauty, but he wasn't entirely successful.

She straightened abruptly and turned to face him. Surprise flickered on her face before it was replaced by feminine appreciation as her gaze lowered to his bare chest.

"You snuck up on me," she accused in a breathless voice.

"I'm naturally quiet. Sorry." In actuality, he wasn't sorry at all. He advanced into the room, stalking her scent. Her natural fragrance was like that of an exotic flower to him. Earthy yet ethereal. Sumptuous and almost divine. "I don't think the cut will require bandages, but it could use some medicine to clean away possible contagion. It burns."

"Oh." She jumped as he neared, focusing on his arm. If not for the burn of what he thought had to be some foreign air that could infect his blood, he would never have distracted her with the injury. But he needed whatever medicine she had in her strange home, to combat what could develop into a life-threatening contagion.

Then he'd take care of what seemed to be a very potent and very mutual attraction.

"Are you sure? I can't find the bandages. I never use them myself. I do have some antiseptic spray though." She turned to pick up a bright white bottle that flexed under her fingers in a rather amazing way. He didn't comment as she moved closer, taking his hand to lift his injured arm to the countertop. "This will sting at first."

The warning was unnecessary. The slight cold of the spray was nothing like the pain he'd expected. He looked at the wound to be sure the liquid had actually penetrated into the raw part that needed healing.

"Are you certain that will work? It doesn't burn."

"Oh yeah. I'm sure. I use this stuff all the time. I bought it specifically because it doesn't sting as much as the other kinds." She gave the wound one more spray and put the bottle down. "That should do it. You can put more on later, if necessary."

"Will I be here later?" All of a sudden, their surroundings disappeared. It was only the two of them, facing each other, alone in the world. The air grew thick as their bodies drew closer. Their gazes met and held.

"Do you want to be?"

"More than anything I can think of." Only inches separated them and Darius took that final step forward, opening his arms and gathering her closer. He held her gaze as he lowered his head, seeking her lips. He would not rush her. If she did not want his kiss, he would back off and try to seduce her another way.

She surprised him by moving closer, reaching up for him and taking his lips with a ferocious intensity he had not expected. After only a slight hesitation he joined in, thrusting his tongue into her mouth and parrying her own forays into his.

She was tuned to him. It felt like she anticipated and

mirrored every one of his needs and desires. She was perfection itself, wrapped up in an explosive, fiery bundle.

He pushed the stretchy fabric of her top upward, and she pulled it off over her head. She was bare beneath, making him groan as he cupped her generous breasts in his palms. Her skin was the most extraordinary thing he had ever touched, like warm satin and as soft as down, yet alive with her own vibrant intensity.

"Darius," she moaned his name as he left her lips and sought her nipples with his tongue. She tasted divine to his dragonish senses. Female and wanton, refined and...perfect.

Josie's senses were on fire. This man burned away all her inhibitions and left her a writhing mass of need. His scent quickened her body in a way she'd never experienced with any male. She licked at his skin, tasting the perfection of their match.

He was her mate.

After all the years and all the turmoil, she'd finally found that one special being meant for her. And he wasn't one of her people. He was...human? He didn't taste like other human men she'd nibbled. No, there was something Other about him. She didn't recognize exactly what it was. At least not yet. But she would know all his secrets before long. Mates could hide nothing from each other—or so it was said.

His merest touch drove her wild, his scent permeated her senses, making her want to wallow in it—in him—for as long as he would let her be near. She wanted to run with him, to have him chase her and capture her and stake his claim. She wanted to be wild and free with him. Only with him.

Darius.

An odd name, but a strong one. She liked that.

She put from her mind the complications this mating would bring her. The family she had forsaken would never have countenanced this match, but destiny could not be denied. She'd learned that the hard way and for all of her grandfather's machinations, she followed her own path in the world. It was a lonely path—or had been until this very moment—but it was her karma.

All that was about to change. She felt it in the air, in every touch of his hands, in every breath she took. Something much larger was in play here. Destiny had come calling, and she had to answer. There was no alternative.

And she didn't want there to be.

She loved the way this relative stranger who commanded such power in her life, made her feel. She loved each caress, each knowing lick, each daring touch. It could only get better from here and she couldn't wait.

She'd never felt like this before—so wanton, so eager to be with a man. Especially one she didn't know. But her inner beast knew this was right. He was her fate, the one she had worked so hard to find. She'd gone against her family and all their traditions to forge a new life for herself. Here and now all her work and soul-searching had come to fruition. He was here. And he would be hers.

He'd seemed a little strange out there in the woods. His words made her doubt his state of mind but the Mother of All wouldn't be so cruel as to send her an addled mate. He'd been in some kind of accident. Perhaps that was the reason for his strangeness earlier. She had no doubt it would all come clear in time. Right now, though, she wanted him with a hunger that was completely overwhelming. Questions could wait.

She attacked the buttons on his soft leather pants, walking him backward out of the kitchen. She wanted her first time with him to be in bed. Luckily he complied with her wishes. He was too big for her to move if he didn't want to move.

Oh yes, he was a fine figure of a man. Tall, black-haired and green-eyed. Muscular and lithe. Fit and handsome. She couldn't have dreamed of a sexier male. He appealed to her senses in every way.

Thankfully the cabin wasn't big, and they reached the bedroom door before she had his pants unbuttoned. She pushed him back against the wooden panel after it banged open and shoved his fly wide, dragging it down over his narrow hips. Sinking to her knees in front of him, she saw him for the first time.

His cock was long and thick. Everything a woman could want...and then some. She'd have to work to take this monster inside of her—in her mouth or in her excited pussy. She reached out to touch him, enthralled when his cock twitched. She smiled as she took him in her hand.

"I think he likes me."

"Of that, have no doubt." His return grin was wickedness itself. "We both like you a great deal." His hips surged forward into her caress. "We'd like it even more if you'd use those luscious lips and hot mouth. Suck it down. Lick it with your tongue."

She did as he asked, drawing out the moment, reveling in the sensation of tasting him for the first time. As she suspected, he was perfect. The little drop of pre-come exploded on her tongue, setting off fireworks in her abdomen as her body primed itself for its perfect mate.

She'd never experienced the mating heat before, but she recognized it for what it was. Her body nearly convulsed with the need firing through her veins for the man who would be her match in every way.

She felt him tremble a moment before he bent and lifted her by the arms, twirling and pushing her up against the wall. She kicked off her shoes and shimmied out of her pants even before he got to it. She wanted him inside her. Now.

"Please, Darius!" She gasped as he supported her against the wall, lifting her clear off her feet with his incredible strength. She cried out as he entered her in one fierce thrust. She was more than ready for his possession. She wanted it. She wanted all he had to give...and more.

He began to move with harsh digs, as near as she was to the breaking point. She felt his muscles bunch under her fingers, felt her fingernails lengthening into claws as the beast within her sensed its mate. She wouldn't change fully, but she'd always heard when the mating heat was upon those of her species they tended to go feral—teeth and nails lengthening so they could mark their chosen mates in the most primal way.

She fought against it. She didn't want to scare him off. He wasn't snowcat. He was...something else. She didn't know what, yet. It wouldn't do to mark him until she knew for sure.

It was hard and fast and just what she wanted at the moment. She made guttural sounds in her throat as he powered into her, supporting her against the wall as he nailed her. She'd never had it so gritty, so hard. It was perfect.

Everything about him was perfect. Her perfect match.

"Darius!"

She didn't want to wait anymore. She had already waited a lifetime. She wanted him to come inside her. To claim her in the most elemental way. To mark her with his seed and begin to tune her body chemistry to his. That was the way of her people.

Darius moved faster and even more forcefully. She was with him, eager for him. He grunted in the sexiest way as he thrust up into her, impaling her so thoroughly she never wanted it to end. But she needed him to come. *She* needed to come, and she couldn't do it without him.

Her inner muscles clenched on him in a rhythm designed to make him give up his seed. The snowcat wanted it. She wanted it all.

"Now, wench. Come for me now."

Darius's guttural order was all it took for her to fly over the edge of oblivion, taking him with her. She felt the spurts of his hot come inside her clenching body, and she welcomed the feel of him claiming her as she claimed him. They belonged to each other—even if he didn't yet realize it.

He soon would.

The snowcat licked the side of his neck, grazing her elongated teeth over his throbbing pulse. She would bite him there. Soon. Josie pulled her back. They had to talk as humans before the Other sides of their nature could come out to play.

Snowcats roamed wild and free, following the most ancient tantric Buddhist principles on their path toward enlightenment. Only when they found their mate, did they change both physically and mentally. The two became truly one and after, they walked their path toward enlightenment together.

She was only half snowcat and raised mostly in the Western world. She didn't buy fully into the enlightenment stuff. Her human mother had been a lot more sanguine about that kind of thing and had passed her beliefs down to her daughter. Had her father lived, she might have learned more about his people's ways. Her grandfather had taught her what he could after her mother had also died. She'd been too old by then to really assimilate into his Tibetan culture, but she'd listened and stored the information.

The bit about knowing one's mate almost instantaneously was certainly true. She just had to find out what kind of shifter he was.

Later. For now, she reveled in the taste of his salty sweat on her tongue, the feel of his cock sliding inside her. As first times went, this one broke all the records. She'd never been so completely devastated by any lover, and they'd barely scratched the surface. The hard, fast quickie up against the wall would be only the beginning, if she had her way.

*"You're fucking her already?"* Connor's voice came to him from elsewhere as Darius came down from the hardest, fastest climax he'd ever enjoyed. *"Aren't you moving fast."* The brotherly observation sounded almost envious.

*"She is amazing."*

*"I know. I felt it too. Do you think she would welcome me as eagerly? I really need to do something about this hard-on."*

Darius felt bad for his twin. At the same time, he wanted to fuck her again. Right now.

*"Deal with it for an hour more, brother. Then you may have her. I will fuck her to sleep, and you may fuck her awake."*

*"You think she'll go for that?"*

Darius hesitated. His plan was simple—and dishonest. They'd done such things before, but never with a woman as special as this one. How she'd become special to him in such a short time, he didn't know. But she was. And he was tempted to do this the honorable way, but that would take too long. Explanations ruined the mood. Better Connor get some of her pussy first. Explanations could come later.

*"She doesn't know there are two of us."*

*"I'm not certain I like the idea of tricking her, but in another hour I'll be desperate enough to do it."*

*"I know."* Darius felt guilty amusement at his brother's

predicament but not enough guilt to switch places now. *"One hour. Be ready."*

*"I've been ready since she sucked your cock,"* came the dry reply.

Darius ignored his twin as he pulled out of Josie's luscious pussy. He let her feet slide to the floor, continuing to support her as he led her to the bed in one corner of the room.

"Hands and knees, wench. I'm going to fuck you."

She grinned at him, firing his hunger higher. "Doggy-style? You read my mind." She seemed eager to try as she scrambled up onto the wide bed, presenting her ass to him as she spread her knees, showcasing her dripping pussy.

She glistened with his come, a sight he relished. Her delicate folds were slightly swollen from his possession, begging for his touch. He knelt on the bed behind her, reaching out to slide his fingers through her wet folds. She gasped as he hit the little button of her clit, circling and pinching as she made little involuntary movements.

When she squirmed too far, he retaliated with a little slap. She yelped and looked back at him over her shoulder in stunned surprise.

"Too rough?" he questioned.

She licked her lips. "Do it again."

Oh, this was a woman after his own heart. He spanked her pussy again, and she pushed back into his touch, wanting more.

"You like being spanked?"

She rubbed her bottom against his hands as he paused. "I never have before. But I like it when you do it."

Their gazes met, and he gauged her reaction to his touch. This wench might be up for more than she thought—more than he'd ever given another woman. He wanted desperately to find out. To test her limits.

"On your back and open your legs for me, puss." He slapped her ass lightly to get her moving. She complied with a confused expression. When she lifted her long, muscular legs and settled them on either side of him, the fire of passion returned to her eyes. "Spread your pussy for me. Use your hands. Show me your secrets."

She made a sexy purring sound as she reached between her thighs and framed her pussy with elegant fingers. A little tug had the outer lips stretched open, revealing the glistening pink heart of her and the excited little clit that stood up for him, begging for attention.

He bypassed her greedy clit, teasing her, circling one finger around the tight hole that still dripped with his come. She shivered at his touch, her eyes half-lidded, watching his every move.

"You have a tight cunt, wench. It grips me hard, heightening my pleasure. Your little clit is provoking. Does it want me to lick it with my tongue?" She nodded, gasping at his imagery. "Does it want me to suck it between my lips?" She clenched her teeth as she nodded again, seemingly unable to speak. "Does it want me to nibble on it with my teeth?" He smiled to show his pearly white teeth, winking at her when her abdomen clenched in excitement. "Does it? Tell me, wench."

"Yes!" she cried out as he drove one finger into her pussy. He curled his finger within her, rubbing gently and trying to find the magic spot that would bring her even more pleasure. He knew he'd found it when her breathing hitched.

"You like that, puss?"

"Yess..." The word was drawn out as she panted.

He leaned down, positioning himself between her legs,

ready to push her even further. He continued the assault with his finger as his tongue licked out to brush against the tight protrusion of her clit. At the first contact, she jumped.

Darius drew back and slapped her pussy. Hard. Not hard enough to truly hurt. Just enough to sting...and excite.

"Now we'll try again. Don't move, wench, or you'll get more of the same." He grinned at her to soften his harsh words, pushing two fingers into her dripping pussy this time before closing his lips around her clit. She behaved while he sucked, teasing the inside of her sheath with two knowing fingers. When he bit down gently on her clit, she cried out and nearly bucked him off.

Darius drew back to be sure he hadn't hurt her, but he could see it was pleasure that had caused her reaction, not pain. Her head thrashed from side to side as he withdrew his fingers from her cunt.

"What did I say, wench?"

Her eyes cleared fractionally as she looked up at him.

"N-not to move." She was adorably incoherent under his touch, which made him feel ten feet tall.

"But you did move. And what did I promise would be the result?"

"That you would spank me." Her expression lit with an eager light as her belly clenched in anticipation.

"Spread your legs, love." He nipped her breast as he whispered the instructions. She complied eagerly, and he knew he had her. She wanted this.

And he was just the man to give it to her.

He pulled back and looked down at her. She was beautifully limber. He'd take great pleasure in testing her flexibility many times over, trying all kinds of positions to take her. That would come later. For now, he had a punishment to administer.

He touched her grooves with his fingertips, teasing and taunting as he drew out the moment. Her gaze followed him, the anticipation growing.

At his first slap, her eyes fluttered closed as she made a little sobbing sound low in her throat. Her abdomen shuddered with ripples of passion. She liked it. The signs were all there.

Darius tapped her again, aiming around the hole that had held him so nicely minutes before. He would cover her entire pussy with little love taps before all was said and done. He had to time it right because she was very responsive. He wanted to see if he could make her come from tapping her pussy alone. He'd bet he could.

She got even wetter with his next smack, and he revised his plan. She was close to coming already. She was even more responsive than he'd thought. The next one ought to do it. He aimed for her clit.


When he tapped her clit, all hell broke loose. Josie came with a scream that shook the rafters, convulsing over his hard fingers as he rubbed her clit throughout it all. His hand rode her pussy, extending the orgasm. He crooned to her, lulling her senses as she climaxed at his command. He owned her.

As it should be between mates.

Before she could even catch her breath, he was on top of her, blanketing her with his massive body, his tangible strength, his masculine protection. He'd punished her in the most delectable way, but he'd also given her more than any man.

Darius thrust into her, his cock finding its home within her warm core. She never wanted him to leave. She wanted this feeling of connection with him, of belonging to him, of bringing him as much pleasure as he brought her. She wanted it forever. She wanted *him* forever.

And she'd have him, if she had anything to say about it.

She'd had a glorious orgasm, but he was still hard as a rock. She wrapped her legs around him and urged him on, grabbing his muscular ass and running her nails down his back. He gave her what she wanted—another hard, fast fuck. There would be time for slow and easy later.

"Give it to me, Darius. Give me all you've got." She wanted him to feel the same unbelievable pleasure she'd just felt.

She got more than she bargained for. As he thrust into her, her senses exploded with a return of passion. She wouldn't have believed it was possible if it wasn't happening to her. Within minutes, she was nearing another peak of ecstasy.

"Stay with me, love."

"Forever, Darius," she promised as her senses spun out of control.

He joined her in a fast, tight orgasm that left her breathless and dizzy. She felt him coming, and her own explosion and then she faded away into blackness as the pleasure ebbed and flowed around her consciousness.

# Chapter Three

Josie woke to motion and light. It was late afternoon judging by the angle of the sun in her bedroom, and Darius was inside her once more. All was right with the world.

He'd lifted her hips while she slept on her stomach, propping her up with a few pillows and spreading her legs. She helped him as he thrust within her, easing backward to meet his long, slow thrusts.

As soon as he realized she was awake, he seemed to catch fire. His thrusts became impatient and harsh, impolite and altogether enticing. His fingers bit into her hips, and she loved every sensation of him losing control.

She loved that she'd done this to him. Her desire rose hard and fast as it always seemed to do with this magical man. She felt as if this was all new. That *he* was new. Though she couldn't explain what that even meant in her own mind. She only knew she wanted him and wanted to claim him as her own.

She pushed back against him, reveling in the feel of his cock thrusting heavily into her body. His balls pressed against her on every thrust, sending her higher. Within moments she was crying out, screaming as she came with him.

His come jetted into her channel, calming the intense need she'd felt for him and restoring her faith that he was, indeed, hers. Finally. She was finally able to breathe easy, secure in the knowledge that she'd taken his come, was transforming even as she lay there, into the woman she'd always been destined to become.

When he withdrew after long, almost-paralyzing moments of pleasure, she collapsed onto her stomach. He removed the pillows and scooped her into his arms, placing nibbling kisses along her neck and shoulder, making her feel precious to him. She felt the emotion coming from him and basked in the way she was already attuning to his emotions and needs. He spooned her from behind and she dozed, secure in his embrace.

When she woke only minutes later, judging by the sun angling through her bedroom blinds, he was asleep. She turned in his arms to look at him, and her breath caught at his perfection. He really was the most beautiful man she had ever seen. And he gave her the most beautiful orgasms she'd ever experienced. It was time she gave something back to him.

Reaching for him, she licked his cock like a lollipop, gratified when it sprang to attention almost right away. She looked up to find his eyes open, watching her.

She played with his balls, caressing him, learning him as she continued to suck until he'd achieved full size. He was impressive. She didn't want to wait to have that giant cock inside her again, though this time the urgency that had driven her before was muted.

She could take her time once she got him inside her. Time to enjoy the ride.

Josie rose over him and positioned him just right as she sank down over his hard cock, pushing downward in one long, smooth, slow glide. She smiled at him as she straddled his thighs, taking him as deep as she possibly could, holding his gaze as she claimed him—body and soul.

She began to ride him. The time for truth had come.

"I am snowcat. What are you?"

"I'm not sure what you mean."

She wasn't fazed by his evasion. Most shifters were loath to reveal their true natures in this dangerous world.

"I share my soul with the Himalayan snowcat. With what creature do you coexist?"

His light green eyes widened as she rode him. She was getting through to him.

"I'm not sure what a snowcat is. We are dragon."

His answer surprised her on several levels. First, there were no dragon shifters to her knowledge. There were ancient legends, of course, but no actual living dragons. At least according to her grandfather. He'd made it his life's work to know such things. Second, he'd said *we*. Was that the proverbial royal *we*? Or was he somehow...

The bedroom door opened, and she turned to look at her lover—standing in the doorway. But he was beneath her, his cock buried deep in her pussy. She looked down at the mirror image of the man in the doorway, naked beneath her, and back again.

"Twins?" God help her, she wanted to feel outrage, but the cock inside her only made her want more. The idea of there being two of her perfect dream lovers was mind-boggling.

She looked from the one beneath her to the one in the doorway again. They were both wearing expressions of chagrin and worry. The one in the doorway had a fading red mark on his arm. He, then, was Darius.

She'd already fucked them both.

Sweet Mother of All.

"You took me from behind, didn't you?" she asked the one

beneath her.

He nodded. "Guilty as charged. You are quite a woman. I could not resist—or wait until you woke." He had the grace to look embarrassed, but the majority of his expression was filled with teasing, sexy amusement. Why she found the sneaky bastard sexy, she had no idea.

"What's your name?"

"Connor."

Another strong name. She liked that one too.

"Do you know what you've done? Both of you?" She saw confusion on their faces and was glad for just a moment. Much would be decided by their reaction to her next words. "You mated me. Both of you. It shouldn't be possible. Somehow, you are both my mate." Relief etched both handsome faces, and it was her turn to be surprised. "Doesn't that bother you?"

"Why should it?" Darius asked, walking into the room and sitting on the edge of the wide bed. He was close enough to touch, and her mouth watered at his nearness even with his brother's cock wedged up high and tight inside her.

"We have always suspected if we found a woman one of us wanted as a mate, the other would too. To be honest, we are relieved such a woman exists. We feared spending the rest of our lives with only each other for company."

"Then you believe I'm your mate too?" This was turning out better than she'd hoped. Although they hadn't admitted what kind of shifters they were yet, they did understand about mating. She wouldn't have to try to explain, which was a relief. "How can a three-partnered relationship work? It's not normal."

"It is where we come from. Two knights will often share a single wife. It is the way of dragons and their families."

"Dragons. You said that before. There are no dragon

shifters. My grandfather would know if any had survived. There are ancient legends, but that's all."

"I assure you, we are much more than legends. Perhaps we should demonstrate how this relationship might work." Connor drew her downward so she was pressed to his chest.

He kissed her and only vaguely did she register the sounds of Darius's leather pants dropping heavily to the floor. When the bed dipped, Connor let her up.

"Ride me, love."

She tried to comply, but Darius distracted her with his hands. He cupped her breasts as his brother rose on his elbows to suck the nipples Darius held up for him. It was wicked. Sinful. And utterly delightful.

Four strong hands roamed her body, tweaked her nipples and rubbed her clit. Darius's hands roamed farther, teasing her ass and the additional entrance between her cheeks. Would he take her there? Would they both fuck her at the same time? Her breath caught at the tantalizing idea.

"Have you ever been fucked here?" Darius bit down on her earlobe as he probed her ass. She nodded, unable to form words. "You have? Hey, Con, our girl has taken it up the ass before. Maybe we should try her together. What do you think?"

She moaned as Connor's grip on her nipples increased. "I think we should. What do you think, sweetheart?"

"Oh!" she cried out as Darius slid one finger into her ass while his other hand teased her clit. Their deliberately provoking talk and teasing words only served to make her hotter.

"I think that's a yes," Darius teased as he penetrated farther. His fingers were wet with oil, and she looked down to see a familiar bottle lying on the bed. She'd last seen it on her bathroom shelf. The trickster had come prepared. They'd planned this all along.

She couldn't find it within herself to be truly upset. This felt too damned good.

"Shh, puss." Darius kept his mouth near her ear, whispering to her as he penetrated deeper with his finger. His brother was pumping up into her from below. She was too far gone to keep up any kind of rhythm. "We'll just go this far for now. Con needs to come and you do too, but we're going to take you together sometime very soon. Both of us. One in your pussy. One in your ass. You'll like that, won't you?"

"Yes." She gasped as his finger slid all the way inside and began a rhythmic counterpoint to his twin's thrusts in her pussy. She sobbed as she came with only a few more pulses. It was all too much. The pleasure overwhelmed her and swept her away on a tide of passion as Connor's cock flooded her insides with his come.

Darius praised her in soft whispers at her ear as she came for them.

When it was over, Darius took care of her. He lay her down on the bed, tucking a blanket around her. At some point, both of the men cleaned her. She felt a return of pulsating sensation in her clit when they bathed her there, but not enough to penetrate the fog of sleep that had fallen over her.

She slept deeply, only to wake up at the sound of thunder.

Darius and Connor slept with her. One on either side of her. Night had fallen long before, and the storm that had been brewing all day was upon them. Rain pelted the cabin roof and lightning sent jagged slats of illumination through the blinds every few minutes.

Nights like these often made her fearful, but with Darius and Connor on either side of her, she felt safe. They were her mates. Her future and her past all rolled up into one. She would never be alone again as long as they lived.

The idea that they were somehow dragon shifters was something she'd have to see to believe. They were magical. She'd felt that from the beginning, when she'd only thought there was one of them. She'd have to get them back for that dirty trick someday. She couldn't get the energy to be truly upset by it now. Her inner snowcat purred for them both. Wanted them both. Needed them both.

She didn't understand it, but there were many things she didn't fully understand about her beast. Her grandfather's lessons were often too complicated for a girl who'd lived most of her life in the West. His talk of enlightenment and the various teachers and schools of thought in his religion had been dizzying for a teenager, suddenly thrust into a new life in a foreign land by the death of her mother.

Her father had died long before, leaving her to be raised by her mother. A French Canadian researcher, her mother had met her father on a trip to western China. They'd married long before he'd ever revealed his heritage. It wasn't until Josie was born that the truth had come out. By then nothing could break the couple apart—except death.

When her father died, Josie's mother went to America. Canadian by birth, she got a position as a university professor in Oregon and had raised her daughter as a suburban kid. When it came time for her first change, her mother had taken Josie to the mountains and had done her best to support her, but she didn't really know much more than Josie had. She'd learned by trial and error.

It was only much later that Josie's mother had confided her grandfather's prediction that as a half-breed, Josie would likely never be able to shift. She'd proven him wrong. Not only could she shift, but the snowcat's influence was strong in her soul.

When her mother died in a car crash, Josie's grandfather had finally showed up to inspect her. A minor with no control over her own destiny, Josie had been obligated to go back to Tibet with him once he evaluated the strength of her snowcat.

It was obvious to her that he'd been prepared to find little of value in his half-Caucasian grandchild. She'd reveled in her beast's power when he'd demanded she shift for him and still remembered his surprise with a feeling of satisfaction. From that day forward, he had treated her with respect and began to teach her about being snowcat.

Aside from his continuing efforts to convert her to his version of Buddhism, they'd gotten along well after that. He was an austere man who was bitter about the loss of his son. Josie made up for it in a small way, he once admitted. She was a strong snowcat and would add to the clan whose numbers were dwindling. Josie had stayed with him until she was eighteen.

She would have stayed longer, but he'd tried to force her to marry. There was nothing wrong with the guy. Her inner cat had been the one to object. He was *not* her mate. She didn't want him.

When her grandfather had tried to force the issue, she'd left. She had never looked back and in the years since, she hadn't heard from her family. She'd been careful to hide her tracks so even if he wanted, her grandfather would have a tough time finding her.

She lay listening to the rain as her thoughts wandered to what had been and could have been. If she hadn't forged her own path, she probably never would have met Darius and Connor. They *were* her mates. The cat knew them immediately. This was her destiny—lying here between them.

Buddhists believed you made your own fate. Josie believed she'd made her own decisions that had brought her to this destiny. A Western girl with Eastern ideas, she found her grandfather's beliefs meshing more and more with her own as she grew older. She was only half Tibetan, but all snowcat and the cat dictated a lot of what she'd come to understand about the world and its people.

Josie fell back asleep, cradled between her two mates, secure in the knowledge that she'd found her destiny with them. Where it would take her, only heaven knew.

When she woke again, the twins were gone from her bed. A quick sniff told her they'd found the kitchen and were in the process of burning bacon, if she wasn't mistaken. Josie found a robe and headed out to avert a fire. Any second now, the smoke detector would start blaring.

When she hit the main room of the cabin, she was amazed to see one of the twins kneeling before her fireplace, the handle of her iron skillet in his hands. He was cooking the bacon in the skillet, over a fire.

"You got something against stoves?" she asked, reaching for the skillet.

"Whoa there." He moved the hot pan away from her grasp. Good thing too. She realized her mistake a second later. The handle was hotter than she could safely handle. She would've burned herself badly if he hadn't pulled away.

"How can you hold that?"

Darius grinned at her. "I'm half dragon, sweetheart. Even in my human form, some things carry over."

"Wow. That must be handy." She looked around the small cabin. There was no sign of the other twin. "Where's Connor?"

"Outside, gathering wood to replace what I used. We didn't want to deplete your supply."

"That's sweet, but not necessary. Why didn't you use the stove?"

Darius looked confused. "I didn't see a stove."

"Bring that skillet and follow me." Josie stood from her crouching position next to him and headed for the small kitchen. She flipped the switch on the gas burner, and the flame ignited. Darius took a step back, his eyes wide. "You've never seen a gas stove before?"

"No. We don't have anything that looks like this where we come from. What fuel is used?"

"Natural gas. Did you see that big metal tank outside the house? The gas man comes every few months and refills it for me. I also have a few solar panels on the roof to help capture the heat from the sun."

"Ingenious. Con, you've got to see this."

The other twin had reentered the cabin without Josie hearing him. One thing was certain, these dragons moved like the wind. Even her sharp snowcat senses couldn't detect their movements.

She spent a few minutes explaining how the stove worked. Then a few more, picking up where Darius had left off with the bacon. She grabbed a half dozen eggs from her small refrigerator and put slices of bread in the toaster. Each time she used a new appliance, she was obligated to explain its workings to the men. They were full of questions and made comments she found hard to understand.

It didn't sound like they were from another country. It sounded like they were from another planet.

Or maybe another time. Medieval times, to be precise.

At least the hot and cold running water didn't seem to faze them, although they were impressed that she had that kind of magic in such a small home. She didn't even begin to know what questions to ask to make their world become clearer in her mind. She supposed given time, they'd come to an understanding.

One thing that couldn't wait much longer was their beast halves. She wasn't sure she bought their claims about being dragons, although Darius's imperviousness to the burning heat of the cast-iron skillet was hard to explain any other way.

They ate breakfast, and the men impressed her with how much food they managed to eat between the two of them. She knew shifters ate a lot, but she was only half shifter and wasn't quite up to their weight.

"Do you feel up to a run this morning?" she asked as she finished her last slice of toast.

"Run?" Connor seemed surprised by the question.

"My snowcat likes to run every other day or so. Living here makes it easy to blend in and as long as there are no hunters in the area, it's relatively safe. Are you up for it?"

"Dragons aren't much for running," Connor replied with a serious mien. "But we'd be glad to fly anywhere you would like to go."

Josie sat back and thought about it. Even if their dragon forms were only as big as their human size, they'd be bigger than any bird. If someone should see them—especially some weekend warrior with a camera—well, it didn't bear thinking about.

"Do you have to fly every few days, or can you go longer without shifting?"

Connor looked at Darius, and they both seemed surprised by her question.

"We don't really know," Darius finally answered with a bit

of puzzled dismay.

"What he means to say is, we've never really had an issue with it. We can be in either of our forms for however long is necessary."

"Really?" Josie was intrigued. "Out of necessity, shifters spend most of their time in human form. To stay too long in our beast forms invites the beast half to take over completely. While it can be a means of getting away from the troubles of our human selves, staying in animal form too long isn't encouraged. At the same time, we need to let the predator run, to ensure the happiness of our inner beast. At least, that's what my grandfather taught me."

"Well, if your cat must run, it must run." Darius pushed his plate away and stood. Connor followed suit.

She hadn't meant to run at that very moment, but she was curious about their beast form. She wanted to see it. Seeing, as they said, was believing. It would be hard for her to buy the dragon thing fully until she got a good look at them in that form.

Of course, they also said curiosity killed the cat. She didn't want to dwell on that little pearl of wisdom. These men were her mates, amazing as that seemed. She needed to know what manner of creature shared their souls, and there was no time like the present to embark on that particular voyage of discovery.

"All right. We can leave the dishes 'til later." She stood and headed for the door, the men following close behind.

Josie paused in the clearing in front of her small house. Normally, she would head into the woods before shifting form, just in case anyone was in the area and might happen to see her. Today, however, she wanted ample room to see what form her new mates would take when they shifted.

"Why don't you guys go first? I've never seen a dragon shifter before."

The twins looked at each other, sharing a sort of shrugging, raised-eyebrow expression that she couldn't quite decipher. She imagined they were curious about her cat. She was doubly so about their claim of being dragons.

A part of her seriously doubted they'd be able to pull it off. Some dark part of her psyche fully expected their lie to be exposed.

And how wrong that part was.

A black fog-like shimmer surrounded first Darius, then Connor and a split second later, two gigantic black dragons stood where the men had been. The only thing differentiating them was an intricate plate of armor that covered Darius's breast and gleamed in the morning sun.

"Sweet Mother Goddess," she breathed, shocked to motionlessness. "You really are dragons."

*"You were expecting something else?"* The voice came in her mind, unexpected and subtly amused. One of the twins was speaking telepathically to her. She thought it was Darius from the teasing tone, but she wasn't sure.

"All this and you're telepaths too?" Josie's knees went weak as the two huge dragons advanced on her position. She was frozen in place, unable to move.

One reached out its long, sinuous neck, its massive head hovering in front of her face. One peridot green eye winked at her with amusement. The same peridot shade the twins shared.

"Guys, you can't fly around like that. If somebody sees you..." It didn't bear thinking about. She began to shake.

The giant dragon tilted his head in question then looked at his brother. Their eyes narrowed as if troubled, and Connor shifted back to his human form. He took her in his arms, holding her close while she clutched his shoulders.

"What's wrong, love? What has you upset?" His concern touched her heart.

"You're so big...and there aren't any dragons here. If someone sees you..." Hiccups interrupted her babbling as emotion threatened to overwhelm her. She didn't know where to begin to tell them everything that was just *wrong* with being a dragon in the twenty-first century. Maybe they really were from another planet. Or another dimension.

"We don't have to fly if you don't want us to." Darius came up beside her, in human form once more. She read concern on his face along with dismay. She was probably freaking these guys out with her violently swinging emotional display.

"I'm sorry," she whispered. She tried to get a grip, but needed a few minutes to come to terms with this revelation. Her cat clawed at her insides, wanting to get out. She pulled away from Connor and looked at both men. "You two stay here, and please don't fly anywhere. Don't do your dragon thing. At least not until I get back."

"Where are you going?" Connor asked. He looked like he wanted to prevent her from leaving, but she couldn't take that. She needed some space.

"My cat needs to run, and I need to think. I'll be back in about an hour, okay?"

Connor watched her go with a sinking heart. She was clearly distraught. Something they'd done had upset her. It didn't sit well.

"Do you think we scared her?" Darius stood beside him as they watched her lope off into the dense forest. She had shimmered with a white cloud of fog—the exact opposite of their dark black shimmer—then turned into a gorgeous spotted white cat. There were legends of such creatures living in the far north of their world, but neither of the twins had ever seen one of them.

"I don't think our lady is frightened by much." Connor thought about her reaction. "She seemed more overwhelmed than scared."

"Well, we are a lot bigger than she is when we shift. Heck—" Darius shook his head, "—even in human form we are much larger than she is."

"Our mate is a tiny thing," Connor agreed. "We must be careful with her both physically and emotionally. I think she is more fragile than she seems."

"What makes you say that?"

"Why else would she be living out here all alone? I fear someone or something hurt her in the past. She is hiding from something."

Darius seemed struck by the thought. His eyes narrowed as he stared after the place she had disappeared. "I'm going after her."

"She wanted to be alone," Connor reminded his twin.

"I'm going to watch over her from above. She'll never know."

"Dar, if there truly are no dragons in this world, I imagine we're going to face some difficulties. For one thing, we're going to have to be very careful about being seen."

"No one will see me." Darius was adamant, but Connor knew Dar had little control over onlookers. He could only be careful and hope for the best. At night they would have a better chance of blending into the dark forest, but the sun was strong today.

"I don't know, Dar. She wanted to be alone."

"You just said she is hiding. What if she is in danger?"

Connor hadn't thought of that angle. "We'll both go. Fly close to the treetops and watch from above."

"It is a good strategy," Darius agreed before shimmering into his dragon form and taking to the sky.

Connor followed in his brother's wake. They stuck low to the trees, using the dense canopy for cover as best they could. All while searching for a furry white cat with dark spots, pointy ears and a long, lush tail.

*"I see her."* Darius was clinging to the top of a sturdy pine, high above the forest floor.

Connor latched on to a nearby tree as lightly as he could, trying not to rustle the leaves or make any other betraying sounds. The big cat prowled over the forest floor, pausing just once, its ears swiveling. Thankfully, she didn't look up.

The cat turned to a streak of white fur as it took off at an unbelievably fast pace through the maze of tree trunks far below. Both dragons took to the air, following close behind, watching over her from above.

*"She is faster than I would have thought,"* Connor commented to his twin.

*"Like a streak of lightning,"* Darius agreed. *"Even flying, it is a challenge to keep up with her."*

*"And she is hampered by the trees. I wonder what speeds she could attain on open land?"*

*"It boggles the mind."*

At length, she paused in a small clearing, climbing on a large boulder to take a look around. She wasn't even breathing hard.

*"That's our mate, Dar. She is something to behold, isn't she?"*

They both heard her surprisingly musical growl just before she looked up. Her tail twitched as she looked directly at the trees to which the dragons were clinging. She knew they were there.

Caught, the dragons drifted to earth in the clearing, shifting when they touched ground. Josie shifted too.

"You followed me?"

"We were concerned for your safety," Darius began as Connor cringed.

*"She will not take that well, brother,"* he sent silently.

*"Why not? Most women would be flattered by an offer of protection."*

*"Have you not noticed our mate is independent to a fault?"*

"I've run in these woods for years and never had a problem." She looked annoyed, as Connor had predicted. "But you two. What were you thinking? You could have been seen. Do you know what would happen if someone with a camera caught you on film or tape? These woods would be filled with news crews and UFO hunters before the day was through."

"What is a camera?" Darius asked.

"Oh Lord." Josie made a face and held one hand to her forehead as if she were in pain. Clearly, she was not pleased with them. "Look, it's dangerous for you to be seen. Let's go back to the cabin, and I'll show you what a camera is."

She shifted and was off like a shot. The twins did the same, following her path as quickly as they could.

The twins were amazed by her photos, her camera and all the other entertainment equipment she showed them over the next hour. They loved the television, as she'd expected. They all watched the news report together, and she had a heck of a time explaining all kinds of things they weren't familiar with including the satellite dish that allowed her to get television way out here in the sticks. Wherever the twins were from, it was very different from here.

"You said dragon shifters were rare in your world. Just how rare?" Connor asked.

"So rare, they are only legend," she admitted. "There are ancient tales about dragons, but nothing more. Snowcats are rare. Dragons are nonexistent. I shudder to think what would happen if somebody actually saw you in dragon form. You'd be hunted. Stalked. You wouldn't be safe."

Both twins seemed to think hard on her words. Neither looked happy.

"Then how are we to stay here? It would be difficult to fly if dragons are never seen in your skies." Connor turned to his twin, dismay on his face mixing with determination to find some kind of solution.

"We could only fly at night."

"With no moon."

"In unpopulated areas."

"It will be difficult, but not impossible."

Her head whirled at the rapid fire sharing of thoughts. As twins they were probably used to finishing each other's sentences. She'd have to get accustomed to the way they worked together. As a rule, she was much slower to process things and habitually methodical. She always thought things through every permutation before voicing her ideas. In fact, she'd been musing quite a bit about the twin dragons and their fate here.

"The more I think about your situation, the more I believe we need to go to Tibet to see my grandfather. He might be able to help us."

"Tibet?" Connor looked at her hopefully. "Is it within flying distance? We could go tonight. There is no moon."

"Flying distance, yes. But not for a dragon. It will take a few hours to get there by airplane and before we can get you out of the country, I'll have to pull some strings to get papers for you. Or something. I've never tried to smuggle non-citizens across borders before. I'll have to call for help."

"Who would you call?" Darius looked suspicious.

"There are other clans of cat shifters in the area. As I said, snowcats are rare and revered by most of the other big cats. If I ask the leader—we call him the Alpha—for help, most likely he'll help, though I've never revealed myself or my clan affiliation to them. I've preferred to be a loner. Being snowcat causes problems sometimes. The younger and smaller felines tend to hang on your every word when they realize what you are, and that's too much responsibility for little old me." She shrugged. She'd never voiced her thoughts on the subject aloud before, but the twins seemed to understand. "And I'm only half snowcat. I wasn't raised fully immersed in the Tibetan culture. I'm not as wise as most of the others. Or half as mysterious."

Darius put an arm around her shoulders. "You are perfect to us, love. Never doubt yourself."

She hugged him back, a little embarrassed at having revealed her secret doubts about herself, but glad to have his understanding.

"Let me make a few calls. We'll probably have to go meet the clan Alpha so he can check us out."

"We'll meet with whoever you wish, if it will help," Connor assured her.

# Chapter Four

They dined that night on venison that had been stored in Josie's freezer. One of the twins held it for a few minutes to thaw it out. It was amazing how closely their dragon power was linked to them, even in human form. Josie had never seen anything like it.

Sure, she had keener eyesight and sharper hearing and sense of smell than normal humans. The snowcat side of her nature seemed to be more separate than either of the twins' dragon sides. Josie had the sharper senses while in human form, the twins could actually call heat and flame. *That* was something more magical than Josie had ever seen, even during her time in Tibet.

Her grandfather's people had nothing on these dragon men. They *were* the dragon, and the dragon was them. It seemed a more intimate twining of soul and identity than she was used to in her own experience. Her snowcat resided in her and when the snowcat came out, she resided in it—separate and distinct.

The dragon twins didn't seem to understand that differentiation. It was alien to them. Which made it fascinating to her.

Connor and Darius were surprisingly good in the kitchen, once they were shown how the appliances worked. Josie lived simply, conserving fuel and battery power. She had to rely on solar energy for her electricity. On cloudy days, she didn't always get a full charge on her batteries, so she had learned to be frugal. As a result, she didn't have a whole lot of appliances that required juice—either electric or gas.

She used the electricity mainly for lighting and entertainment, but she did have a few small electric appliances like her toaster and microwave. The stove was gas, and she had unpowered backups for almost every necessity. Hurricane lamps with full reservoirs of lamp oil stood ready should she need them, along with cords of wood for the fireplace. She could cook over it too, in a pinch, as the twins had tried to do, but she left that for true emergencies. So far, she'd never had to try it.

Leaving the kitchen with dinner preparations well underway, Josie placed a call she never thought to make. She'd had the man's number for over a year, just in case, but hadn't planned to call. Tonight, it seemed, would be a first.

She called the Alpha of the local cougar clan.

Getting through to him was easier than she'd expected. Cougars, being native to North America, affiliated themselves more with the *were* population than the exotic cat shifters. They kept themselves somewhat apart from the *were*wolves and other *were*creatures, straddling the line between the cat shifters and the *weres* in a delicate dance of dominance.

The leader of the small group of cougars in the area was located a few hours from Portland. They had a house and property on one side of the Columbia River Gorge and it was there, they agreed, that Darius, Connor and she would meet the Alpha the next day. She'd had to out herself in order to gain an audience with the man. She'd resisted alerting any shifters to her presence in the area for as long as she'd been here.

This Alpha knew she wasn't cougar. She didn't have an affiliation among the North American clans she could claim. In order to establish herself, she'd had to tell him exactly what she was. Subterfuge was not welcome by most Alphas. He had accepted her claims with guarded interest and seemed willing to meet to discuss her problems further. Unspoken was the knowledge that if she proved she was who she said she was, her life here would never be the same. The cougars would talk. She may have just given up her privacy for the twins' sake, but what was done was done.

Josie disconnected the call with mixed feelings. She knew she needed help if she was going to get the twins to her grandfather, but she wasn't sure of this Alpha. She'd never met the man, though he had a good reputation. She hoped she could trust him.

She also hoped he and his clan members would be able to handle having a snowcat among them. Once other shifters found out what she was, they tended to get weird around her. Snowcats had a reputation for being closer to the spirits and more magical than most other shifters. It was something her grandfather and his followers did their best to encourage and maintain. As far as Josie was concerned, the reverence in which snowcats were held was only partially earned.

It was true that her shift was more magical than others, but Josie didn't particularly think that made her any closer to heaven, or enlightenment, or whatever you wanted to call it, than any other being. Just because she had a little more magic than most was no reason to idolize her. When other shifters started acting weird around her, Josie felt uncomfortable in the extreme.

If they couldn't handle her—a mere snowcat—how in the world would the locals deal with two dragons in their midst? Now *there* was some serious magic. Josie had felt it tingle through the air as her men shifted and ever since, she had noticed it around them. They were never entirely free of it. The magic buzzed around them in a low-level hum. It was a comforting sort of hum she hadn't noticed until she'd felt it escalate into a symphony as they shifted form.

It was actually kind of beautiful. And very, very magical.

If snowcats were revered, these two dragons ought to be deified.

Firming her resolve, she turned toward the kitchen. The smell of sizzling meat and vegetables tantalized her nose and made her stomach growl as she walked into the small room. The kitchen table was set as if for a state dinner, except of course for her paltry stoneware dishes and mismatched utensils. The men apparently had good manners and knew how to set a table. Maybe their world wasn't so backward after all.

The roast sat in the center of the table, just waiting to be carved. Heaping plates of mashed potatoes, green beans and other vegetables she'd had in her freezer sat around the main platter. Her mouth watered.

"This looks delicious." She tried to keep the surprise out of her voice but saw the smirking grins on the twins' faces. They knew darn well that she'd expected far less when they insisted on cooking dinner for her.

"Allow me." Darius pulled her chair out for her. Connor moved to carve the roast while Darius brought each of the side dishes to her, spooning servings onto her plate at her direction.

Connor served the roast in thick, savory slices while Darius took his seat. Solicitous didn't even begin to describe the way they treated her. Unctuous might be closer, but it didn't quite capture the very real concern for her comfort that she saw in their eyes.

After she was served, the men took huge portions for themselves. Josie had been surprised by the sheer amount of food they'd prepared, thinking perhaps they'd overdone it. Now she began to understand just how much these two men could eat.

"This is really delicious," Josie complemented them both as she sampled everything. They really were good cooks. "Where'd you learn to cook like this?"

"We don't often get the chance to prepare meals indoors," Connor began.

"When we're on patrol, we often shift and cook outside rather than eat game raw in our dragon forms." Darius finished his twin's thought. "Our brothers laugh at us sometimes, but I think they all prefer cooked meat."

"Though they'll never let on." Connor picked up the thread again, grinning at his brother and then at her. "They enjoy teasing us too much."

"How many brothers do you have?"

"Eight," Connor answered. "Roland is the eldest, then Nico, Hugh, the other twins Collin and Trey, Trent, us, Jon, then the baby, Wil."

"Although, since his adventure on Gryphon Isle, Wil is closer to our age now."

Josie didn't understand how that could be, and the look on her face must've telegraphed her puzzlement.

"Wil was kidnapped by servants of the wizard Gryffid and taken to him on Gryphon Isle. Gryffid did something to change the way time flows on the island and Wil spent five years there, learning from Gryffid and training with the fair folk warriors before our people got to him and brought him back. Only a week passed for us while Wil aged five years."

"It was quite a shock. He'd been captured a gawky teen and came back a man grown." Connor raised his glass and took a long swallow of water. "At first we didn't believe it was him."

"I can see why. That's...amazing." Josie was more than a little alarmed at the idea of such magic. Things like that just didn't happen. For that matter, a girl didn't have dinner with two *dragons* every day either. She felt hysteria loom near the surface again, but tamped it down.

She'd seen magic. Hell, she *was* magic. She knew its flavor and understood as much as she could about it, having lived with it her whole life. This was something else altogether. What they were talking about in such a matter-of-fact way, was impossible in her world. The stuff of legend only. And there it should remain, as far as she was concerned.

"I fear we are distressing you again," Connor said in a tight voice. "Please forgive us. It is hard to know what topics will cause you discomfort."

"No, it's okay. Really. I'm just a little... I guess overwhelmed would be a good word. The kind of magic you're talking about doesn't exist here. Not to my knowledge at least." She firmed her resolve and her backbone. "Which is all the more reason to get you two to my grandfather. If anyone will know about this kind of stuff, it's him."

"It will be an honor to meet your grandsire," Connor said formally.

They finished dinner in silence, only talking again as they cleaned up the kitchen. Darius and Connor wanted to do it by themselves, but Josie insisted on helping. She didn't want to be left alone with her thoughts. They were too disturbing.

When Darius came up behind her at the sink and slipped his arms around her waist, she didn't object. In fact, she felt a wave of relief come over her. This, she could focus on. The passion that was between them would take her mind off her worries and allow her to be at peace—if only for a little while.

Connor joined them as Darius moved to her right, crowding

close. Her men surrounded her, buffeting her on both sides so that she was pressed into the counter in front, with one of them on each side.

"Do you want us, love?" Connor whispered in her ear, his tongue slipping inside to tease the whorls and make her squirm.

"Yes." Her voice was a mere gasp of sound, but they heard it. She reveled in the fire of their touch, the way they grasped her and moved with her toward the kitchen table, shedding clothes as they went.

Darius tossed Josie's jeans under the table as Connor kissed her. They took turns. One twin would distract her with kisses and heated touches while the other removed another piece of her clothing. She tugged at their shirts, but aside from those being loosened, the men were clothed while she was...well...naked.

She had to hand it to them. They were very efficient when they worked together toward a goal.

"I want to touch you," she complained as Darius placed nibbling kisses down her throat. He straightened.

"Your wish is my command, sweetheart." He tugged his shirt off over his head and let it fall on top of the pile already on the floor. The medallion around his neck flashed in the kitchen light, catching her eye. Unconsciously, she reached out to touch it and was jolted by the buzz of magic that leapt from the metal to her hand and up her arm.

"Whoa." She pulled her hand back quickly while Darius frowned.

"Are you all right?" He took her hand, examining it for injury. "It's never done that before."

"It's okay. Just a sizzle of magic. Or something. That thing really packs a wallop."

Darius tilted his head as if trying to decipher her words, but grinned as he moved close once more. "So do you, my love."

She laughed at his outrageous tone. Darius was the ultimate rogue, she was learning, while his brother was more like still waters that ran very deep, indeed. They looked so alike, yet they had unique personalities that made each stand out in her mind. She liked them both and needed them with a biological compulsion. The mating call was strong. It would not be denied.

Love, though, was something else. She needed them. She wasn't quite sure about the love part yet. What she felt seemed like love, but it was new, fresh and…scary. She couldn't really be certain.

Her mind was in turmoil about taking two mates. Heck, she figured she'd have a hard enough time finding one man to put up with her mixed parentage and odd ways, let alone two. While three-partnered relationships weren't unheard of among shapeshifters, she'd never even entertained a fantasy that such a life could be meant for her.

The way they made her feel was starting to make her a believer, though. She was swept away by their arousing touches, their attention to every last detail of her pleasure.

Darius distracted her while Connor lifted her off her feet, positioning her near the kitchen table. He bent her over a chair, then stepped away, making room for his brother. They worked well together, and she reaped the benefits.

Darius stroked her bottom while Connor moved to stand off to one side, as she leaned over the chair's back. She looked up at him, meeting his gaze as he reached out to caress her shoulders, then moved lower, to cup her swaying breasts in his big palms. She loved the way he stroked her, gentle one moment, rough the next, then soothing and always considerate.

Darius's fingers moved downward, sinking into her wet heat. He didn't play games, but went straight for her clit, tickling the aroused flesh with a knowing touch as she gasped. Connors fingers pinched her nipples while Darius slid two thick fingers into her pussy. She needed them, and she needed them soon. She couldn't take much more of this without exploding and she wanted them with her when the climax hit her.

"Fuck me, Darius. Fuck me now." She was a cat-shifter in delicious heat. The snowcat inside didn't understand why its mates were making it wait. It screeched inwardly, willing them to fuck her.

"As my lady wishes." Darius's words brushed past her ear in a breathy whisper as he leaned over her, removing his fingers. She felt him lift away only to replace his fingers with something much bigger. He paused at the mouth of her pussy, one hand on her ass and one hand between them, guiding his way, she imagined. But she couldn't imagine why he was waiting. Didn't he know she was desperate to be fucked?

Then Connor got her attention with a soft touch to her cheek. She opened her eyes to find his bare cock bobbed right in front of her face as he stepped forward.

"Take me in your mouth," he ordered, and she liked the rough edge to his voice.

"Do it. I want to watch you take him," Darius cheered her on. She knew why he'd waited. He wanted to watch her swallow his brother's cock before he got inside her pussy. It was just kinky enough to set her on fire.

Josie opened her mouth and received the tip of his massive cock on her tongue, taking a moment to swirl around him a little before she took the rest of it. He was big, but he was also considerate. He never gave her more than she could comfortably handle.

"Look at me, baby. I want to see your eyes while I'm in your mouth." Connor's guttural words turned her on even more as she did as he asked.

Without warning, Darius shoved home, pushing her forward a bit, onto his twin's cock. It was sheer heaven being stuffed from both ends by them.

Darius began a fast rhythm that made her want to cry out. Instead, her cat alternately purred and growled, the vibrations working up through her throat to surround Connor's cock and making him groan.

He pulled out completely as Darius began to pound her in short digs. Connor fondled her breasts as he watched his brother make her come so hard she cried out. She climaxed over and over around Darius's thick cock. He gave her his warm come in powerful spurts that only heightened her pleasure. She was dripping by the time he was done.

She trembled, her arms barely supporting her as Darius pulled out. She only had a moment's rest before Connor slid a soft cotton kitchen towel between her wet thighs, cleaning her with a few impatient strokes.

Josie saw the striped towel join her clothes on the floor a second before Connor lifted her like a rag doll and sat her on the kitchen counter a few steps away. He really was incredibly strong.

He positioned her just the way he wanted, her pussy at the perfect height as her ass slid forward on the polished countertop. Without preliminaries, he shoved into her, parting her slick tissues with little difficulty. This time, his rhythm felt like one long, orgasmic climax that started when he began to move. He was already primed. It wouldn't take long. She'd already almost blacked out from the sheer force of the pleasure he gave her.

Josie could see Darius over Connor's shoulder, watching. She'd never thought of herself as an exhibitionist before, although she knew all shifters were to some extent, but seeing the rapt look on Darius's face sent her over an even higher cliff of ecstasy as Connor fucked her on the kitchen counter.

She'd never seen or done anything as raunchy as this in her life, but she already wanted everything they could give her. The spasms of pleasure hit her again as Connor pushed hard into her in fast jabs that made her whimper and moan. She screamed when he came, his hot spurts of come sending her into the largest tremor of completion yet.

Connor and she gasped for air. Darius looked ready for action again as he stalked toward them. He looked deliberately at the place where she and Connor were joined.

"I want more," Darius said simply. The growl in his voice stoked her fire once again. She wouldn't have believed it if she wasn't living it.

Connor pulled out slowly, letting the sensations linger, then stepped away as Darius lifted her into his arms and headed toward her bedroom.

She looked around quickly at the kitchen to make sure nothing potentially dangerous had been left unattended.

The rest of the kitchen cleanup could wait.

There were much more important things to do at the moment.


Stewart Mathieson and his mate Cindy greeted them as they left Josie's Jeep in the parking area a few yards from the big main house. Several of the cougars were outside, preparing a barbeque pit. It looked like the Alpha and his mate were overseeing the setup when Josie pulled in. They walked forward to meet her with cautious smiles on their faces.

*Bianca D'Arc*

Stewart held out his hand to her first. Josie knew it was because he knew she was snowcat and despite the fact she was only half, it was enough to draw unwanted attention—even reverence—from other cat shifters.

"Greetings, Alpha. I'm Josephine Marpa. We spoke on the phone." They shook hands.

"It's an honor to meet you, Ms. Marpa."

"Please, call me Josie. And these are Darius and Connor. My mates."

Stewart's eyebrow rose. His wife, bless her heart, gave Josie an envious wink.

"Are you also snowcat?" Stewart asked as he shook hands with the twins.

"No. We are dragon."

An uncomfortable silence stretched as the Alpha pair looked at the twins in confusion.

"Dragon?" Stewart echoed finally.

"That's one of the things I came here to talk to you about. You see, Darius and Connor aren't from around here."

"Not from Oregon?" Cindy asked hopefully.

"Not from this world," Connor answered politely. "We were brought here from our own world during a magical storm."

Stewart backed up a step and grinned. "You're kidding, right? This is some kind of joke."

"I assure you it is not." Connor tried to be polite. Josie could tell both twins were near to losing their temper. Apparently dragons didn't like to be questioned.

"We have no time for this. I will demonstrate." Darius stepped away and headed for the fire pit the cougars were trying to light.

Josie wanted to stop him, but he was too fast even for her. Between one blink and the next, the walking figure of Darius was replaced by a hulking black dragon that sent cougars in human form scurrying in fear as he breathed a stream of fire into the prepared coals. They burned to perfection in five seconds flat.

Darius, in dragon form turned to look at them, propping one clawed hand on his hip as if waiting for their reaction, and Josie couldn't help but be amused. A single hiccupping giggle turned into outright laughter as Connor grinned with her. She turned back to the stunned Alpha pair.

"I'm sorry. I know it's a lot to take in." She talked as she tried to stop laughing. "They really are dragons, and they really aren't from this world."

"I believe you." The Alpha turned back to her, his jaw slack with shock. "You're a dragon too?" he asked Connor.

"Yes. Darius and I are twins in every respect, though I am a few minutes older."

"Son of a gun." Stewart watched, transfixed as Darius walked back toward them, shifting form as he moved. The black dragon was replaced by a man wearing black clothing in a matter of moments. "Your clothes go with you?"

Connor seemed surprised by the question. "Is that not how it is with you?"

"No. We can't take anything into the shift with us. We go in naked and come out the same way."

"That would cause logistical problems if you did not have clothing handy wherever you landed. Or is public nakedness acceptable in this world?"

"It is among shifters, for the most part," Josie answered. "Not among humans. You could get arrested for appearing nude in public. Shifters have to plan ahead or stay in animal form until they get someplace safe."

"That must be very limiting," Connor agreed. "I know for a fact Darius could never plan that far in advance. He'd wind up being naked wherever he went."

Josie thought privately that with a body like his, very few women would mind, but wisely kept the comment to herself. Slowly, the scattered cougars crept back toward them. Josie looked up to find they were surrounded by curious cats in both human and cat form. Connor seemed to recognize it at the same moment.

"This is a cougar?" he asked, pointing to the nearest feline. "They look very much like the mountain cats of Shindar, though their ears aren't as pointy."

"Another name for cougar is mountain lion." Josie supplied the information, surprised to hear of any kind of similarity between Earth animals and those from their world.

"I hate to ask this of you, especially after seeing that, but we need to see you are who and what you claim to be." The Alpha gave her a serious look that she understood. These people didn't know her. They needed some kind of proof before they extended the full hand of friendship to her.

"Of course." Josie stepped back and let the change come. Her cat rejoiced at being let free and rubbed up against Connor and Darius, twining about their legs as they reached down to stir their fingers in the tufts of white fur around her ears. She sat on her hindquarters, allowing the Alpha and his people to see her, waiting.

"Forgive me for doubting you, my lady. It's an honor to have you with us." The Alpha made a sign of respect, as did his people, the ones in cat form, vocalizing with welcoming screeches and growls.

Josie let the cat bask in their greeting, then shifted back to human form. Like the dragons, her clothing came with her. It had always been that way for her, and she hadn't questioned it until she'd met her first non-snowcat shifter. That sort of shifting was definitely not the norm. Only the most magical of beings could do it.

"That must be nice, to not have to scrounge for clothes," Cindy said as Josie came back to her human form. Her voice held a hint of good-natured envy.

"I'd heard that about your kind, but I've only ever seen it once before today. I knew a snowcat named Tzu once."

Josie recognized the name. "A great teacher among my grandfather's people. He taught me forestry, and how to find and use medicinal plants."

"You grew up in Tibet?" Cindy asked.

"Only for a few years. My mother was French Canadian. I'm only half snowcat."

"Only half?" The Alpha male seemed truly surprised. "Then the Goddess is definitely smiling on you. I've never seen a smoother shift or felt more magic in the air—except for your dragon friend. Thanks for getting the barbeque off to a good start. I don't know about you, but I'm famished. Will you three join us for dinner?"

"We'd be delighted." This was going even better than Josie had hoped.

They were introduced to the other cougars, and then the men headed over to the barbeque pit to work on spitting the pig they intended to roast. Cindy took Josie over to the picnic tables where the women were setting things up much earlier than they'd originally planned, thanks to the dragons in their midst. They asked her a few questions about being snowcat, which she didn't mind, and other questions about Darius and Connor, which she did mind. Apparently the ladies didn't realize she was mated to both men, and some were eyeing them with a predatory gleam. Josie straightened them out as politely as possible, and after that they seemed to rub along better. At least on her end.

The picnic tables were on the side of the house with a gorgeous view of the gorge through the trees. The lush vegetation appealed to her senses. The fine mist that was habitual in this part of Oregon kept everything green and growing most of the time.

When Connor shifted to dragon form, Josie halted in her tracks, fearing something was wrong, but she shouldn't have worried. The cats stood back and allowed him to roast the pig with just a few breaths of flame. It was clear he'd done this before. In dragon form, he stepped back to consider the roast as he worked on it, twirling the heavy spit in one giant clawed hand as if it was as light as a toothpick. He really was something to behold.

"Well would you look at that." Cindy and the other women seemed as transfixed by the sight as Josie was.

"We've apparently got the dragon," one of the other ladies commented. "Now all we need are the knights in shining armor."

As the women laughed, no one heard Darius approach. Several of the women jumped when he spoke right behind them.

"There are many knights in my land, but few wear armor that shines. It is best to dull down any metal surfaces lest they make better targets for archers."

"There really are knights?" Cindy was a little less obvious in her awe than the rest of the women, but then she was an Alpha female and leader of the rest. "I thought knights were supposed to slay dragons. Yet you sound like you admire them."

Darius scowled. "I don't know how it was when dragons roamed your world. In our land, knights partner with dragons. They live with them and fight alongside them."

"Do you have a knight partner?"

Darius laughed but caught himself when some of the ladies bristled. "Your pardon, please." Oh, he was charming when he tried. Heck, even when he didn't, he could charm a female of any species with one hand tied behind his back, Josie thought. "Black dragons are like you—shapeshifters. We do not partner with knights. We lead both the humans and dragons."

"There are other dragons? Ones that don't shift?" Cindy seemed truly impressed by the idea, and Josie was enjoying hearing about their world, so different from hers.

"Many. Of every color of the rainbow. Most live within the borders of our land. Some, like the wild Ice Dragons, live where they choose, usually in the coldest places, and they go their own way."

"That is amazing." Cindy spoke for the rest of the women, who wore varying expressions of awe and rapt attention on their faces.

Until a big black dragon loomed up behind Darius. Connor had arrived, with the entire pig on the spit in his claws. Stewart was at his side, grinning from ear to ear.

"We dine early, thanks to our guest."

The ladies rushed to finish laying out plates and utensils while Connor began slicing the pig with his razor sharp talons. Josie watched, amazed at how precisely he worked with such large...well...knives on the ends of his fingers. That's what they amounted to. Sure, she had pretty sharp claws when she shifted, but they were at most a few inches long. Connor's were over a half a foot—maybe longer—and they looked much sharper than her own claws ever were.

"Connor is showing off for your friends." Darius sidled up beside her. "He wanted to impress them."

"He's doing an awfully good job." She watched as the cougar men helped the dragon by holding up plates for the slices of pork.

Darius chuckled. "Good. We want to help in any way possible, and I'll admit it's hard to know what to do in this world. If we were home, we'd be able to handle everything. Here, we're at a loss. It's not a comfortable feeling."

"I can imagine. But don't worry. So far, everything's under control. As long as we stay among shifters, you'll probably be welcomed—or at least respected. Out among the non-magical population, you're going to have to be very, very careful. Actually, you're going to have to let me do most of the talking."

Darius nodded gravely and it was the most serious she'd ever seen him. "We are familiar with covert operating in foreign lands. You are our guide, love. We will do our best not to increase your danger."

They ate dinner and sat around outside until long after dark. It was the first time in a long time that Josie had enjoyed the company of a group of shifters. It was good to see the way this clan worked. The Alphas ruled the rest with a fair hand if she was any judge of character, and the rest of the clan—those who were present—seemed happy and relaxed in the presence of their leaders. It was a very good sign.

As the younger members of the clan were sent off to bed, the Alpha male came to speak with Josie.

"You and your friends are welcome to bunk here in the clan house for the night. My mate and I will arrange for transport and let you know what we can work out. I have some friends at PDX." He named the international airport by its call letters. "I don't think it'll be too hard to get your friends out of the country. Shifters and other magical types often need to travel on the down-low, so we've done this kind of thing a few times before."

Josie felt a weight lift off her shoulders. "Then I did the right thing in calling you. Thank you, Alpha. I can't tell you what a relief that is to hear."

"I hope that if and when you return, you'll consider running with our clan from time to time."

Josie understood what an honor the Alpha was bestowing with the invitation. She bowed her head in acknowledgement. "Thank you, Alpha. If I return here, I think I'd like that very much."

# Chapter Five

"Will you join us for a quick run before bed?" Cindy extended the invitation to Josie. It was only polite to agree to a quick run with her hosts, but she worried about what her mates might get up to while they were gone.

"I'd be honored," Josie replied, then shot a worried glance at the twins, standing near the fire pit with Stewart and a few other men as the women finished clearing the tables. "Um...what about them?"

"Well, the clan owns this side of the gorge for about a mile either way. We only allow other shifters to live on our land, and we're quite a ways from the city or even the suburbs up here. Still, we should check with Stewart and see what he thinks."

After consulting the Alpha and talking it over with the twins, they arrived at the conclusion that as long as they stuck to cover, the moonless night would be enough concealment for a short flight. Josie wasn't convinced, but the men outnumbered her. It seemed the cougars wanted to watch their new dragon friends fly, and nothing Josie said was going to stop it.

She couldn't blame them really. It wasn't every day a creature straight out of Arthurian legend showed up on your doorstep for a barbeque. If she wasn't so worried about them being seen, she would have agreed wholeheartedly.

When the small group assembled by the back porch and

the cougars started disrobing in preparation for shifting form, Josie politely turned her back and called on her snowcat. The twins followed suit, and the trio waited for their hosts to join them.

The cougars were a little smaller than Josie was in shifted form. They also blended into the forest night better than she did. The snowcat's white fur sparkled against the dark greens and browns of the forest. Josie knew the snowcat's natural habitat was high in the mountains of the Himalayas. Her patterned coat was meant to blend in with snow and gray rock. Plus, she, well, for lack of a better word, glowed.

The snowcat's greater magic lent her a somewhat-ethereal glow that surrounded her like an aura and at times, made her seem almost translucent. Her grandfather had explained the phenomenon as residual magic leaking around the snowcat's form. She wasn't sure exactly what it was. She only knew it was part of the reason most other shifters thought of snowcats with an almost-godlike awe. That, and the fact that they were rare and seldom traveled beyond their village in the Himalayas.

The cougars surrounded her, watching her as if to see what she'd do. The dragons launched into the air and took everyone's attention off Josie, for which she was grateful. In the tumult of two sets of dragon wings causing a small gale, she set off into the woods, alert for any scent trails that would allow her a small chase, though she wouldn't hunt to kill this night. Her appetite had been satisfied by the delicious barbecue. No, this hunt would be for fun and as a test of skill only.

Josie knew she'd be easily seen in the dark forest. She wasn't trying to lose the cougars. She just didn't want them deferring to her. By taking off on her own, she'd made it clear that they could do the same or join her. It was up to them.

Stewart and Cindy did join her after a few minutes, where

several scent trails converged. Josie was following a fox and after a few seconds of sniffing, it was clear the other two were on the same trail. With an eager lope, they set off together taking turns ranging to the side of the small game trail while one or the other would follow the scent.

About a hundred yards later, they saw the little red vixen. And more importantly, she saw them. The chase was on.


Darius and Connor flew carefully at first, following the collection of cougars and their brightly shining mate as they prowled through the trees.

*"She's not very good at blending in, is she? Why does she glow like that?"* Darius asked his brother in the privacy of their minds.

*"Magic, I presume. Chances are, with a name like* snowcat, *her people are bred for colder climes. I bet she'd blend right in on a field of snow and ice. Those big paws would do well on such terrain."*

*"Good point. Sad that she sticks out like a sore thumb here. This forest is too moist and rich. Too green and brown for her to blend in any way."*

They watched her catch a scent, then they followed as she began chasing a small red blur. That thing was fast, whatever it was. Josie and her cougar friends were even faster, for all their larger size. The twin dragons admired the skill and speed of the cats below as they ran their prey to ground with a triumphant howl.

The little red creature was allowed to run away, to live and be hunted perhaps, another day. The twins decided they liked the fact that the cougar shifters were able to refrain from killing something they didn't need for sustenance. Killing for killing's sake was never a good sign in people or animals.

As the group ranged back toward the house, Darius and Connor decided to stretch their wings a bit. They passed a small clearing where some of the cats had claimed a high perch on an outcropping of rock and Darius did some maneuvers to give them a bit of a show.

*"Where are you going?"*

*"They can see us from there if we take a turn over the water."* There was a wide river with little water traffic at this time of night.

*"Josie will not like it if we are seen by others."*

*"There is no moon, Con. No boats on the water near enough to see us, and only shifters on this side of the river. With their eyesight, they will be able to see us, but not much else will. They seem fascinated by dragons, so why not show them a little bit of what we can do. It'll feel good to stretch our wings."*

As usual, Darius talked his brother into doing something against his better judgment. They winged away and swooped low over the water, skimming their talons across the murky surface, then rose in a practiced swoop and dove again heading the other way.

As they neared the clearing on the side of the gorge they could see the ghostly white shape of their mate in shifted form. She was surrounded by the other cats, watching them with gleaming eyes. With unspoken agreement, they headed toward the shore and the cover of the trees to shadow the cats' path back to the house.

Darius and Connor shifted back to their human forms as they walked into the backyard area. The cougars were already there, in various states of furriness and undress. Josie waited, facing the woods, as if looking for them.

Darius walked up to her and bowed low. "You are magnificent on the hunt, my lady. It was a privilege to watch."

"I'd imagine," Stewart said as he joined them, tugging on the hem of his shirt as he approached, "she'd be even better in snow."

A white shimmer surrounded her. Seconds later Josie appeared in human form, fully clothed with a smile on her face as she turned to their host. "I do enjoy the colder climates, and the snowcat likes the feel of snow under her paws. She's a good climber and likes to test her agility on rocky slopes."

"A bit of a daredevil, then?" Stewart asked with a lopsided grin.

"Just a bit," Josie agreed as they began the trek toward the house as a group. The group of cougars had diminished in size. Connor assumed the rest would follow along later, either still on the hunt, or perhaps engaging in some activities best done in pairs.

Their host walked with them back toward the house. "I'll finalize the arrangements in the morning for your flight. For now, you're welcome to the hospitality of our house. I hope you'll have a good night."

He left them at the door with a slight nod of his head. It was the deference of one Alpha to another. High praise, she knew.

The room they were given for the night was luxurious compared to the bare necessities in her cabin. She lived simply up in the high country, and she didn't mind it at all, though she enjoyed creature comforts like any woman. The big bathroom was something she wanted to explore...with her mates.

She sent them a come-hither look as she dropped her clothes and turned on the taps. Darius and Connor weren't far behind. Both were undressing at record pace as the tub filled with hot water. They didn't bat an eye at the modern plumbing.

"You have hot water and baths where you live?" She looked

at them over her shoulder as she ran her fingers through the steaming water, adjusting the faucet to get it to be just the right temperature.

"Of course," Connor answered. "Being dragons, we often heat the water ourselves, but some Lairs keep a communal cistern that feeds into the pipes that lead to each chamber. If the Lair is big enough, there are hot and cold cisterns kept ready at all times."

"Then there are the larger baths fed by hot springs. Everyone uses those for both cleansing and recreation." Darius gave her a saucy wink. "Dragons, as a general rule, have exhibitionist tendencies that rub off on their knight partners from time to time. It's not uncommon to find a set of knights frolicking in the baths with their mate while their dragon partners enjoy a mating flight."

"Your world sounds very different from this one." Josie marveled at the images he inspired with his words while Darius took her in his arms. Connor came up behind her, boxing her in with their warmth and masculine hardness. "But many shapeshifters have exhibitionist tendencies. They spend a lot of time either naked or in their beast forms. They've been known to get it on in the forest regardless of who might be looking."

"So shapeshifters in your world like to be watched?" Connor's deep voice made his wicked words even more enticing.

"I guess so." Her voice was breathy with rising desire as they crowded her. Both men were naked, hard and oh so desirable. "Snowcats, however, are a little more circumspect."

"Hmm...we'll have to see what we can do to change your mind," Darius teased her even as he dipped his head close to steal a kiss. She fell deep under his spell as Connor's hands came around her waist and moved lower to delve between her legs.

She widened her stance, helping him achieve his goal. She was sure he found her wet and wanting as she arched her back, rubbing her ass over the delectable hardness of his cock. Oh yeah, that was what she wanted.

"Do you think this tub is big enough for the three of us?" Connor whispered in her ear.

She looked down at the small swimming pool, filled with heavenly warm water. "It's a Jacuzzi. It's meant for more than one."

"What's a—?" Darius asked as she bent to flip the switch that turned on the jets. "Ah, now that's different. We don't have anything like that outside the hot springs."

Both men seemed interested in the motion of the water, watching it instead of focusing on her. She'd see about that.

Josie slipped out of from between them and stepped into the huge tub. That seemed to wake them up, and they quickly followed her in. Water sloshed. She'd intentionally filled the tub only halfway, knowing the three of them would be moving around. Vigorously, if all went as planned.

She smiled secretively as she lured her men to her side. The huge oval tub was made for up to four. There was enough room to squeeze all three of them together on one side, if they didn't mind bumping against each other intimately.

No, she didn't mind that at all. Not one little bit. In fact, she intended to get a whole lot closer to them both before the night was through.

Apparently Darius and Connor were thinking the same thing. Darius grabbed her around the waist, lifting her in the water until she sat in the V formed by his legs at one end of the oval tub. She could feel his cock bobbing against her ass and suddenly she didn't want to draw this out any longer. She wanted him. Now.

Josie tried to turn in his arms.

"Whoa, where are you going?" Darius's big hands stopped her movement.

"I don't want to wait, Darius. I want you now."

He leaned close to her neck, speaking against her ear. "Then now you shall have me." He lifted her as easy as if she weighed nothing at all, settling her slowly on the hard rod of his cock. The slick water and her own eagerness allowed deep penetration with little effort.

"Yes," she groaned when he was seated fully within her. The sound echoed off the gleaming tile of the bathroom. She tried to move, but he held her still.

"You've got what you want," Darius purred in her ear. "This time we take it slow and easy. You think you can handle that, little girl?"

Slow and easy would kill her. She just knew it.

Connor sat back at the other end of the tub, watching them with hooded eyes. Darius lifted her up slowly, then lowered her on his cock, all while Connor watched. The sensation was wickedly stimulating.

"I think she likes being watched after all, Dar." Connor licked his lips as he watched his twin finger her nipples. When his gaze rose to meet hers, Josie felt a small explosion of need in her body. She whimpered as Darius lifted her and lowered her again. It was an agonizingly slow motion that made her want to scream—both in pleasure and frustration.

Darius rocked her on his shaft, drawing out her pleasure. Connor watched it all, rubbing his cock beneath the surface of the sloshing water. She could see the motion of his hand and the rippling of his tight muscles as he worked himself. It made her want more.

"Please, Darius." She didn't really know what she was asking for. Thank heaven Darius seemed able to read her mind. He began to thrust harder and faster, causing the water to ripple violently around them. She didn't care. They could flood the whole damned house as long as Darius kept doing what he was doing.

Connor leaned forward as his twin repositioned her. They caught her between them, Connor holding her by the shoulders as Darius maneuvered for more leverage. It was worth the slight wait. When Darius pushed in again, he went deeper and more forcefully than he had before. The change of angle also hit something inside her that made her entire body clench in need. She couldn't take much of this.

She began to moan on every thrust as her completion drew near. Darius increased his pace as Connor murmured encouragement. He watched every sway of her breasts with an avaricious glint in his eye. She held his gaze, promising him without words that he was next...if she survived. The way it was looking, she might not.

Darius pushed her higher, the water around them swishing in counterpoint to his harsh movements, driving her onward. Connor's hands held her steady, suspended between her men.

"Almost there, my love," Darius whispered, his ardor intensifying that last little bit.

"Darius!" She felt the climax looming in his possession, heard it in his voice. He was close and so was she. So close, in fact, that all he had to do—

"Come for me, Josie. Come now."

That was all she needed. He commanded her response, and she gave it to him. Shudders shook her body as orgasm hit her like a tidal wave. Darius followed a heartbeat behind, filling her body and soul.

When the storm dissipated they were both breathing hard. Connor was there to catch her, lifting her in his arms as he stepped from the giant tub. He rubbed her sensitive skin with a heated towel, caring for her as if she were the most precious thing in the world to him.

She felt cherished. Pampered and spoiled by two of the most delectable men she had ever known—or would ever know. After these two, she knew she would be spoiled for anyone else. They were her mates. The only ones for her. If she succeeded in helping them find a way back to their own world, she didn't know if she could go on living without them. That was a bridge she would have to cross when they got to it. For now, she intended to bask in their attention and lavish her love on them as well. For as long as it lasted.

Connor carried her to the bed after drying her with pleasant thoroughness. He'd only swiped the towel at his own aroused body, but he'd taken time with her, rekindling the fires that had only been banked, never put out. By the time he joined her on the big bed they'd been given for the night, she was purring, ready for more of her men.

This time, Darius watched from the sidelines, and she suddenly realized they were as good as their word—they were trying to see if she could enjoy being watched. The very idea spiked her arousal.

She liked it when either of her mates watched her being pleasured by the other, but she wasn't sure how she might deal with a stranger's eyes on them as they made love. As in all things carnal, she'd let her mates guide her. These two rascals no doubt had vastly more experience than she did in such matters. Jealousy wanted to take hold, but it was impossible to be mad at them for things that had happened before they ever even met. Now that they were mates, the twins' prowling days were over.

Connor made love to her hard and fast. He couldn't wait after watching that steamy scene in the bath. Neither could Josie. She welcomed him into her arms and between her thighs with abandon. He pounded into her, making her come hard and fast, screaming his name as ecstasy took her.

When he was done, Darius climbed over her once more. He hadn't been unaffected by watching his twin. And so it went for most of the night.

Josie was sore when she woke, but she couldn't disguise the grin of utter satisfaction on her face. Her men wore identical expressions. The three of them no doubt looked smug when the joined the cougars for a quick breakfast before the Alpha arrived to take them to the airport.

They took their leave of the cats with genuine warmth and invitations from the cougars to return anytime. Josie felt truly welcome among them without the usual pressure of being snowcat. With her men around there was something far more interesting for the cougars to focus on. What was one half-snowcat when compared to two fire-breathing dragons?

Josie hadn't seen the guys since early that morning when Stewart had escorted them to the charter portion of the big airport. She would board the usual way, assured by the cougar Alpha that he would be able to smuggle the twins aboard the aircraft via some friends in the charter area. She didn't know how it all worked, but she trusted the Alpha to do his best.

She only hoped it was good enough. Josie was a nervous wreck when the time came to board the jumbo jet that waited on the tarmac. She'd watched out the windows while various service vehicles docked with the aircraft, delivering all kinds of supplies. Crew members had come and gone while she watched and, though she'd strained to catch some glimpse of her men, she hadn't seen any sign of them anywhere.

Josie jumped in her seat when the boarding announcement for her flight was called. If all went as planned, the twins would be waiting for her on the plane. If they weren't there, with security the way it was today, she'd be stuck on a plane bound for China with no idea of their fate. They were taking a risk, but there seemed to be no other way.

She was the first in line to board when the gate attendant started taking tickets. She rolled her carry-on bag up the ramp toward the hatch and was relieved to smell a hint of cat up ahead. Cougar, if she wasn't mistaken. The blonde flight attendant who waited to welcome her was most definitely a shifter. The knowing smile clinched it as the woman pointed her toward the back of the plane.

Josie went as fast as she could through the tight space between the seats. It was supposed to be an aisle. It was more like a very narrow gap between the rows and rows of seats on the big plane. Nerves assailed her as she made her way out of first class, then business class and into the main cabin where everyone else would sit.

Her heart started beating again when she saw two figures waiting for her in the last row. Darius sported a hooded sweatshirt that he wore with the hood pulled low over his head as he slouched in his seat. Connor waited for her, appearing wide-awake and watchful. It was probably wise to hide one of their faces. At least during boarding. They were handsome enough to draw attention from every female on the flight without there being two of them. Better to only let one be seen at a time. Twins were much too memorable.

Josie went to them, and Connor helped wrestle her bag into the overhead compartment. She smiled, thinking how impressed he'd been by her wheeled bag and the fabrics from which it was made when she'd packed it the day before. Wherever they were from, they didn't have technology like they had on Earth. What little they'd told her about their world made it sound vaguely medieval.

"Any problems?" Connor gave her a quick peck on the cheek as he settled in the seat beside her. Darius had the window seat, and she was between the twins, in the middle. The flight wasn't full. The empty seats meant they might have room to stretch out later, but for now, she liked the security of sitting between her two mates.

Two mates. She still couldn't really wrap her head around that idea.

"No problems. I was worried about you two, though. Was it okay?"

"Your friends took us in a large, square vehicle from the building where you left us to here. We went across a vast distance of what he called a runway, though we saw no creatures running there. And the stone was surprisingly flat."

She stifled a giggle. They really had no technology. "First of all, it's not stone. Well, not really. It's cement—a mixture of rock, sand and other stuff with water that we spread to make the roads flat. When it dries, it's hard like rock and lasts for years. Like the roads we were on yesterday." She'd had fun trying to explain macadam to them, though her knowledge of construction was sadly limited. Connor nodded, so she supposed her explanation was good enough. "As far as what a runway is..." She tried to think of a way to prepare him for what was to come, but was at a loss. "This plane needs room to get up to speed before it can lift off."

"Then the wings do not flap?" Darius asked from beside her, though he appeared to be asleep, slouched against the hull. "They looked rather stiff when we saw this vehicle from the outside. I'll admit, I have my doubts about it being able to fly."

"No, the wings don't flap. The engines propel us at such high speed, lift is created under the metal wings that allows us to fly." She wasn't much better at explaining aeronautics, but the men didn't seem to mind. "You'll see. Once we get up to speed we'll shoot upward, and you'll be pushed back in your seats. You can watch out the window as they use the little flaps on the edges of the wings to change the shape of the wing and get airborne. It's pretty cool."

"If you say so." Connor looked uncertain. "I'd prefer to fly myself, but I'm willing to give this method of flight a try. We looked over the skin of this vehicle and if it begins to fall, we can always tear it open and shift in the air."

"Planes seldom fall out of the sky. Not unless something catastrophic happens, like losing cabin pressure. So don't tear anything open, all right? The metal skin on this thing needs to stay intact so everyone can stay safe."

"We have done nothing," Darius protested. "We merely have reconnoitered the situation. It is useful to be prepared for all contingencies."

"Well then, tell me this. Can dragons fly at heights over thirty thousand feet? That's where we'll be, and that's why this cabin is pressurized. The air up there is too thin to breathe and freezing cold."

"How big is a foot in your measurements?" Connor looked skeptical.

"About like this." She held up her hands to give them an approximate size.

Connor looked to Darius, and both looked back to her hands, surprise on their faces. Darius was frowning, but neither twin answered her.

As the cabin filled up, the flight attendants started making their rounds, helping people get their gear stowed and find their seats. In addition to the cougar up front, two more of the stewards smelled like shifters to Josie. The Asian stewardess seemed to be some kind of raptor—probably an eagle, judging by her tawny hair and piercing eyes. The black-skinned male steward smelled distinctly of lion shifter.

It was odd to see a lion in such a subservient role. Lion shifters had a reputation much like that of their animal cousins. The king of the jungle was a fierce predator and cunning protector. Many lion shifters fulfilled the same kinds of roles, often in the military, and particularly in Special Forces.

Josie watched the man as best she could through the crowd of boarding humans. He caught her eye and winked with a bright grin. He was well aware of her interest and seemed comfortable with it, which was strange.

"Why is Duke smiling at you?" Darius actually sounded jealous.

"I can't figure him out, and he caught me staring at him. A smile is better than a roar, I always say. Especially from a lion shifter."

"Lion? Is that what he is? Big cat. Golden ruff around his neck?" Connor looked at the man with interest in his gaze. "We have heard of such creatures living in the deserts to the south, across the great sea, but I have never seen one."

"Lions are known as the king of beasts for good reason. Lion shifters are rare, but mighty. It's just strange to see one employed as a flight attendant."

"He was introduced to us as an air marshal, though we are not familiar with the term," Darius supplied.

The big man's presence made sense to her after hearing that. "Air marshals protect passengers from those who would cause mischief on airplane flights. Terrorists, hijackers, criminals and crazy people have caused airplanes to crash in the past, killing many people. As a result, a lot of flights have undercover marshals hidden in plain sight—either as passengers or as crew—ready to stop any trouble before it begins."

"A Guard, then." Connor's expression held new respect. "It is a worthy occupation if he is as mighty a warrior as you believe."

The safety briefing began, all passengers having boarded. Connor jumped slightly when the marshal's voice first sounded over the intercom. They could see him speaking into the phone attached to a nearby bulkhead, so it was clear who was speaking.

Josie pulled out the safety card from the back of the seat in front of her, and the twins followed suit. They looked at the pictures of possible disaster scenarios, and she could feel their agitation. After that, their attention was focused on the lion shifter and the safety demonstrations given by the other crewmembers.

Safety instruction finished, the plane began to pull away from the terminal. Darius had his nose pressed against the glass, watching everything that went on outside. Connor's eyes were closed as if he were in some kind of trance.

"Are you okay?" She touched his hand.

Connor nodded. "I am watching through my brother's eyes. It requires concentration."

"That's amazing. You can really do that?"

"Yes. Though we do not do it often. In this case, Darius grabbed the window seat before I could get to it. We are very curious about how this metal tube will fly." His eyes were closed, but he seemed able to converse with her normally. "There is a lot of equipment involved. We have nothing like this in our world."

"Neither did we, until the past fifty years or so. Technology has really come into its own over the past century. Before that, we probably lived much like you do." Glancing over Darius's shoulder, she saw that they were lined up for takeoff near the end of the runway.

With a roar of jet engines, the plane in front of them started its roll down the runway. It leaped into the air moments later, shooting upward in a beautiful display. Then it was their turn.

Josie took Connor's hand as she rested her head back against the seat. The plane's engines whined as they went to full throttle and in a burst of speed, barreled down the runway. She squeezed Connor's fingers as the wheels left the pavement, and they shot into the air. The noise level increased as the engines strained. A thunk told her the landing gear had retracted into the belly of the plane, and they were on their way.

As the plane began to level out from its takeoff climb, Connor's eyes opened and he turned to her. A frown creased the space between his eyebrows.

"All in all, I prefer to fly on my own."

"But the speed, Con." Darius tore his gaze from the window to protest. "We can't attain speed like this unless we're in a dive, and only for short periods. And we're so high."

"Be we are not in control. The metal tube decides where we will go," Connor argued.

"Actually, there are two men up in the cockpit who are flying the plane. They're called pilots," Josie put in.

"Like sea captains? We have pilots who navigate coastal waters, guiding larger ships through dangerous areas." Connor seemed to grasp the idea easily enough and if Josie wasn't mistaken, there were seafaring pilots on the coasts of many nations to this very day, doing the same duty Connor described.

"So then, it is they who decide where we go. That's better, I suppose, but I still prefer to choose my own path."

"We are flying so high and moving so fast, it almost feels like standing still," Darius observed. "No wind reaches us inside this metal tube. If it weren't for the noise and small drops of water streaking against the glass porthole here, I might not know we were actually moving."

"The water is from going through clouds on our way up," Josie supplied. "It's said if a pilot flies high enough, they can actually see the curvature of the Earth. I don't think we'll get that high, but we'll be above the clouds and sometimes you can see the lights of other planes out the window at night."

"They pass close enough that you can see them?" Connor asked.

"You can see the lights. As a rule, they keep a safe distance between planes. People on the ground keep track of every airplane in the sky and plan out courses for the pilots to follow so there's no danger of collision or getting caught in dangerous turbulence. The pilots are in radio contact with the ground and can speak to other planes in the vicinity."

"What is radio? Some kind of telepathy?" Darius asked.

"No. Few humans have any sort of psychic abilities. For that matter, few shifters do. A radio is a piece of electronic equipment that allows us to transmit messages from one place to another, within a certain range. It's technology. Not magic or any kind of psychic ability. Telepathy is rare in my world."

"Interesting." Connor's answer was casual as he watched the flight attendants deploy with their funny looking rectangular carts. "All dragons can speak mind to mind. Because of the way our mouths are shaped, it is impossible to speak aloud when in dragon form, so we use telepathy, but not everyone can hear us. Only knights and a very few women in each generation are gifted with the ability to communicate with dragons in their minds."

*"Can you hear us, mate?"* It was Darius's voice, but his mouth hadn't moved. She'd heard him in her mind.

*"She can,"* Connor's voice answered in her mind. He sounded both pleased and amused. *"It may take some time before you figure out how to speak back to us in this manner. We can help you learn."*

"Amazing..." Josie's voice trailed off, letting the idea sink into her mind. They were implying she could talk back in the same telepathic manner. The idea was tantalizing—like everything else about her new mates. Their world must be so cool.

The twins let her guide them through the refreshments and meal, which she could only guess looked vastly different from what they were used to. They seemed intrigued by plastic and amazed at how easily she threw everything away. Paper napkins seemed to surprise them as well, and she began to wonder if their world wasn't a bit barbaric.

What did they wipe their hands on? What did they eat with? Cloth and metal or carved wood, most likely, like they had in olden times on Earth. But she was a thoroughly modern girl, used to the modern North American culture. She'd spent time in Tibet and liked it, though life was a little rougher there—lived closer to the land without all the trappings of Western high-tech life.

If they made it to their destination, the twins would do better there. Of course, their Western features would make them stand out. They had dark hair and striking green eyes, two sides of the same coin and that coin was gorgeous. Yeah, they would stand out wherever they went.

# Chapter Six

Once the meals had been served and the plane settled down for the night's sleep period, the lion shifter and his raptor friend took seats near them. The back section of the plane was relatively empty and they could talk quietly and not be heard by the humans. Shifter hearing was much better than any human's.

"I am Ndukwe," the man introduced himself to her. "I did not have much time to speak with you before, but please pardon our curiosity." He looked from them to the female flight attendant and back, as if hesitating. "We hear you are snowcat." The inflection of the statement made it a question.

Josie nodded. "I am." She didn't see the need to go into detail about her mixed parentage. "And you are leo."

"Yes, cousin. Yuki is a golden eagle. And are your men truly...dragons?" The man's dark eyes held wonder as he gazed at the twins.

"I see word has already spread." Josie tried to suppress a chuckle.

"This kind of secret will be hard to keep, cousin." Josie liked the way the lion shifter claimed kinship with her snowcat. Both were among the most powerful cats in the world, and it was good to have the respect of equal footing. She knew the leo would give few others that honor. "So it is true?"

Connor offered his hand to the leo. "We are black dragons from the land of Draconia."

Ndukwe shook hands with Connor, then Darius, leaning across her to do the job right. She didn't mind. It was good to see the leo treat them as equals—even superiors—as well. She was able to observe them and realized they were used to such respect. They expected it. But they weren't obnoxious about it.

"Where is your land?" Yuki asked in a melodious voice.

"Nowhere we can explain," Darius said. "We were blown into a magical storm and the next thing we knew, we woke up in Josie's forest. It is similar, but not the same as the forests of our homeland. Or any land to which we have traveled."

"We believe powerful magic brought us here. And indeed, our journey was envisioned by someone we know to be a gifted seer. We didn't believe her when she warned us this was coming, but we certainly do now." A wry twist of Connor's lips was echoed by Darius's quiet guffaw.

"When you shift, you are black?" Ndukwe grinned, obviously pleased by the thought.

"All of our family is. Black dragons are the only ones who can shift form from human to dragon. All other dragons are just dragons," Connor said matter-of-factly.

"There are other kinds of dragons in your land?" Yuki seemed enthralled by the idea.

"Many." Connor seemed pleased to tell them about his world. Josie wondered if he'd ever see his home again, and if so, what that would mean to their relationship. Would she go with them? The thought boggled her mind. "There are dragons in every color of the rainbow and many combinations in between. Then there are wild Ice Dragons whose scales shine like mirrors, reflecting all colors back at you in a sparkly display. Our new sister-in-law adopted a baby Ice Dragon named Tor, and he is absolutely breathtaking after a roll in the sand to polish his scales."

"And though we've never seen it, there are tales of Snow Dragons even farther north. They are thought to be wild. We don't know much about them. They are supposed to be sparkly white, their scales like glistening snow."

They spent an hour or more talking with the flight attendants. Ndukwe, it turned out, was from Nigeria and Yuki was Japanese. Both were clearly in awe of the dragons in their midst and happy to help smuggle them on and off the plane.

When the flight ended, they were met by two shifter escorts at the terminal. The escorts had some sort of official capacity and were able to get them onto a smaller plane without any of the usual hassle imposed by the Chinese government. The two shifters—one was a tiger and one a wolf—asked for her to give them the traditional snowcat blessing, and she did so only feeling partially like a fraud. To them, she was snowcat. Nothing else mattered. Not her heritage or her Western looks.

When the twins stepped forward to add their own formal words to hers, the two shifters seemed to regard them with awe and a sort of stunned amazement. They had heard the rumors. Word had spread fast through the shifter community. Everyone seemed to know there were dragons in the world, heading for the snowcat sanctuary in the Himalayas.

Josie only hoped her grandfather didn't know yet. There were few phones anywhere near the snowcat village, so perhaps he hadn't heard. If so, she'd be lucky. She wanted to surprise him with the twins. She wanted to see his first reaction—not the one he'd had time to think about.

The plane to Tibet was much smaller and made funny noises she preferred not to think about. Safety standards in the Communist country weren't quite what they were in the West.

Connor took one of her hands as Darius took the other.

"Don't worry. This craft flies at a height we can handle with no problem. Should it falter, we can fly you to safety easily enough."

It comforted her to know they could rescue her should the plane take a nosedive. It also warmed her to know they were attuned to her moods already. They knew when she was scared out of her wits and why.

"It'll be okay," she insisted, but she didn't let go of their hands until they landed on a narrow runway high in the Himalayas.

Darius and Connor looked around with interest as they disembarked from the small plane, directly onto the tarmac. A small building in the distance was the airport terminal. As with their arrival on mainland China, a shifter escort was there to meet them. This one spoke only Tibetan and bowed in greeting, which Josie returned. She struggled to remember the language of her youth and was startled when Darius addressed the escort—a nervous-looking leopard shifter—in perfect Tibetan.

"Where did you learn this language?" Josie asked him in the same tongue.

"Am I speaking a different language?" Darius looked truly surprised.

"You are."

The leopard escort's eyes widened, and he began to pray.

"It could be the magic trinkets Shanya gave us," Connor observed, pulling the necklace from an inside pocket of his leather tunic. He held it in his hand, and Josie recognized it as a twin to the one his brother wore. It had the mark of a dragon chased in gold and silver. Handsome work in the shape of a small shield. Connor too, was speaking the native dialect.

Darius moved the collar of his tunic aside and displayed the matching necklace he wore. It gleamed against his bronze skin.

"One of the fair folk gave these to us before we departed on our journey. She was a seer and warned us that we would be making a quest to a far-off land. She was right about that part, at least." Darius raised an eyebrow in the direction of the surrounding snow-capped mountains.

"Fair folk? That's what Irishmen call elves, but they're just a myth." She waved one hand in dismissal of the idea.

"Like dragons, eh?" Darius grinned at her.

"All right, you have a point," she had to concede. Josie looked at the frightened escort who had retreated a few steps. She smiled at him, trying to ease his fear. He was young and untried, more frightened than he should have been. "What is your name?" She tried to speak softly, to encourage his trust.

"Zhao. I was sent to escort you, but I am not a true escort. I fear my skills will not be up to your standards, blessed one."

Oh, boy, this one had it bad. The snowcats liked to cultivate reverence among the other shifters, and this youngster had bought her grandfather's mumbo jumbo hook, line and sinker.

She took his arm and began to walk away from the plane. They couldn't stand on the tarmac all day. People were beginning to wonder about them.

"Don't worry, Zhao. I'm sure you'll do fine. My name is Josie. Do you have a vehicle?" He seemed to come out of his daze and nodded eagerly, gesturing toward the parking area.

They walked companionably toward the dilapidated van that waited. Darius and Connor took charge of her carry-on bag while she did her best to calm Zhao's nerves. They piled into the van and the young leopard got behind the wheel, more at ease with each moment.

"I can take you to the base of the mountain. We were not able to get word to the snowcat patriarch of your arrival. Sometimes we don't see anyone from the mountain for months at a time. I am sorry."

"Actually, I prefer to surprise my grandfather," Josie admitted.

"The patriarch is your grandfather? Then you are the ghostcat."

"The what?" Even Josie was surprised by the name. She had no idea the villagers at the base of her grandfather's mountain even knew of her existence. Of course, she had snuck down the mountain often enough as a youngster, seeking friends her own age. She'd even found a few among the village children, but her grandfather always came and got her, demanding she follow him back home.

"Forgive me." Zhao seemed embarrassed. "It is what some of us called the pale young girl who visited our village many years ago. We thought perhaps she'd died. It's good to know she lives and has fulfilled such a grand destiny. You walk with dragons, they say."

Josie was impressed the leopard had figured out and heard so much. The shifter grapevine must really be working overtime.

"Darius and Connor are dragons brought here from another world. We've come to see my grandfather to learn what he knows about where they come from. As you can imagine, it would be hard for dragon shifters to live in our modern world."

Zhao's eyes flicked back and forth between the road and his rearview mirror, in which he could see the twins. He looked awe-struck once again.

"It is hard for any shifter. I can only imagine how hard it would be for a dragon to hide his presence in this age of technology."

Zhao fell silent and Josie turned to the twins, who sat on the bench seat in the back of the small van.

"The village is used to shifters. It is one of the few places in the world we can roam, but even here, we have to be careful not to be seen by outsiders. If humans see us in our animal forms, we could be shot at or hunted. At least we look like animals people are used to seeing. There are no dragons in this world. If you two were seen, it would cause big trouble."

"It's kind of hard for us to hide, considering how big we get in our other form." Darius laughed, but she felt his unease. How would they live in this world? Josie only hoped her grandfather could offer some good advice.

Zhao stopped the van at the base of a trail that led up the mountain. The men got out and surveyed the area, looking upward with calculating eyes. Connor stowed the handles on her carry-on and adjusted the straps, sliding it onto her back.

She hadn't expected that. Sure, she could carry the thing, but she'd thought the twins would have a little more chivalry than to make her carry the bag when they had no luggage of their own. Then Connor walked off, away from the trail without so much as a word.

"Where are you going?" she called after him.

He didn't answer as a black fog surrounded him. A moment later, the dragon stood in his place. Darius took her hand and led her to his brother.

"He gets the honor of carrying you this time, but it's my turn next." Darius showed her where to place her foot on Connor's bent knee to climb up onto his back.

"We're flying up there?" She was shocked by the idea, surprised she hadn't realized what the twins intended.

"Of course. No sense walking through knee-deep snow when you can fly. It will be quicker and warmer this way." Darius turned to Zhao and shook the young man's hand, thanking him for the ride before he too, shifted shape into a black dragon.

Connor took a running start, expanding his wings and in two great sweeps of his tar black wings, they were airborne. It was like nothing she'd ever experienced before. Within moments, they were high above the ground, Zhao and his van turning to insignificant specks below.

Darius followed behind, bringing up the rear. Only seeing the glint of the sun off metal did she realize the intricate necklace had transformed into a plate of armor that covered his chest with a gleaming design. He was magnificent as he gained on them, flying beside them and winking one huge, jeweled peridot eye at her.

*"How do you like it?"* Josie jumped a little, realizing it was Darius's warm voice in her mind. Experimentally, she tried to send a message back.

*"I love it!"*

Whether he heard the words or not, she wasn't certain, but he seemed to get the gist of her feelings.

*"Is that the snowcat village?"* Connor's voice felt slightly different in her mind, distinctly unique.

She looked upward, realizing they'd covered the distance that usually took a full day to climb on foot, in less than a few minutes. Sure enough, she saw the curving lines of the dojo's roof in the distance.

"Yes! That's it!" she shouted aloud to be heard above the wind. It was cold up here, but with Connor's dragon warmth beneath her, she didn't really feel it. His dragon body was like a furnace, warm and toasty where they touched, even through

116

her layers of clothing. They drew nearer to the village, and she felt an odd sense of triumph that was quickly doused.

With dawning horror, she heard an alarm being sounded through the village. Bowmen appeared on the rooftops, and a few eager arrows were loosed.

"Stop!" She screamed over the wind, and pounded her fists on his hide, but Connor ignored her. Tears came to her eyes as she saw the glint of arrows flying toward them.

Connor seemed to hover, caught one tiny arrow in his claws, looked at it then threw it away in disgust. He veered away from the village, putting his body between her and the rain of arrows aimed their way.

*"Never fear, sweetheart. Darius will talk to them."*

"But the arrows!"

*"Such arrows cannot pierce our hide. They could damage your lovely skin however. We will wait in safety while Darius does his best to make them see reason."*

"Darius?"

Already some distance away, they flew well out of range of the village's weapons but were able to see the black dragon with his gleaming chest plate of armor land in the snow. People scattered and arrows flew, bouncing off his coal black hide. Flame came from his mouth. Josie could see he was careful not to hurt anyone or burn anything of importance. It was merely a show of his power.

A dragonish chuckle drifted from Connor's mouth. He aimed the stream of smoke away from her as they flew, gliding now as he followed a path back and forth in the sky so they could keep an eye on his twin and the village.

*"Dar is not the most tactful in our family, but we all had lessons in diplomacy as we grew up. He'll bring them around."*

"But their weapons. Won't they be able to hurt him now that he's so close?"

*"Such weapons as I just saw cannot hurt us."*

"But others can?"

*"As our mate, you will learn all our deepest secrets in time, my love."*

"How can I be sure he's safe unless I know what can hurt you? I know the kinds of weapons they have in the village. You don't."

*"A good point. Do they have diamond blades in that village?"*

To say she was surprised would be an understatement. "Not to my knowledge. Maybe on some rock cutting tools, but not on the weapons."

*"Then there is little to fear. Diamond blades are the only things we know of sharp enough to pierce dragon scale. Of course, some things like skith venom can hurt like the dickens and do major damage if we don't wash it off quickly."*

"What is a skith?"

*"Worm like creatures as big as me and Dar. They squirm along the ground and live in rocky places eating anything that comes by, including people. They spit venom that is as corrosive as the strongest acid. You do not have such creatures in your world? If so, you are fortunate. They were created to be a dragon's worst enemy and inhabit the neighboring land of Skithdron."*

Josie was intrigued, but her attention was split between his words and the action on the cliff. The arrows had stopped, and she saw her grandfather walk forward to meet Darius, who remained in dragon form. Perhaps they were ready to calm down and see what the dragons wanted.

"That's my grandfather," she whispered, but apparently

Connor heard her soft words.

*"Good. Dar is more likely to make headway with the leader. It is a good sign that he came out to parlay."*

Connor flew a little closer on the next pass, and she could see the old man's eyes turned toward her.

*"The old man wants to know if the daughter of Marpa has come home to stay?"* Darius's voice sounded through all three minds.

"To stay?" Josie was suddenly frightened. She didn't want to stay here. She wanted to be with her mates—wherever that led her. "I don't know. I go where you go. He needs to understand that."

*"I'll make it clear,"* Darius assured her. *"They've put their weapons down. I'll shift, and we'll see how that goes. If they don't attack me as soon as they think I'm vulnerable, chances are it'll be safe for you to land."*

"Be careful," Josie whispered, hoping Darius would get the message. She wasn't sure how this telepathy thing worked, but it was a handy gift. She'd learn, if at all possible, so she could talk with her mates the way they talked with her.

On the ledge, Josie saw the shimmering black cloud envelop the dragon for a split second before Darius, the man, appeared in his place. He was clothed in black leather and the gray hooded sweat jacket he'd worn on the plane, his gleaming dark hair vibrant in the sun. He was taller and broader than the men who surrounded him, confident in a way few men were.

God, how she loved him.


Connor flew closer, going in cautiously. The entire village, it seemed, watched their progress as he alighted on the snowy edge of the small town.

*"Slowly now, my love. Use my knee to step down and do it with the dignity you wish to portray. Remember, you are a princess among these people. Do not let your grandfather intimidate you in any way. You are our mate now. He has no power over you except that which you give him."*

The pep talk was exactly what she needed. "I love you." Josie bent to kiss Connor's sinuous neck before stepping off, just as he'd instructed, with as much dignity as she could muster.

*"As I love you,"* Connor said in her mind just before he shifted form. Warm hands came down on her shoulders as he stood behind her. Darius joined them, taking her hand as he walked her forward to face her grandfather in a grand show of ceremony. These guys certainly had the theatrics that her grandfather liked down pat.

"Sir, may we present your granddaughter, our mate." Darius sensed there would be outrage from some of the villagers.

"Both of you?" The elder seemed surprised by his own outburst, but the anger in his eyes demanded answer.

Connor moved from behind her to stand beside her, one twin on each side. In such a position it was easy to see the men were as identical in human form as they were as dragons. More shock passed through the villagers, and her grandfather's eyes widened.

"It is the way of dragons," Connor said with a careless shrug, though she knew he watched every nuance of reaction carefully. "There are few women willing or able to partner our kind."

"Granddaughter, is this true?" The old man spoke to her directly for the first time in years.

"Yes, Grandfather. This is Darius, and this is Connor." She

gestured to each in turn. "Both are my true mates, as I am theirs."

The man seemed stunned, as did the villagers. The elder recovered first. He stepped forward and offered her a surprising hug.

"Welcome home, child. And welcome also, to your mates. It has been many centuries since dragons graced our skies."

They were ushered inside the main hall in short order, those who could, crammed in behind them. The place was filled with curious snowcats, but they kept a respectful distance from Josie, her grandfather and the twins.

The old man invited them to sit, and refreshments were served by some of the other villagers at his command. Josie knew the ceremonial greetings had to be done before they could get down to business. She shot the twins a look that begged them to follow her lead. A tiny, almost imperceptible nod from each of them reassured her somewhat. Connor's steady voice in her mind went even further to calm her nerves.

*"You are our guide in this strange land, Josie. Don't worry. Remember I told you we were taught diplomacy in our youth? We won't shame you in front of your grandfather."*

*"You could never shame me."* She thought the words, hoping they made their way to his mind. She still wasn't very comfortable with sending her thoughts to them, though she heard theirs just fine. She hoped it would get easier with practice.

Her grandfather began the ritual of greeting, and she sought the bag at her side. She had some things she'd thought to pack in there to ease their way. Reaching inside, she pulled out a lovely white silk scarf. It had white-on-white patterns in the fabric of twining dragons. She'd bought it on impulse many years ago and realized only now how prophetic a purchase it had been. She presented the gift to her grandfather, and it was received with a welcome smile.

"It is good to see you remember the old ways, child."

"Grandfather, we come seeking your counsel. Darius and Connor are not from this world. They were brought here through a magical storm and awoke in the forest near my home. I was the first person they met, and I shudder to think what would have happened if they'd crossed paths with anyone else on their first foray into this world, or worse, landed in a city."

"They did not," the old man said in his quiet way. "They could not. Such is not their karma. They arrived just where they were supposed to arrive, to meet just the person they were supposed to meet—you. It is the way of things."

She had never gotten used to his philosophical outlook on the world. The Western side of her just couldn't deal with his casual acceptance of things. Especially astounding things like dragons landing in her backyard.

"As you can imagine, I don't know how they will survive in our world. It is likely they'll eventually be seen in their shifted form, and that will cause all kinds of trouble."

"Not trouble, child. Revolution." A militant light entered the old man's eyes. "The people of Tibet are already talking of the return of dragons to their land."

Oh, she didn't like the sound of this.

"Your pardon, revered elder," Connor said with great respect in his deep voice that Josie couldn't fault, even though he was speaking out of turn. Still, she needed a minute to regroup. Her grandfather's implications had stunned her. "We are already embroiled in a great war in our own land. If at all possible, we must find a way to get back home to help our brothers and our people."

Well that was news to her, but then, they hadn't had much time to talk about these kinds of things. Even though the idea of living in their medieval-sounding world was frightening, Josie already knew she would go anywhere they went. No matter the cost, she had to stay with her mates. But fear rode her hard.

*"We haven't had time to tell you about the situation in our land,"* Darius's voice came to her in the privacy of her mind. *"For that we're sorry. Our brothers need us. If there is any possibility of returning home, we must search for it."*

*"We can talk about it later,"* she tried to send, though she wasn't certain he could hear her.

"You are twins, yes?" Her grandfather distracted her from her worries with such a strange, obvious question. "Identical in every way. Buy why does only one wear armor in his dragon form?"

Connor shook his head and reached into his pocket for the necklace she'd seen once before. "That's because I decided not to put this around my neck. My brother is the more impetuous of the two of us. A strange seer, newly arrived to our land gave us these trinkets a few days ago and Dar put his on right away. When he shifts, it shifts into the armor you saw. I am more cautious. I've kept it in my pocket all this time."

The snowcat elder leaned in to look at the amulet in Connor's hand with something approaching reverence.

"You should put it on, dragon lord." The old man leaned back and breathed a heavy, cleansing sigh. "And now that I have seen this—" he looked from the necklace in Connor's hand to the one now displayed at Darius's throat, "—I understand what must be done."

Josie was glad somebody seemed to understand something around here.

"There is a mountain called Gang Rinpoche, sacred to

123

Marpa, a great wizard of antiquity who brought enlightenment to our land and was the progenitor of our family line. On the sacred mountain there is an ice cave, accessible only from the air, or so it has been told from generation to generation of snowcat elders. In that ice cave is a talisman like the one you have just shown me. I have seen a drawing of it in an ancient text available only to the elders of each generation. That talisman waits for the one who will travel between worlds. It waits for you, granddaughter." His pale gaze pinned her, and a chill ran down her spine. "When the three become one, the heavens will open in the blink of an eye. Magic that has not been seen in this world in many generations will be unleashed for the good of both worlds."

"What does that mean?" Josie was at a loss.

Her grandfather smiled craftily. "I begin to understand the ancient puzzle. All will become clear as it was meant to be. Tomorrow, if the dragon lords allow, I will take you to Marpa's sacred ice cave. There we will find the talisman and take the next steps on your journey."

Connor and Darius bowed their heads, keeping eye contact—a show of respect among her clan and theirs too, apparently. It was amazing how easily they fit in here, among her father's people. Heck, they fit in better than she did.

"It would be our honor to fly you to this sacred cave," Connor answered formally.

Nosy clan members crowded into the great hall began to murmur among themselves. Tension filled the air as momentous events began to unfold. Josie was at the center of it. Either she was growing used to the tumult of her life since the twins entered it or she was just too tired from all the traveling to care. Her eyelids drooped as her grandfather arranged for refreshments.

"First you will eat, then you will be shown to your quarters for the night. On the morrow, we will undertake our quest." Her grandfather's eyes sparkled like a youngster. There was no doubt the old man was looking forward to flying. Or maybe he just wanted to get a good look at Marpa's sacred ice cave after all these years. Probably a little of both, she figured.

"You have our thanks. As you can probably tell, the journey to get to you was lengthy and tiresome." Darius put one arm around her shoulders, supporting her sagging spine. She was beat, and it probably showed.

"The shifters we met on our path were nothing but kind to us," Connor was quick to add. Of the two, he was the more diplomatic. "They have our thanks for easing our way in this strange world. Where we come from, only dragons and birds fly." Connor laughed as he lifted a morsel of food to his lips.

"And gryphons," Darius added as an afterthought.

"Gryphons? Truly?" Josie's grandfather beat her to the question, and all the snowcats waited to hear their answer.

"They are newcomers to our land, but yes, there are gryphons in our world. They are not numerous. Or perhaps I should say, we do not really know their true numbers. When we left our brother's kingdom, two mated pairs had sought his permission to nest in the cliffs above the royal palace. It was the seer who accompanied the newest pair who gave us these trinkets and warned us of our impending journey. We, foolishly, didn't believe her."

Darius laughed with his twin. "We owe her a big apology when and if we return."

"Your brother's kingdom?" Josie repeated the part that had really caught her attention.

"Yes, my love." Connor took her hand in his, looking deep into her eyes, audience be damned. "This is one of the things we have not yet had a chance to discuss with you. Our eldest brother, Roland, rules over both humans and dragons in our land."

# Chapter Seven

Darius took her other hand, drawing her attention. "We are members of the royal family and as such, you will be a princess in our land. Roland recently married, as did our next oldest brother, Nico. The rest are bachelors—excepting me and Con, now." Darius winked at her. "You will have sisters-in-law and even some youngsters flying around should we find a way to return to our land."

"Flying?"

"Roland's wife bonded with a baby Ice Dragon. He is still quite young," Darius went on. "Really just a toddler, though he flies like a dream and is larger than most full-grown dragons. You'll love him. He's the darling of the castle."

"He's *just* a dragon, right? Not a shapeshifter?" She wanted to be sure she had that part right.

"Yes. Most dragons are only dragons. It is a trait of the royal lines that we are both human and dragon. Our ancestor, Draneth the Wise, made it so," Darius reassured her, and she knew he spoke to the audience that listened as well. Connor then picked up the tale.

"Draneth was one of the last of the great wizards of old. He struck a deal with dragonkind. By making himself and all his descendants both human and dragon, they were deemed worthy to rule both races. In our land, the dragons are equal citizens with the people. Both follow our brother, Roland."

"There is a Council of Advisors, of course," Darius put in. "And a Dragon Council, as well. But Roland is the one who will lead us all into battle, if battle is truly in our future."

"Why? Do you expect a war?" Fear made itself known, tickling the edges of her spine as she waited to hear what they would say.

"We have already had battles—some major, some minor—with our neighbors to the north and east," Connor confirmed with narrowed eyes.

"The king of Skithdron is mad," Darius said with conviction. "He attacked us along the border and we pushed his forces back. He held our new sister-in-law prisoner in his castle, and she told us of the horrors there and the deal he'd made with the barbarians in the northlands. The next attack came from the north, with weapons supplied by Skithdron. We almost lost Roland in that battle, but his wife was able to find the dragon within herself at the last moment and she mounted a rescue with her cunning baby Ice Dragon and our youngest brother, William. It was insane of them to even try, really. But it worked, so we can't complain."

"What is the fighting about? Do they just want to conquer territory?" Josie was aware of the silence and the snowcats absorbing every word, but the twins didn't seem to mind.

"If only it were that simple." Connor sighed. "No. We believe King Lucan of Skithdron plots to free the wizards trapped in ice millennia ago."

"Wizards?" Josie's grandfather joined the conversation, drawing their attention.

"Yes. As in your world, wizards are the stuff of legend. Generations ago, there was a mighty war among them where those on the side of good—those who did not want to enslave all other races to do their bidding—eventually won the day, but at great cost. Most died. Others chose exile."

Darius picked up where his twin left off. "Of the evil ones, most were killed in the battles. A few remained and were imprisoned for all time in the ice at the farthest reaches of the northlands. There they remain to this very day. Or so the legends say."

"If King Lucan proceeds with his plans, we will fight him until he is defeated. When you come back to our world with us, your life will be rich, but it may also come with danger." Connor cupped her cheek, holding her gaze. "We would not put you in peril for anything, but you need to know that our world is not a peaceful one at the moment."

Josie smiled. "No world is as peaceful as it seems. Life is inherently full of danger, especially for a shifter. You are my mates. Wherever you go, I go. For your sake, I hope we find a way to send you back home. Nothing will change my mind. When you go home, I will go with you if possible."

"The Mother of All would not bring you together only to part you at the first possibility." Her grandfather's tone reassured her.

Like most shapeshifters, snowcats believed in a female deity. The snowcats called her the Mother of All. She who gave life to all there is and all there will be. They were Buddhist in many ways, but the snowcat form of Buddhism was different than that practiced by the majority of Tibetans. Just like the shifter forms of many common religions around the world differed from their human counterparts.

They ate with her grandfather and the audience of snowcats, then were shown to the best guest quarters the village had to offer. Josie had never been more grateful to see a bed than she was at that moment. Jet lag had caught up with her in a big way.

She stumbled to the low sleeping platform and tumbled onto it face-first. She snagged a pillow and tugged it under her head, shutting her eyes and wishing she didn't have to move from that position for several hours, at least.

Her wishes were granted in the form of two sexy hunks who undressed her where she lay, manipulating her limp body with skill and caring as they removed her clothes. They rubbed her tired muscles, one starting with her feet, the other at her shoulders. Before long, she was moaning in bliss, relaxed as a wet noodle and purring for her lovers.

The purr only grew louder when they rolled her to her back and switched places. Connor moved to massage her aching breasts while Darius settled between her spread thighs. After a few experimental forays of his talented tongue, he got into a rhythm that revived her and made her want to participate fully in their love play, but they wouldn't let her. When she tried to reach for them, they politely removed her hands and placed them at her sides.

"This is for you," Connor said as he kissed his way down her collarbone to her breast. "All for you, my love."

"But I want to touch you." Even to her own ears, she sounded whiney. Connor held her hand away from him, pressed to the mattress.

"Later, dear one. Let us do the touching for now."

Connor sat behind her, cradling her upper body with his while his twin lapped at her center like a cat with cream. Her body began to shiver with arousal, desperate for her men.

"Please don't make me wait," she panted.

Darius looked up, holding her gaze as he slipped two fingers into her wet core. He began to stroke, holding her hips down when she wanted to squirm. When he dipped his head once more to take her clit between his lips it only drove her higher—but not high enough.

"I need more, Darius. I need you." She was panting in time with the shallow thrusts of his fingers. She needed deeper penetration. The kind she knew he could deliver with his cock. An indecipherable look passed between the brothers as Darius rose above her.

"Are you certain, love?" Darius asked, his voice laced with concern. "We wanted to give you pleasure."

"You have, but I need you, Darius. And you, Connor. Don't make me wait. I always need you." She sounded as desperate as she felt, and she could see her words affected her men.

"Then you shall have us." Connor spoke from behind her, nodding to his brother.

"Sweet Mother of All, how did we get so lucky to have you as our perfect mate, Josie?" Darius rose over her, replacing his fingers with something much more satisfying.

He slid home in a powerful stroke that left her breathless. As he began to thrust deeply within her, Josie turned her head, taking Connor by surprise. His hard cock was within easy reach, with a little twisting and stretching that came easily to a nimble shifter like herself. She took Connor in her mouth as his twin claimed her pussy with ever-deeper strokes.

All three of them gasped as the flames licked higher between them. They were locked in passion. Three as one, the twins pleasuring her as she pleasured them. The moment stretched, perfect in its intensity. The bubble of her love rose to encompass them all. The three who would face whatever came in these uncertain times...together.

Josie cried out when she hit her peak. The twins weren't far behind. Both of them gasped as their bodies joined hers in the ultimate bliss, bathing her in their come, lifting her away from this Earth to a place only the three of them could reach. Together.

At dawn, the village around them began to stir and Josie woke, realizing just how thin the walls of the guest cottage they'd been given really were. A blush stole over her features as she thought of their cries of passion the night before. Her mates had pleasured her several times before they fell into an exhausted heap on the wide bed.

A satisfied smile licked over her lips as she looked at Darius and Connor. They were down for the count. She'd done that to them. She'd given them the peace they needed to sleep deeply. Not even the noises of the bustling village beyond their door disturbed them.

Josie slipped from the bed, intending to rustle up some breakfast for her men. She remembered the communal cafeteria at the center of the village. She would go there and get a decent meal for them, bring it back and serve her very first breakfast in bed.

That thought in mind, she dressed quickly and headed outside. The guest cottage was on the outskirts of the village. Walking in the cool morning air was invigorating. She passed a few people on her way to the cafeteria. Most nodded in greeting, saying nothing.

Not so, when she came face-to-face with a man she'd hoped to avoid.

Jet, her grandfather's chosen successor—the man he'd wanted her to marry—blocked her path. His face held no welcome, only an angry sneer.

"I heard you with them last night. Half the village did." Jet looked angry. Truly upset and out of control. This was not the cool-headed warrior she remembered from her youth. She had to be strong in the face of his anger.

"They are my mates. It is my right to behave however I wish with them in the privacy of our bedroom. This is none of your business, Jet. Now let me pass."

He leaped in front of her, barring her way once more. "Not so fast. You were promised to me, Josephine. Me. You should have been mine, as leadership of the clan will be mine. But you had to go and ruin it all. Now you will pay for your willfulness. Your grandfather should have disciplined you long ago."

He raised his hand to strike her. The blow never fell. Darius was there, holding Jet's wrist with deceptive ease. Josie knew how strong Jet was. Darius had to be even stronger to hold him without any apparent effort on his part. Josie was impressed again with her amazing mates.

"Leave now, and we will forget this foolishness. You are never to approach our mate again. Do you understand?" Connor spoke from her side as he pulled her against him, to safety. Only when she was out of range did Darius release Jet's wrist, but he didn't go far.

"I do not take orders from you, *lizard*." He made the word an insult. Neither Darius nor Connor seemed to care. It was clear they were superior. Too bad it looked like Jet needed to learn that lesson the hard way.

Connor took her another few steps away, and then time seemed to slow for Josie. Jet was as fast as any snowcat, which was to say *fast*. He reached into his jacket and pulled a gun.

That in itself was shocking, for firearms had never been part of the snowcat world. They were not part of the ancient teachings, and her grandfather upheld prior rulings to outlaw them in the snowcat village.

Josie ducked, trying to drag Connor down with her, but he stayed upright. He must've perceived the danger though, because he shifted to his dragon form in the blink of an eye.

The sharp report of the gun made her gasp, and then she heard a pinging sound. Josie looked to see what had happened as the acrid smell of burned gunpowder hit her nose.

Where Darius had been standing was now Darius's dragon form, his chest encased in that shiny metal armor. Jet dangled, unconscious, from one front claw, the gun lying on the ground several feet away.

Darius was unharmed, as was Connor, and Josie breathed a sigh of relief. Her men were safe.

"What happened? I know he got a shot off, but what did it hit?" Josie searched for the bullet and answers as the villagers gathered to discover what the commotion was about.

Jet was in deep trouble. He'd broken their laws and accosted not only her, but the dragon princes, their honored guests. He'd just guaranteed his own exile, the fool.

"It hit me," Darius said with disgust as he lowered the unconscious man to the ground where several big men waited to take him into their custody. Then Darius turned toward them and shifted form. "Or rather, it hit the breastplate. Right about here." He held his hand over his heart, and Josie sagged in shock. She'd come so close to losing him. "What was that thing, anyway?" He rubbed the area over his heart as she ran to him, sobbing.

He looked confused, but she was too overcome to explain anything at that moment. Darius had almost died. She threw herself into his arms, touching him all over, making sure he was really okay.

"That was a firearm. A gun. Very common in the world outside. They are outlawed here in our village. Jet deceived me." Her grandfather walked up to them, an equally grim-faced Connor at his side. "He deceived all of us. He will be dealt with.

Have no fear on that score."

"What is a firearm? It sounds magical, like a firedrake," Connor asked innocently. Josie sobbed anew, knowing beyond the shadow of a doubt that these special men could not survive in this world of technology. They were totally unprepared for it.

"It is not. It is merely technology. The smaller ones fire small projectiles, but they are still enough to kill a man, or a shifter. The speed with which these projectiles fly can penetrate almost anything—probably even dragon scales, I'm afraid. The larger weapons can kill huge beasts or blow up vehicles. Some can blow up entire cities."

"That sounds like magic to me," Darius said with a dark frown.

"It is not. It is the ingenuity of man alone. Something even more fearsome in this world than magic." Josie's grandfather shook his head in apparent disgust with the entire situation as he turned to go.

"Darius." She found her voice at last, the sobs receding. "That bullet could have pierced your heart. You would have died." She hung on his shoulders as his expression went from disbelief to concern. He was beginning to understand. "The armor saved you. It protected your heart."

Darius hugged her close. "You are my heart," he whispered, holding her gaze. "You're right, it did protect my heart."

She kissed him, relieved and charmed at the same time. Only Darius could be gallantly charming while simultaneously scaring her to death.

When she rose from the drugging kiss, she turned to Connor. "Please put on the amulet. I want you to be protected too. This world can be a dangerous place."

Connor reached into his pocket and took out the necklace, weighing it in his hand as she walked over to him. He looked down at the metal in his hand and then up at her face.

"For you, my love. I'd risk anything to make you happy."

"Risk?" She was confused.

Darius encircled her waist from behind. "Con is the most cautious man I know. He wanted to see what the necklace did to me before he took the chance and put his on."

"It saved his life, Connor." She tried to hide her exasperation. "I think that's proof enough it's a good thing, don't you?"

Connor gave her a cunning smile. "I suppose you could be right."

Holding her gaze, he slipped the necklace over his head, and she watched it gleam in a sudden shaft of sunlight. A single chiming note sounded in her ear so fast, she might've missed it, but it sounded like the purest of crystal, the most colorful of rainbows, the most powerful of magics.

"Did you hear that?"

"What?" Connor shrugged, and she got the idea he hadn't noticed the short, high-pitched sound.

"Just a tone of magic when you slipped that on." She gestured toward the amulet resting over his heart. "Don't worry. It sounded really good. Peaceful. Pure."

Connor looked at her strangely, seeming willing to accept her word for it but curious about the occurrence.

"What's a firedrake?" She remembered the comment that had piqued her interest a few minutes back.

"A person who has the ability to direct magical flame," Connor answered. "They can burn evil and control their fire. It is said they are descended of wizards and very rare."

Darius picked up the explanation. "Some have come to light in our land in recent weeks. My brothers worry that it is a further sign that dangerous times are coming to our land."

"We will go to Marpa's mountain today." Her grandfather spoke into the silence, drawing all eyes. "Break your fast, then meet me by the ledge where you arrived. It is as good a place as any to begin our journey."

"Do you really mean to take them to Gang Rinpoche?" She used the local name for the holy mountain also known as Mount Kailash. Climbing the mountain was forbidden. It was considered a sacred place by five different religions.

"Marpa had a cave on the crystal face of the mountain. It is there you must go to seek your answers. I will guide you there, if you will allow me to fly with you? The mountain cannot be climbed." For the first time in her life, Josie saw her grandfather look hesitant. It was a revelation. Even her fearsome grandfather respected the abilities of her new mates.

"Do you want to go there, love?" Darius asked in a soft voice.

Gathering her courage, she nodded. "If Grandfather thinks we should, then we should. It's a holy place. One where nobody is allowed to go."

"Except the snowcat elders," her grandfather chimed in. "Though no snowcat elder has made the journey in millennia. The time was not right. I have seen the signs. The time is now. Will you take me?"

"We will go anywhere our mate needs to go." Connor's voice was firm, his resolve clear. They were going to fly to the sacred mountain. May the Mother of All watch over them.

They arrived at the departure point a short while later. They'd eaten, bathed and Josie had dressed in her warmest clothing. It was bound to be cold on that peak. Her men were dragons and impervious to the cold, but she clung to her jacket as closely as she clung to the warmth of her mates.

Her grandfather was waiting for them when they arrived, and Connor went over to him, speaking in respectful, low tones. She couldn't hear what they were talking about and made to move closer. Darius blocked her path with a devilish grin on his face.

"I get you this time." Darius snagged her around the waist and led her a short distance from his brother. "I've been waiting to feel your legs wrapped around me, sweetheart." His whisper in her ear made her shiver. "Don't worry, I won't let you fall. I'll never let you fall."

He dropped a devastating kiss on her lips and then stepped back. He'd shifted shape before she'd even caught her breath. Of the two men, Darius was definitely the one who liked to live dangerously.

"If you weren't covered with impenetrable scales right now, I'd scratch you for teasing me, Darius." She winked to let him know she was only kidding, but he seemed to understand. A dragonish chuckle, complete with pleasantly cinnamon-scented smoke, erupted from his lips and she got a gander at his foot-long fangs for the first time. He had some serious chompers in dragon form.

*"Climb aboard, my love. Show your grandfather how it's done, and we can be on our way."*

Darius's voice rumbled through her mind. She glanced over to find her grandfather standing next to Connor, who had just shifted into dragon form. She stepped on Darius's bent knee and swung her leg over his back as her grandfather watched, then copied her moves. Within moments, they were both mounted and the dragons took gracefully to the sky.

Darius followed Connor's lead. The old man was giving Connor verbal direction to the sacred mountain and the ice cave he'd been told lay hidden near its summit. It was an easy trip for a dragon that would have been impossible for anyone on foot. Even someone in a helicopter would not have been able to find the hidden entrance to the cave.

When they came upon it, it was clear the entrance had been constructed in such a way as to be visible only to those who knew where to look and what to look for. It was an optical illusion. The entrance appeared as one flat face of snow and ice, but was really a sliver of an opening in the sheer mountainside.

Josie felt the tingle of strong magic against her skin as they passed through the tight opening. Connor and her grandfather were just ahead of them. Connor had landed inside the cave and her grandfather had already dismounted when Darius slid to a stop, his claws scraping on the ice floor. She slid off his back and joined her grandfather as the twins shifted shape, unable to go farther into the cave at dragon size.

"This is amazing." She dared not speak above a whisper. Something about this place felt sacred. Like the inside of a cathedral. In a way, it was a kind of cathedral. A cathedral of ice.

The entryway widened into a massive chamber lit from within by sunlight that filtered through the solid ice of the ceiling, walls and even the floor. The ice had a tint of blue in one area, copper in another. Everything sparkled, and there was quite a bit to see.

Far from being empty, the chamber was filled with carvings on the walls, the high, domed ceiling and the small bumps and recesses scattered around in a roughly geometric pattern. At the center of the wide, circular room was a flat-topped, round pillar that made a waist-high table. Vines twined around the base of the cylindrical column in an artistic, natural motif, rising slowly toward the center of it, where the vines ended and clouds began.

Flitting among the clouds were two dragons. Dragons carved in pure ice, they looked exactly like the twins in their shifted form. Only these dragons were tiny carvings in pure white and reflective prisms of light, while the twins were massive and had a coal black sheen when they were in dragon form.

Josie got her first good look at the carved walls as she moved farther into the room. All the species of shifters she knew were represented in the carvings and some that were only legend. Snowcat was prominent throughout, but there were others as well. All the big cats were there, as were the wolves, the raptors and so many others she lost count.

She turned her attention back to the center of the room and the ice table. Her grandfather stood before it solemnly. Josie moved closer, as did the twins, to see what her grandfather was up to. He bowed in respect, touching his fingertips to the edge of the table, motioning for her to do the same. She did as she was told and bowed low, feeling a magical thrill of energy shoot from her fingers to her toes as she touched the flat-topped pillar of ice.

She rose from her bow, and then she saw it.

An amulet almost exactly like the ones around Darius's and Connor's necks. Only this one showed a snowcat, not the dragon that graced their medallions. Her grandfather lifted it reverently from the sparkling ice surface, holding it in both hands as he turned to her.

"It has come to pass. The daughter of snowcat joins with the dragon. This, I believe, was meant for you." He held out the amulet, and she took it with trembling fingers. She could feel the magic of it buzzing through her skin. She didn't have to be told that this was an object of immense power.

Darius and Connor flanked her, one on each side, looking over her shoulders, down at the silver and gold necklace.

"It's just like ours, except it has a cat on it instead of a dragon." Darius stated the obvious.

"What does this mean?" Connor asked her grandfather.

"It means that you are the ones who were foretold in the most ancient scriptures of the snowcat. It was said a daughter of snowcat would join with the dragon. I didn't know what it meant until I saw you two." Her grandfather looked very old and weary all of a sudden as he stepped away from the altar. "I can tell you what teachings have survived the centuries. This place is known only to the elders of our tribe, though none I know of have ever been here before. Snowcat alone is not able to reach this high on the mountain." The old man began walking around the chamber, looking at the magnificent carvings. "The amulet and other things, it is said, remain locked away here in the ice, waiting for those who need them."

"But I only see this amulet. Besides the carvings, this place is empty." Josie was confused.

"You see the amulet because it is meant for you. It is Marpa's gift to you, child. The snowcat daughter destined to join with the dragon. I wonder if even Marpa could have foreseen that you would bring not one, but two dragons?" A faint smile touched the corners of the old man's mouth as he continued his progress around the room.

"What is she meant to do with the amulet?" Connor asked. "Do your legends say anything more?"

Grandfather turned just his head to give Connor a quizzical look. Oh, the old man knew something. Josie was familiar with that raised eyebrow and the inscrutable expression. Her grandfather knew much more than he was telling. Perhaps he was drawing out the tale to buy time. Chances are, without the twins' help, he would never see this cave again. He had to get a good long look while he could.

Josie sent him a small, knowing grin that was answered with a slight, approving tilt of the old man's head. Even after all these years away from his influence, she understood her grandfather.

"I don't know that she's meant to *do* anything with the power of the amulet, but I do know the artifact has immense power of its own, imbued to it by the great wizard, Marpa, eons ago. Josephine is a daughter of the line of Marpa. Some of his blood flows in her veins, all these generations later. She should be able to tap into the magic he left behind for his granddaughter many times over. It was left for her. It was meant for her."

"But what can it do?" Darius insisted.

Her grandfather turned fully to face them. "I believe it is the key, along with your dragon amulets, to crossing the boundary between our world and yours."

# Chapter Eight

The men looked stunned. Darius and Connor looked at each other with expressions that went from shock to hope to eager anticipation in the space of seconds. Then they turned that intensity on her.

"We can go home?" Darius asked, his voice barely a whisper.

"I don't know," she answered honestly. "I guess so. If that's what Marpa intended."

"It is." All three looked at her grandfather. His voice echoed through the ice cavern with strength and surety. He knew something she didn't. There was no doubt. "It is part of the teachings that have been preserved. The daughter of snowcat will join with the dragon to defeat Marpa's enemies in the dragon realm."

"If Marpa was a wizard, his enemies would be..." Darius began.

"...other wizards." Connor finished the thought.

"*Evil* wizards," her grandfather confirmed, nodding sagely. "Marpa was on the side of light, of good. He passed his teachings to us. He gave us instruction on how to live to achieve enlightenment. Few know that before he passed down his teachings to the mortal world, he fought great battles against the evil ones of his own kind. In the peace that followed the victory of goodness over evil, those who were left began to teach the lesser beings the path of truth and light." Her grandfather began to examine the carvings once more. "Marpa and those like him brought peace to our world but in winning the battle, most magic was dispersed. Except for creatures like us—those who can tap into the magic that was left to shift form—there is little real magic in this world anymore. Not like it was when Marpa and his fellows battled an evil as great as their power for good. Their battles fractured the magic in this world. I imagine, from your words, your world is not like this."

"No, it's not. Our wizards battled too, in the distant past, and were thought to be extinct," Connor told him. "Only recently have we discovered, at least one of the prevailing good wizards went into seclusion after the last great battle. The wizard Gryffid is alive and well in his island fortress, living among the fair folk and his creations, the gyphons."

"These fair folk," Grandfather repeated the strange name as if tasting it. "Are they magical folk? And the gryphons?"

"Yes, very magical. Fair folk live in hidden enclaves, it is said, all around our world. They often go out into human society, disguised as warriors or bards. They have sweet voices and lightning reflexes, enhanced by their own intrinsic magic," Connor explained.

"And gryphons are as magical in their way as dragons," Darius stated. "Our dragon friends have their own kind of magic and can heal others when they manifest the Dragon's Breath. They also speak mind to mind with those who can hear them and can detect many kinds of magic."

"Are there many other creatures and peoples in your world that make such light use of magic?" her grandfather asked. He was driving home a point, and she knew he wouldn't relent until they all saw it and understood his meaning.

"Yes," Darius answered carefully. "I only know for certain about those I have encountered myself, but there are stories from other kingdoms and lands. Magic is an integral part of the fabric of our world."

The old man sighed heavily, and his heavy brows drew together. "Sadly, it is not here. Surely you've felt the lack since you've been in this world. Whatever magic there once was has been scattered and submerged, hidden by the last of the great wizards. They probably thought it was too dangerous to leave lying around for those who came after them. Who knows if their decision was correct? We only must deal with what we have." His spine straightened. "So now we have a very powerful magical artifact with everything but your name on it, granddaughter. It is for you to discover how to use it, and for you to decide when, and if, to use it."

Josie didn't like the heavy feeling in the pit of her stomach as the responsibility settled squarely on her shoulders. Suddenly, her grandfather stopped moving. She didn't have time to worry more about her troubles as he motioned them to draw near.

The twins went first, protecting her in that old-fashioned way of theirs. She'd have to break them of the habit, but for now it was oddly comforting.

"What is it?" she asked from behind as three big men blocked her view.

Darius and Connor parted silently, and she faced her grandfather and the ice wall that was ice no more. Behind an elaborate dragon carving was a clearly visible line of some sparkly metal. As she looked up and down its length, she realized the thing had to be about seven feet long, with a larger piece on either end that she couldn't make out through the ice covering.

"Touch the dragon's heart and all will be revealed," Grandfather instructed.

"Which one of us?" Darius asked, looking confused.

Connor grinned challengingly at his twin. "How about both?"

The twins reached out together, and as they touched the heart of the dragon—a dragon that was wearing the armor she'd seen them wear, now that she had a better view of the carving— the ice disappeared.

Not one, but two gleaming spears were revealed.

"Take them. They are yours," her grandfather intoned as she moved away, standing off to one side. "These are the Wizard's Lances, once used by the elite leaders of Marpa's armies, now passed to you who battle evil in another realm."

Josie got her first good look at the gleaming silver and gold lances. They were basically three-pointed spearheads on top, with a counterbalance on the other end that looked like the ball of a giant mace, with lethal, sparkling sharpened spikes.

"I feel the magic in this weapon," Darius commented as he hefted the center of the staff, moved into the open part of the chamber and gave it an experimental twirl.

"It is perfectly balanced," Connor agreed, on the other side of the chamber, going through some practice moves with the glittering weapon.

They were impressive. Not only were they dragons with superior strength, but they were students of the fighting arts who had superior skill in their human forms as well. She saw her grandfather watching them with a critical but approving eye as they tested the new weapons and put them through their paces.

"Your mates do you proud, granddaughter," he told her as

she stood by his side. They watched the twins perform mirror versions of some strange but clearly advanced staff *kata*. They were both acrobatic and strong with near-perfect balance and absolute concentration. And they were perfectly matched.

"They're amazing, aren't they?" She couldn't help the bubble of pride that entered her voice.

"Two more talented masters I have never had the privilege to see," he agreed quietly. High praise indeed, from a snowcat elder who had studied and taught martial arts his entire life. "They bring honor to our clan, as do you, granddaughter."

Josie felt a tear gather in the corner of her eye, but refused to let it fall. She'd always craved her grandfather's acceptance. To have it, when she was about to embark on the most uncertain time in her life of uncertainty, meant more than he would ever know.

The twins came to a halt at the end of their *kata*, facing each other at exactly the same moment. Then grins spread across their faces.

"I think they like the gift, grandfather," Josie joked as the twins walked slowly back toward them.

Before anyone could speak, Josie's grandfather moved forward, to face all three of them. "I believe I understand the meaning of the ancient teachings. From what you have told me, there is war against evil in your world. You must return to fight it and with you, must go my beloved granddaughter. She is the key. With her power, and your own, when the three amulets are joined, you may travel between our worlds. It cannot be done lightly, but it can be done. And you will take with you the gifts of Marpa, the Wizard's Lances, so that you may defeat your enemies, the enemies of light and goodness."

They stayed in the cave until the light began to fade so

Josie's grandfather could take a good long look around and say a few respectful words in thanks to Marpa and those who had come before. Darius and Connor, surprisingly, added their formal words of thanks for the gift of the Wizard's Lances, the amulets and their mate. That final bit touched Josie's heart and she echoed their prayers, following the example set by the men.

The dragons were welcomed this time as they returned to the village, and the elders gathered to hear what Josie's grandfather had to tell them about their pilgrimage. They didn't go far, though. It seemed everyone else had been busy while they'd been away and a sort of feast was waiting, at which Darius, Connor and Josie were to be the guests of honor.

She was flabbergasted by the idea. Only half snowcat, Josie had never been feted by these people in her youth. In fact, more often than not, she'd gotten the idea that they disapproved of her Western ways, even her Western face.

That all seemed to be in the past. At least for the villagers. They had rolled out the figurative welcome mat for the dragons and their new mate, and the cynical side of Josie wanted to sneer at their sudden change of heart. The little girl inside who'd wanted their approval so badly felt different.

Josie tried to strike a happy medium, smiling through the meal and the celebrations that followed. Most wanted to talk to Darius and Connor, of course. A few of the more polite souls inquired after her with real interest. She'd had *some* friends in the village, after all, it seemed.

As Darius and Connor discussed their land and its troubles, Josie started to feel the same urgency they felt. She knew they wanted desperately to go home, but she was scared. There was no question she wanted to be with them, wherever they ended up, of course. Still, the idea of leaving her world behind completely to enter a realm in which she had no experience, no knowledge, with a war going on was frightening.

Her mates would be by her side. She had to keep reminding herself of that. They would help her as she learned about their world.

"Rest easy, granddaughter." Josie's grandfather had snuck up on her while she'd been engrossed in her thoughts. The twins were busy talking to a small group of elders, and she'd been momentarily left alone.

"I'm not sure I'm strong enough to start a new life in their world, Grandfather." She needed his guidance. She needed his counsel, more than ever before.

"This is the fate your karma has brought you, child. Believe it or not, you have done this before. It is something you are good at. Have no doubt. This is what you are meant to do. To bring light to a threatened world and the magic of the snowcat that is strong within you."

"What do you mean, I've done this before?" She was truly puzzled by his words.

"Think back to when you were a child. When your mother died and I came for you. That lonely child was brave enough to follow where I led, though she had never seen me before. You started a new life in a new land with strange customs and people who were not entirely ready to accept you. Yet you prospered. Then, a few years later, you did it again by striking out on your own and making a life for yourself in America. You prospered there as well, without the help you could easily have gotten from other cat clans. They would have revered you. They would have given you any assistance you needed. Yet you forged your own way and made a success of it. Why do you think you will fail now?" He gave her a kind smile. "Especially with two warriors of such caliber beside you. Two warriors who love you. Two warriors who would give their lives for you."

Her eyes teared as she looked at her men, so strong and supportive, so loving and gentle, so fierce and magical. Her grandfather was right, as he usually was. Darius and Connor would be there for her in their land. They would be together. That's all that really mattered.

Impulsively, she leaned forward to give her grandfather a hug. He returned it, squeezing her close and placing a kiss on her cheek. She felt the emotion of the moment and knew she had finally achieved one of her childhood goals. She had her grandfather's approval. It meant more than she would have believed.

"Thank you, Grandfather." They broke apart, and she saw his aged eyes glistening with emotion. Her own eyes welled with more tears, but smiles wreathed both faces.

"You will go tonight. After the feast." Josie was stymied by her grandfather's abrupt words. "The longer you delay, the harder it will be to leave and the more desperate the situation in their land will grow. As snowcats, it is our sacred duty to oppose evil wherever we find it and seek the goodness in men, show them the light. We use our magic to foster enlightenment. You must now do the same. You must carry our banner into your new world to fight at your mates' side."

She felt at sea. She'd just really found peace with her grandfather, and now he was sending her on her way.

"Will I ever see you again?"

"In time, child. So the ancient teachings say. The voyage between our worlds cannot be made lightly. You hold the power—along with your mates—to do so at will. After the crisis in their world is resolved, you will return here. So the snowcat decrees. And I will be here to welcome you and hear of your adventures."

She thought she read knowledge of the future in his canny

expression. "You know more, don't you?"

An inscrutable smile graced his lined face. "That is for me to know, and you to find out. Of course, I am not a snowcat elder for nothing."

"I thought so." She hugged him, laughing with him as her heavy heart lightened. She would see him again. For now, it was enough to know that as she embarked on the next part of her life. The life of a mated woman with two handsome men as her partners on their journey. It would probably be a perilous journey, at that, but with Darius and Connor at her side, she could do almost anything.

It was Darius's turn to act as her ride this time, since Connor had shuttled her back down the mountain earlier that day. The amulets had turned into gleaming armor breastplates on each black dragon. They posed for pictures, adding to the surreality of the moment as Josie said farewell to her grandfather. She had the snowcat amulet around her neck and felt it tingle and hum against her skin.

"When you get far enough away, you must call the storm, child." Her grandfather's urgent tone made her pay attention.

"Call a storm? How?"

"Do you remember your mantra? The one I taught you as a child."

"I do." She wasn't sure where this was leading, but it sounded ominous.

"Repeat your mantra. It is yours alone. It will call the storm, if your will is strong enough. Center your thoughts and say your mantra. Do not lose focus."

She thought she understood. The words to the mantra her grandfather had taught her were more complex than such things often were. He'd also told her never to practice it around others, though she did not understand why at the time. Now it all began to make sense.

"You taught me a magic chant, didn't you?"

He grinned. She would remember that grin, whenever she thought of him. It was a much different image than the one she'd held in her mind in years past. She liked this one much better.

"I suspected you were meant for great things, even when you doubted yourself."

"I never knew."

"I know, child. Such is the way of life. The young never see what is right before their eyes. With age comes knowledge, and sometimes wisdom. I believe you are on the path toward wisdom."

"I'm not so sure," she joked, giving him a final hug. "I'll do my best to make you proud."

"I have always been proud of you, granddaughter." His words rocked her to her core, and a warm feeling spread from her heart throughout her body.

"I love you, Grandfather."

"As I love you."

They said their final farewell, and she turned to mount. Once she was on Darius's back, seated securely, everyone stepped back. Only her grandfather stayed near, his eyes trained on her.

Just before Darius launched into the sky, she heard her grandfather's final words of advice for her.

"Remember what I taught you and don't lose focus. No matter what, don't lose focus."

His words followed her into the air and she had no chance

to respond. She would remember his advice. She would do her best to remember everything he had ever taught her.

The night was black as pitch. As black as the hides of the dragons. Snowcapped peaks surrounded them, but the three who flew through the night sky had superior vision and were able to see obstacles before they became a problem.

When she could no longer see the village behind them, Josie began to chant. It drew the dragons' attention, and they broke her conversation with their questioning thoughts.

*"What are you doing, sweetheart?"* Darius asked in her mind.

"I'm trying to call the storm that will bring us to your world." There was just a hint of frustration in her tone. She'd barely gotten into the rhythm of her mantra before she was interrupted.

*"Can we help?"* Connor asked politely, flying closer.

"I don't think so. Grandfather said I needed to concentrate. For now, just let me say my mantra and see what happens. Please don't interrupt. If this works, I'll need to stay focused. You guys fly. I'll hold the storm—or whatever it is—as best I can."

*"We will do so, but if at any time, it looks like you are in danger, we reserve the right to interrupt."* Connor veered off to fly a few feet farther away, in what must be a more comfortable distance for the two dragons.

"Fair enough." Josie breathed as deeply as she could and began again.

It took a while, but she felt the wind begin to pick up as the clouds began to swirl. Moments later, she saw an eerie green glow from within the clouds just ahead of them as it began to snow and sleet, soaking her in seconds. The icy precipitation melted and steamed against the dragon's warm hide, keeping her warm, even in the deluge.

She fought against the fear that threatened to choke her, overcoming it with the discipline taught her as a youngster. She was able to watch and observe, as if from afar as the storm swallowed them. She stuck to her mantra, focusing the magic of her words in the magic of the storm as the dragons labored on.

The violent green of the storm enveloped them, and that was the last thing she knew.

*"Where are we, do you think?"* Darius asked his twin as they awoke in a forest for the second time. This forest, unlike that other one, at least looked familiar.

*"I believe we are somewhere near the Northern Lair."*

*"Thank heaven for that, at least. We are back home. In our own world."*

*"Is she awake yet?"*

*"Not quite."* Both had changed to human form upon waking, and Darius took charge of Josie's still form. She'd been on his back when they came through the storm and aside from the faint they had all suffered, she looked as if she had come through it well.

*"Someone comes,"* Connor warned his twin.

Both men were armed with the Wizard's Lances should there be trouble.

Darius carried Josie farther back, under cover while Connor took point, jumping up into a tree to see if he could get a better vantage point. Even in human form, they had superior agility and were able to make the leap from ground to limbs several man-lengths in the air with little difficulty. Darius looked around for a suitable tree should it become necessary to hide Josie aloft.

*"Northern barbarians. I can see a troop of them behind their scouts. The two scouts are heading right for us. You'd better get our mate under cover."*

*"Way ahead of you, brother. I've already got a tree picked out."* Darius broke cover for a quick moment, making the leap upward to a lower branch with Josie hoisted over his shoulder. He worked his way up the tall pine until he was hidden by the boughs, then found a little crook where he could stash her. She would be safe there until she recovered.

Darius tucked her into the tree, making her as secure as he possibly could. Seconds later, the sounds of skirmishing came from below. Connor had engaged the enemy, which meant he'd seen no other way. The scouts had found him.

*"I need you, Dar."*

*"On my way. Josie's safe for now."*

*"Good."*

And then there was little time for thought as Darius dropped out of the tree and into the fray. The scouts hadn't been that far ahead of their troop, and a real melee was in progress as Darius fought his way to his twin's side. They stood back to back, the Wizard's Lances effective in keeping a wide perimeter around them clear. The three-bladed ends of the Lances were sharp as dragon talons and just as lethal as the twins wielded them against inferior fighters.

*"We could go dragon and fry their asses,"* Darius mused as he took down another opponent. *"It would be faster."*

*"We would also betray who and what we are. Obviously we landed on the wrong side of the northern border. These heathens probably once belonged to Salomar."*

*"Good point, brother. It would be good to learn what we can while we're here so we can report back to Roland."*

*"True, but how are we to learn if they are Salomar's lot or some other group? These brigands don't wear uniforms or signs of office."*

*"Mayhap we should just ask them."*

Darius's teasing tone was typical of him but very often, his direct approach yielded unlooked-for results. As Connor expected a moment later, Darius spoke aloud to his latest opponent.

"I say, did you lot used to fight for Salomar?" The teasing tone and haughty words made Connor snicker even as he noted the anger on his current opponent's face.

"I don't think they like Salomar, Dar. The one I'm fighting made a face when you mentioned his name." Connor taunted the enemy with his words.

"Good thing we killed him then, isn't it," Darius shot back, then returned his attention to his opponent. "So who do you fight for now, eh?"

Only three men were left of the group. Most were out cold, some dead. Darius and Connor each faced one and the remaining brigand held back, as if watching. Connor saw his opponent's eyes flicker to the one who observed.

*"Did your man just look at the gawker over there?"* Connor asked his twin privately.

*"That he did,"* Darius agreed.

Connor observed the observer as best he could while keeping his guard up. This last opponent was the best of the bunch so far. That wasn't saying much.

*"He doesn't look like a barbarian leader, but he could be a lieutenant, put in charge of this lot. Chances are, he'll have the*

*information we want and more, if we can capture him. Once we dispatch these two, he'll make a run for it, I'll wager."*

*"Then we need to try to down both our opponents at the same time and make a dash for him. If one of them goes down, he'll start to run."*

*"Agreed."*

Through careful maneuvering, Connor and Darius timed their blows. Connor's opponent went down only seconds before Darius's and then both men were off, after the sole remaining brigand, who was swifter on his heels than they would have credited.

"Stop, damn you," Darius grunted as he ran at Connor's side after the bastard, both hefting the metal lances.

The man looked back at them, already far ahead, then dove into a thicket, out of view. Darius and Connor chased after, arriving in the thicket only to find the man cornered by a glowing white snowcat, her claws unsheathed and pining the man's arms to a large tree. The big pads of her feet were on his, preventing him from kicking and his sword lay several feet away, out of range.

Darius let out a long whistle as a grin split his face. Connor wasn't far behind as Darius sauntered up to the cat and the man. Making a show of it, he pet the snowcat's neck, and she rubbed her head into his chest.

"That's a good kitty," Darius said with approval. "Now let's find out a little more about you, my friend," he addressed the captive. "Before I let my pet nibble on your bones. She hasn't been fed in a while."

# Chapter Nine

"I'd say we got more out of that bastard than we'd have ever gotten under normal interrogation. You, my love, are a wonder." Darius was chipper as he walked arm in arm with Josie. Connor scouted ahead as they neared the northern border of Draconia.

They could have flown, but both were tired from the storm and the fight shortly after returning to their world. For now, they were better walking until they reached the river. They'd have to fly then, but it would be a quick jaunt across the water and then to the Northern Lair where they could recover in relative peace.

"We have to talk to Lana and find out who this Gebel person is," Darius kept talking, though he was careful to keep his conversation low, so that only they could hear him. They weren't out of the woods—so to speak—yet.

"And Lana is you brother Roland's wife, right?" Josie asked in low voice. They'd tried to tell her all about their family, and who was who. Even Connor admitted it wasn't easy to keep the whole crowd straight.

"Yes," Darius answered, patient with her in a way he seldom was with others. "She was stolen from her family as a girl and sold as a slave to these Northern barbarians. She served in Salomar's hold until she was tasked to tend a dragon egg."

"Tor was in the egg, right?" Josie asked, proving she had retained some of their stories.

"That he was. When he was old enough, Tor and Lana escaped to live in the wild, but Lana knows a lot about the Northerners. If anyone in Draconia knows anything about their new leader Gebel, I'm betting she does."

Connor saw the spark of light off water as he topped the hill and knew they didn't have far to go. They'd found the river. The trees thinned here, and only a wide expanse of green stood between them and the river.

"I think we should fly from here," he said, stopping as the others caught up with him. "We can be across the river in less than an hour and then make our way to the safety of the Northern Lair."

"A good plan," Darius seconded.

"Are you two recovered enough?" Josie seemed worried about them. "That passage through the storm took a lot out of me. It had to be even worse for you two, since you had to fight those winds."

"Which is why we walked this far." Connor bent to kiss her quickly, unable to resist her allure. "We're all right to fly this short distance. Actually, the first time we crossed—when we ended up in your world—we were in much worse shape. Perhaps it gets easier with experience."

"Well if my grandfather's right, we'll get a chance to test that theory sooner or later," Josie quipped as she stepped next to Connor to get a better look at the river. "I have to say this, your world is really beautiful. The air is so crisp and pure. That river sparkles, and it's actually blue. I've never seen a blue river before."

"Many rivers are brown with stirred sediments. The bed of

this river is rock and stone, and there is a special kind of fish that thrives here. It eats plant and organic debris before it can accumulate," Connor informed her. He, too, liked the look of this river, but it marked a very dangerous border.

Connor got to carry Josie across the border into Draconia. They crossed without incident, though they did see another small party of brigands patrolling the border farther away. The dragons could see the patrol, but it was doubtful the humans who made up the patrol could see them in the descending twilight.

Both twins were truly weary when they made their final approach to the Northern Lair. An honor guard of patrolmen and dragons had come to escort them. They landed, to be greeted by Hal and Jures, the leaders of this Lair.

"It is good to see you, Prince Darius and Prince Connor. We thought perhaps something terrible had befallen you when you did not arrive as scheduled," Jures said, looking from one twin to the other as they shifted to human form.

Josie had already dismounted and stood between them, an uncomfortable look on her pretty face. Connor put his arm around her in a show of support as Darius stepped forward to exchange greetings with the knights who ran this Lair so well.

"We have quite a tale to tell," Darius informed them. "Have you news of our brothers?"

"Roland is overseeing the search efforts from the castle. Collin and Trey are out looking for you along the eastern border. Trent is watching over Jon and Wil, who insisted on searching to the south. And Nico is—"

"I am here."

Connor was never so glad to hear his older brother's voice. Nico seemed to be buttoning his shirt as he made his way onto the landing ledge, his new wife, Riki, just behind him. Apparently they'd been caught off guard by Darius's and Connor's return.

Darius turned to meet Nico and was caught in a bone-crushing hug. Connor could see the emotion in Nico's expression as the Prince of Spies let his guard down for just a moment. He'd been truly worried about them.

"How long have we been gone?" Connor asked, stepping closer with Josie by his side as Nico let Darius go.

"You're three days overdue." Nico looked from Connor to Josie and back again and jumped to all the wrong conclusions. "If you had us in an uproar just so you could hare off with some girl—"

"Hold, Nico." Darius slapped his palm on Nico's shoulder to halt his forward progress. "That's not it at all. We've been..." Darius looked to Connor for words, but Connor didn't know how to describe where they'd been either.

"They were transported through a violent, magical storm, to my world." Josie saved the day, standing forward to face Nico's fury on her own, not giving an inch. Not for the first time, Connor admired her courage. "I am a snowcat shapeshifter from a world where magic no longer exists in abundance. What little there is resides in a few supernatural races that must live in secret from the rest of humanity. My world runs on technology, not magic."

"And it is a wondrous place, brother." Connor moved to stand beside her. "We traveled great distances by air, but not under our own power. We rode with a hundred other humans in a hollow, metal craft with a giant wingspan. It flew high above the clouds at heights dragons cannot dream of and speeds we can only achieve for short bursts when in a dive."

Nico's head tilted as if he were testing the truth of Connor's

161

claims. He didn't look angry anymore, which was a good start.

"It's called an airplane," Josie put in helpfully.

"And why could you not fly yourselves to wherever you needed to go?" Nico asked, suspicion clear in his tone.

"There are no dragons in my world. They are legends out of the distant past. Once I realized what they were, I knew they needed to talk to my grandfather, the leader of the snowcats, but we couldn't let anyone else see them who wasn't already aware of the existence of supernatural creatures. Ninety-nine percent of the people in my world are totally unaware of magic of any kind."

"I would hear more of your tale before I decide if you're telling me the truth or just making up some fantastical lie to get yourselves out of trouble." Nico turned and led the way off the landing ledge, leaving the twins no choice but to follow.

"He really was worried about you," Riki said as she took Darius's arm, and they followed in Nico's furious steps.

"That's your big brother, huh?" Josie asked in a whisper as Connor escorted her after them. "He doesn't seem too pleased with you."

"Nico's usually the more lenient of our elder siblings. I would have expected the anger from Roland, but not from Nico. Of course, things have been different since our youngest brother, Wil, was kidnapped."

"Did you get him back?" Josie looked shocked.

"Yes. As a matter of fact, those who took him, sent him home a week later. The only problem was, he was five years older. He'd been kidnapped by servants of the Wizard Gryffid and taken to his home on Gryphon Isle to be tutored and trained. Gryffid didn't ask permission, he just stole Wil and returned him an older, wiser...stranger. It's been hard getting to know him again. He is much different than when he left."

"Are you...are you certain it's really him?"

"Quite certain. The dragons know the truth. There's no way to fake what or who we are to them. All of us are half dragon. No one else in this world, besides those of the royal family, can make that claim. And dragons recognize their own."

"Royal family?" Suddenly their claims of being princes in their world came back to her. Was that for real?

"There are several lines descended from Draneth the Wise," Darius told her. "We are the main branch, descended from the eldest son of the eldest son, going back to Draneth. There is also the House of Kent, from which Riki and her twin, Lana, descend."

"They're dragons too?"

"Black dragons," Connor corrected her. "Only black dragons are shapeshifters. And actually, it's rare for Riki and Lana to be able to shift. Most females of the royal lines cannot. Their younger sister, Belora, and their mother, Adora, cannot. Both Riki and Lana came to their powers late, as it is said, most females do. If they can shift at all, it usually comes upon them after full adulthood. Perhaps Belora might discover the talent at some point in the future."

"You really are princes? That wasn't just a line?"

"A line?" Connor looked as if he didn't quite understand what she meant.

"You know, something you say to impress the girls."

Darius laughed outright while Connor looked affronted. "No, it is true, I assure you. Our eldest brother is king of this land."

"We are just lowly princes," Darius added with a teasing look. "And you are our beloved princess."

"Princess Josie?" The thought of it was a little heady, to be sure. She was still just plain old Josie, no matter how many people wanted to deify her in different ways. "Nah, that just sounds silly."

"Silly or not, it is the truth of the matter. Among our people you will be treated with the respect due a Princess of Draconia." Connor's tone told her there would be no further argument on the matter.

Josie decided to let it drop for now. The middle of a family squabble was no place to be worrying about her new title, real or imaginary. Nico looked older and more world-weary than the twins, and he definitely had that older-sibling disapproval vibe going on. Josie didn't envy her mates having to face this man's anger or accusations. She'd stand with them regardless. She could do no less. They were her mates.

Eventually they reached a round chamber with a giant sand pit in the middle. The whole place looked like it had been carved out of rock. Slabs of the stuff formed the floors and walls she'd seen so far, though the furniture—what little she'd seen— seemed to be made of wood and other common materials.

The people dressed in natural fibers dyed various colors and leather. Lots of leather everywhere. Especially on the men. There were few women here. She did see one or two in the halls along their path. One wore a dress that could have come out of Camelot, the other was in leather pants and tunic. No one seemed to mind either clothing choice, which was a relief to Josie. She liked skirts well enough, but she was no medieval maiden content to wear such things on a daily basis. If she had to give up blue jeans, she was darn well going to wear their Draconian equivalent.

Nico spun on his heel as the door shut behind them, facing his brothers. Ricki stood beside him but was much less upset.

If anything, her expression looked reserved. Darius and Connor tried to stand in front of Josie, possibly to shield her from their older brother's wrath, but she was having none of that. She shouldered between them, to stand with them, between them, facing down the dragon alongside her mates.

"Now do you want to go over that again? The truth this time, if you please." Nico's raised eyebrow told them he hadn't believed anything they'd told him so far.

"It was the truth," Connor defended them. "Everything we've told you is true. Josie is a snowcat shapeshifter, blessed with a strong dose of what little magic is left in her world."

"Her grandfather helped us get back here. He led us to this talisman. See?" Darius lifted the chain around Josie's neck and she helped him, holding out the snowcat emblem for Nico to see. "It matches the amulets Shanya gave us. With the three amulets used together, Josie was able to call the storm that brought us back."

Nico still didn't look convinced.

"Look. I think it's pretty obvious, I'm not from around here, but my snowcat recognized my mates as soon as they landed in the forest and walked up to my cabin."

"Mates?" Nico's eyebrow rose even higher, if such a thing were possible. "You're mated?" He looked at his brothers for confirmation.

"Yes." Connor put an arm around her shoulders.

"She is ours." Darius put an arm around her waist.

"This is ridiculous." Nico threw his hands up in disgust and turned away, stalking off a short distance around the chamber.

Riki seemed embarrassed. "Congratulations," she offered with a wry smile. "Don't worry, he'll come around. They've all been worried sick about you two. Tensions have been running very high since Wil's kidnapping. To have another disappearance in the family so soon was more than they could really take. Roland is half convinced you're Lucan's prisoners in Skithdron. He'd have been likely to mount a major assault before long, but thank the Mother of All, that won't happen now that you're back."

Connor sighed heavily and let his arm drop from around Josie's shoulders. "I had no idea it was that bad. We were only gone a few days, but with everything that happened to us and all that we saw of Josie's world, it feels like a lifetime."

"Is it true there's no magic in your world, Josie?" Riki offered an olive branch, and Josie took it gladly.

"Not much. No dragons, certainly. My grandfather knew legends of the times when wizards fought among themselves. He said their battle fractured the magic in my world, dispersing it. Only a few races of supernatural beings can claim and use magic. The rest of the people rely on technology, and few now believe in magic."

"How sad, yet, it must be quite a different place than what you see here. I bet you'll have a big adjustment ahead of you." Riki looked sympathetic, which Josie appreciated.

"As long as I have my mates and I can run free every once in a while, it'll be all right." She tried to sound brave. Still, the little things would take a hell of a time getting used to. All those dragons, for one thing. There must have been fifty of the creatures in every color of the rainbow along their path, and every one bowed to her men as they passed. *That* would take some getting used to.

"Run free?" Riki asked.

"I'm a snowcat. I shift form into the cat and back again, much like you can become a dragon. The snowcat enjoys a fast run, particularly on rocky, challenging terrain. I live—used to live—high in the mountains with no close neighbors so I could let the cat run every day or two without worry about being seen. It would have raised quite a few eyebrows if a Himalayan snowcat were seen prowling in the Pacific Northwest. I had to be cautious about where I chose to hunt and run."

"What is a snowcat? I don't think I've ever heard of such a creature." Riki seemed interested, and even Nico had stopped muttering and pacing to stand at the far end of the chamber. He had his back turned to them, but it was clear from his posture that he listened.

"A big cat, like the Mountain Cats of Shindar, but white, with black and grey markings," Connor supplied.

"And huge paws with curving claws sheathed within to help her gain purchase on snow and ice. She glows with magic in her cat form." Darius gave her a squeeze, smiling in that roguish way he had.

"Truly?" Riki seemed eager. "Can you change form at will? Is it draining? I'll freely admit, when I first started shifting, I couldn't do it more than once a day. It was too tiring."

"Adolescent shifters often experience a drain, but I've been shifting for more than a decade. I can do it pretty much whenever I feel like it." Riki seemed receptive, so Josie offered more. "I can show you, if you like."

"Would you?" An eager light filled Riki's eyes, and Josie thought she just might have found her first friend here in Draconia.

Without thinking further on the subject, Josie called her cat and felt the white mist of magic envelop her. Darius's hand sank into the fur around her neck and scratched, just as she liked it. A purr welled up from deep in her chest as he stroked her and her ears swiveled to catch the soft gasp that issued from Riki's mouth. Nico turned to stare at her from across the chamber, and she decided to tweak him a little bit, padding toward his wife on silent paws.

"You're lovely, Josie. And you do glow with magic. It's like nothing I've ever seen before and quite stunning."

"Stand away from my mate," Nico ordered, suddenly next to Riki, facing Josie down with angry eyes.

Josie bared her teeth at him and growled low in her throat. Darius and Connor came up beside her, and she sat back on her haunches between them, almost daring Nico to say more. In the blink of an eye, she shifted back to her human form.

"I wouldn't hurt her. She's at least been nice to me." Josie's dry tone said clearly that Nico hadn't.

Finally, the older brother cracked a smile. Josie saw in that moment, his angry stance had been part of an elaborate test. Oh, he'd started off angry enough, but he was more relieved than anything else to have his brothers back. The show was to teach them a lesson and also to test the mettle of the stranger they'd brought back with them. Josie understood why they called this brother the Prince of Spies.

"Good one, Nico. You certainly know how to welcome a girl into the family." She shook her head at him while he grinned. One corner of his mouth tipped upward in acknowledgement, and she knew she'd read him right.

The twins didn't seem to get what had just happened for a minute until sudden understanding dawned and varying expressions of frustration, annoyance, relief and humor crossed their faces.

"Nico, for heaven's sake." Connor stepped forward for the hug of welcome he hadn't gotten on the landing ledge. The brothers pounded each other's backs as Nico finally relented and welcomed them home.

"Messengers have already been dispatched to Roland and the other Lairs," Hal reported. The leaders of the Lair had arrived in the round chamber a few minutes later, along with two dragons who immediately waded into the sand pit and sat as if they were part of the conversation.

It turned out this chamber was part of the leaders' suite of rooms where they lived with their dragon partners.

"They will no doubt be relieved to find you both returned to us safe and well. And there will be much rejoicing in the fact that you have taken a wife," Jures added as he joined them at a small table set at the far end of the chamber.

"I wonder what they'll make of your snowcat?" Riki mused. "I doubt there's been such a union of different kinds of magic in recent history. From what I've learned, the descendants of Draneth the Wise usually marry humans, or as in our case, distant relations who share the dragon legacy."

"We'll no doubt have someone search the archives," Nico agreed. "I suppose the Mother of All had some reason for it, which will come clear in time." As he spoke, the Lady Candis brought out some refreshments from a side room and served them to everyone, then joined the discussion.

"Nico," Connor began. "When we came out of the storm, we were on the other side of the Border. There we met and fought a group of men that used to be loyal to Salomar. We learned they have a new leader. A man called Gebel. Do you know of him?"

"Gebel?" Nico's eyes narrowed. "Are you certain?"

"That was the name we were told," Darius agreed.

"And how came you by this information?" Nico looked suspicious.

Darius grinned and took Josie's hand. "Our cat cornered the last man standing. Actually, he was trying to run away, but she's awfully fast on those pretty paws. When confronted by her teeth and the threat of us letting her eat him, the man was very forthcoming. He said this Gebel person has taken over where Salomar left off. He regrouped the armies and is working again with Lucan of Skithdron."

"This is very bad news, indeed." Nico scowled. "Gebel was the sorcerer Salomar relied on when Loralie was out of reach."

Riki picked up the tale. "Lana told me that Loralie would be absent for long periods of time, yet she always came when Salomar called. He had something that drew her, held power over her. Lana didn't know what it was, but he used it sparingly. When Loralie wasn't around, Gebel took her place at Salomar's side. He wasn't much of a magician, but he was clever and sly. Lana hated him."

"Then the counselor has now become king," Connor said with grim finality. "If he manages to solidify as much power as Salomar had, we could have trouble in the North once again."

A sudden commotion among the dragons had all the men alert. The trumpeting of dragons could be heard all around the Lair and the sound of feet pounded in the hall.

"Roland comes," Nico said, tilting his head and listening to the dragons' cacophony. "Judging by the uproar."

"The messenger couldn't have reached him yet." Jures seemed surprised.

"The king has his ways," Nico sounded mysterious as he grinned and stood, heading for the doorway. Hal and Jures stood as well, accompanying him.

"I bet Shanya saw something," Darius said to Connor in an aside just loud enough for Josie to hear as they too stood.

Josie joined them. "Who's Shanya?" And why was Josie suddenly jealous of what sounded like a girl's name being spoken so familiarly by her mates?

"She's a seer. One of the fair folk," Connor told her offhandedly, which reassured her. He wouldn't speak casually of her if there had been something between them.

"Fair folk? You mean like a fairy? A little pixie with wings who plays tricks on people?"

Both men looked at her strangely. "Fair folk are the same size as us," Darius clarified.

"They do not have wings, and Shanya seemed a very serious girl when we met her. I don't believe she is the kind of woman who enjoys tricking others," Connor picked up the explanation.

"My mistake. We have legends about fair folk in my world. There are many different stories, of course. Some describe them as cute little fairies with wings flitting about like little birds, full of otherworld magic."

They walked together toward the doorway, but were far behind their hosts and the Prince of Spies. Riki had stayed with them and the dragons remained in their wallow, though they seemed to be spiffing themselves up in preparation to receive visitors, if she was any judge. Josie noted absently that the abrasive sand seemed to do a heck of a job polishing their scales. The dragons were starting to really sparkle as they rolled around in the sand, getting it everywhere in the process. That explained the brooms placed strategically along the walls around the circular chamber.

"To my knowledge we do not have such creatures here. The fair folk are not common in our lands either, but we do know they exist. Wil told us there's a whole tribe of them living on Gryphon Isle. Shanya is one of those. She came to us only a short time ago, in the company of two young gryphons who had mated against their elders' wills. They were having a hard time finding a place for themselves among their disapproving elders, and decided to strike out and try to forge a new path here, in our land. Roland allowed them to nest in the cliffs near Castleton, and they act as envoys, of a sort, between us and the gryphons," Connor added as they ambled closer to the big, arched doorway.

"Actually, there are two sets of gryphons living with us," Riki clarified as the men nodded. "The first pair is slightly older and came from Alagorithia. We have representatives from two gryphons clans and so far, they're getting along well with us and with the dragons. It's fun to fly with them. The feather wings gives them a whole different dynamic in flight, and it's interesting to note the differences."

"It must be amazing to fly like a bird." Josie was entranced by the idea. She'd gotten used to her mates being dragons. To realize there were women out there—that Ricki could in fact, shift into a dragon—blew her mind.

"Like a dragon," Ricki teased. "And yes, it is an amazing feeling. I never thought I could do it. I never even knew my heritage, until Nico found me."

Josie would have asked more, but her mates seemed to straighten as footsteps thundered down the hall toward them. A tall, dark-haired man rounded the corner. Josie could see immediately that this was another brother. An older brother. No doubt, the king.

"Rol!" Darius rushed forward to meet him. Connor followed his twin. Both were gathered up for back-pounding hugs of welcome, and Josie could see the very real relief on their big brother's face.

"You two had me worried," Roland said as he let them go. He put one arm around each of the twins' shoulders and walked with them toward the chairs they'd just left. "Shanya said you'd be all right, but I refused to believe it until I saw you again for myself. You don't look any older, thank heaven." The brothers laughed at that, and Josie knew they must be referring to the way their youngest brother had been returned to them—five years older. That had to have been a shock.

Josie saw Nico bringing up the rear with Hal and Jures. She joined the group as Roland paused to say hello to the dragons in the sand pit. They bowed their long necks low to him, and he returned their greeting with what appeared to be genuine affection as they preened before their king. So far, Josie was getting a good impression of the king of Draconia.

He seemed more open, more accessible, than his spymaster brother. And he loved Connor and Darius. That much was clear. He'd been worried for their safety and had rushed to make sure they were all right. Anyone who cared so much for her mates, was okay in Josie's book.

Connor held out a hand to her when they were near the chairs once more, and she went to him. Darius took her other hand.

"Rol, this is our mate," Darius said, his gaze holding hers.

"Josie, this is our brother, Roland, King of Draconia." Connor finished the introduction, and Josie wasn't sure what to do. She remembered how the dragons had greeted their king and decided to give him a sort of bowing curtsy, though she didn't lower her eyes. She was too good a martial artist to lower her eyes to an opponent.

She read approval in Roland's smiling face as he stepped forward to meet her. The twins released her hands, and Roland took them, drawing her upward to stand before him.

"I am pleased to meet the woman who can tame two of my wildest brothers." The teasing twinkle in his eye made her laugh. "I wish you luck with them. Remember, now that they're yours, you cannot give them back."

Josie and Roland hit it off and though she was at first a little nervous about his being the king, his easy manner and obvious love for his family set her at ease. They reviewed the information they had already gone over with Nico, talking about Josie's world and the twins' travel through the storm to get there. Roland examined Josie's amulet with great care and also looked at the weapons the twins had brought back with them.

"Wizard's Lances, eh?" Roland asked again, verifying the name Connor had given him for the odd weapons. "I believe I have seen drawings of something like this in the ancient archives. We'll have to send the archivist on a search through the library. I don't recall at the moment where I saw it, but I do know it was there somewhere. The trident shape intrigued me when I was a lad."

Roland was less pleased with the news from the north. Nico introduced the topic, then let the twins give their report, with some input from Josie.

"I need to talk to Lana about this," Roland thought aloud as the twins finished speaking.

"That's what I thought," Riki agreed. "She knows more about the Northlands than anyone."

"For now, I suggest we adjourn to the main hall for dinner, then spend the night here. I deemed Shanya's vision reliable enough to recall our brothers to the palace. We'll fly there tomorrow for a reunion, strategy session and celebration. You'll have a full-blown wedding feast to attend by the time we arrive. You had best prepare Josie for what to expect." Roland winked and led the way out of the chamber, into the large hallway that was big enough to accommodate two dragons walking side by side.

"What did he mean by that? What's to prepare?" Josie grew concerned as she walked between her mates.

"Do you dance, Josie?" Darius asked with a twinkling smile.

"Yes. Most shifters like to dance."

"That's good," Connor took her hand in his as they walked along behind Roland, Nico and Riki, with Hal, Jures and Candis bringing up the rear. "Part of the traditional wedding feast is a series of dances. We'll explain them to you tonight...in our room."

From the banked flames in his eyes, Josie suspected the dances were more risqué than formal.

"I'll look forward to it." She squeezed his hand as he led her into another chamber. This one was huge, and full of people. A cheer went up as Roland strode into the room and many of the men bowed and smiled at the royal party.

"Are all these men knights?" There had to be well over a hundred brawny men in the room and maybe two or three dozen women scattered around among them.

"Yes. The Northern Lair houses about two hundred dragons and their knights," Hal answered from behind. She could hear the pride in his voice as he talked about his home. "We have quite a few families with youngsters—both children and dragonets—as well. The men are knights, the women you see are each partnered with a pair of knights and any youngsters are members of those families."

"Sadly, we have many single knights as well," Jures added.

"Why is that sad? I'd think any woman would jump at the chance to marry a knight and live here with all these wonderful dragons." Her answer drew smiles that brimmed with approval, but she still didn't understand.

"It's good you feel that way. Many women are afraid of the dragons and lack the ability to bespeak them. It is a rare female that can live among knights and dragons," Connor said.

"And a rare woman who won't mind when the dragon side of the family gets frisky," Darius put in with a sly grin.

"What do you mean?" There was something she was missing here.

"The dragons bond on a very deep level with their knight partners. In fact, dragons are not allowed to mate until the knights who partner with the dragon pair have found a woman willing to marry them," Connor clarified. "You see, if the dragons were to mate before their knights had a woman of their own to love, the need inspired by the dragon's lovelust would drive them mad. At such times, only a passionate encounter that mirror's the dragons' mating flight will do, and only with a woman the knights both love. Love is at the heart of such partnerships and only a true and abiding love can share in the magic of a dragon mating flight."

"So anytime the dragons in the family have sex, the knights and their wife have to follow suit?" That sounded potentially inconvenient to Josie. "What if they're in the middle of something else?"

Darius burst out laughing. "Many's a time I've seen newlyweds running half-dressed through the halls of the Castle Lair, racing to get to their mate in time."

# Chapter Ten

Later that night, when they returned to their room, it was clear someone had been there. Items appeared that hadn't been there before. Connor took a bundle of cloth from the bed with a huge grin and placed it in Josie's hands.

"What's this for?" She held up the odd bits of clothing he'd handed her.

"We're going to walk you through some of the dances you'll be expected to perform with us tomorrow." Connor seemed perfectly serious, but she could feel the purr of excitement simmering just below the surface. "Candis loaned us this for now, but I'm sure there will be fancier clothing waiting for you at the castle. Shanya is probably ordering it made, based on her visions of the future."

Josie was intrigued again by talk of this girl who saw the future, but the jealousy had passed. She was secure in her feelings for her mates, and secure in her knowledge of their love.

"Put that on, and we'll start the lessons." Darius came up behind her, wrapping his arms around her waist and placing a quick nibble in the crook of her neck that made her squirm. "The sooner we get started, the sooner we get to fuck."

"Darius!" She slapped at his arms and scooted away from him in mock outrage. In truth, she didn't want to wait any longer to have them inside her. This dancing thing had better be simple. She didn't have the patience to learn anything complicated at the moment.

She dressed quickly, wanting to get this over with. When she turned, she realized that both of her men were watching her. They'd removed some of their clothing. It wasn't enough. She wanted them naked. Now.

Dancing first, she reminded herself. She had to learn this stuff or she might look like a fool tomorrow in front of their family and half the kingdom. She owed it to them to make an effort. She didn't want to shame them or make a bad first impression on the people among whom she'd be living.

Josie forgot her annoyance after the first few minutes of the lessons. The dances were like nothing Josie had ever seen before. They were designed for three partners and involved a lot of touching, a lot of bumping and grinding that perfectly matched her mood. Each round grew progressively more daring and involved the removal of clothing until they were each clad in only thin strips of cloth and leather. It devolved from there into a Bacchanalian kind of encounter that left her breathless.

"Don't tell me we're going to be making love in front of everyone?" Her voice was a husky whisper as the twins held her between them. All three were naked and sliding skin on skin, torturing her with the hard contours of their bodies against hers. Darius was in front, Connor behind, teasing her with long strokes of their hands, their rough skin against her.

"No, love," Connor breathed into her ear, making her shiver with need. "The public part of the dancing ended a while back. This is the part we'll be doing in private, in the bower they'll have set up just for us."

"Thank the Lady for that." She dragged his mouth closer so she could kiss him.

When Connor broke off, Darius turned her head and captured her lips with his. The kiss went on and on while Connor's hands stroked down her back and into the crack of her ass. He touched lightly, then his hand went elsewhere for a few moments, only to return coated in something warm and slippery. She purred when he began to prepare her back entrance. Whatever he was using made her temperature spike and her need rise to an unbelievable height.

She reached back, clutching his ass with one hand and squeezing until he grunted and nipped her shoulder.

"No more teasing. I need you both!" Her demand was met by growls of approval as Darius picked her up and carried her to the decadently large bed. No doubt about it, this bed was made for three.

Connor took her from his brother and turned her on her side, positioning her body just the way he wanted. She was too far gone to complain. In fact, she would have applauded his take-charge attitude if she'd been able to do more than moan in ecstasy when he slid into her from behind.

Darius lay in front of her, watching his brother's claiming with a heated expression.

"How does that feel, love?" Darius asked. "Does he make you burn?"

"So good..." she managed to get out before Connor began to move. His rhythm destroyed her sense and turned her into a quivering mass of feelings. That's when Darius struck.

He suckled her breast with hard lips, using his tongue in an almost-rough motion that set her on 'fire. He switched to the other side, using his fingers to pinch the wet nipple just hard enough to make her squeal with delight. He knew just how far to push her. Just how far to torment her responsive body.

"I need you, Darius. I need both of you," she panted as

Connor picked up his languid pace.

Darius slid closer with a grin. "As I need you, my love." He fit his body to hers, coordinating with his twin. Connor held still while Darius entered her, carefully testing her receptiveness until he was certain she was with them. She loved the way they were so careful with her at all times. Even when things got a little rough, she could always trust them not to hurt her.

"Move. Please. Move." She needed them to come, to push her over the edge, to bring them all to ecstasy.

Darius growled as he complied, setting a harsher pace with Connor's full cooperation. She loved the way they worked in tandem.

One stroked inward as the other pulled out. She was never free of the sensation of thick cock filling her. Just the way she liked it. The way she needed. The way she was coming to crave.

A little more. That's all she needed. A little more and she'd be over the ledge, over the edge, into the oblivion she'd found only with her mates.

"Darius," she pleaded, tears in her voice, on her face. She gripped Connor's hand where he clutched her hip. "Connor," she whispered as the twins sped their pace. She moaned as the passion rose between them, enveloping them in a fog of desire.

"Now, baby." Darius rested his forehead against hers as the tide broke over her. She came with a strangled cry, feeling her mates join her a split second later. Together, the three of them spiraled to the highest point, riding the wind currents down. Slowly. Their pleasure lasting an eternity that blended into blissful sleep.

When Josie woke again, it was just after dawn. Someone had taken care of her in the night, bathing her and slipping her beneath the blankets. Darius and Connor were gone from the bed. The fading warmth on either side of her told her they hadn't been gone long.

She got up, slipped on a borrowed robe that lay at the foot of the bed and went in search of her mates.

The sound of running water drew her to a side chamber. Inside, she found Connor, bending over a huge stone tub that was rapidly filling with water. He looked up and smiled when he caught sight of her in the doorway.

"Good morrow, my love. I was just preparing a bath for you."

She stepped into the stone chamber, intrigued by the amenities. It was an honest to goodness bathroom, but instead of porcelain fixtures, everything was carved from stone and polished to a high gloss.

"This is really beautiful." She ran her fingers along a countertop that had a border of leaves and vines carved around it.

Connor shrugged. "It's not as fancy as the bathing chambers you'll find at the Castle Lair, but it'll do. I'm glad you like it."

"And there's hot and cold running water?" She joined him by the rustic-looking tap mechanism.

"Cold, for certain. Hot is a little harder to manage in this climate without a dragon's help. Luckily, you have two dragons at your beck and call." He grinned as he leaned in to kiss her lightly.

"No time for that." Darius bustled into the room. "Rol's got us on a tight schedule. He wants to be back at the castle by mid-day. We have just enough time to bathe and break our fast." Darius stripped as she watched, enjoying the view.

He dipped a toe into the giant tub and pulled right back out, making a face at his twin.

"You didn't even heat it yet? Come on, Con," Darius chastised his brother even as he reached out with one hand and touched the surface of the water. Within seconds, steam began to rise from the deep tub, wafting into the air with aromatic freshness.

"Now you." Connor lifted her to her feet and slid the robe off her shoulders before pushing her into the steaming water.

Much to her disappointment, the boys really did mean it when they said they didn't have time for much more than bathing and breakfast. Though they didn't rush her out of the deliciously warm water, they also didn't allow themselves to get too distracted, not matter how much she wanted to play. Well, not much anyway.

They dressed and rushed out of the borrowed suite at a fast clip. Josie was starting to get to know her way around the Lair and knew when they hit the main hallway that led to the great hall where they'd had dinner the night before. The arrangements for breakfast were a lot less formal and Roland, Nico and Riki were there before them.

The twins grabbed some food from the buffet and led her over to the king's table, seating her before grabbing their own chairs on either side of her. All three of them ate heartily, which didn't seem to raise any eyebrows here. Everyone at the table after all was a shifter and was probably used to the higher metabolism that required so much more food than regular folk. Josie was glad to be among them. She felt like part of the group rather than an interloper, even if she couldn't fly. Her cat was content, basking in the ambient warmth that seemed to always surround the dragon shifters.

"Before we set off, would you grant me one small favor, Josie?" Roland addressed her directly as the breakfast party began to break up.

"Sure. What is it?"

"I have yet to see this magical cat of yours. Would you mind shifting for me?"

Josie grinned as she used the napkin to rid herself of crumbs. She'd finished eating and was ready to go when everyone else was. She stood and faced the king, who was also standing in preparation for departure.

"No problem. I'd be happy to show you my other side." Josie called the cat and in a shimmer of white, she shifted form.

The king walked up to her, and the cat bowed its head to the monarch, without lowering its gaze. Josie's ears swiveled as she caught murmurs from those around them. It seemed her shift had caused a bit of a stir among the other people in the hall.

*"Don't worry, love. Roland must have a reason for doing this,"* Connor reassured her silently, and she realized she was being put on display deliberately.

*"Roland always has a reason,"* Darius seconded in her mind. *"If you think Nico is bad, Roland plays even deeper games of strategy. Don't ever let either one of them sucker you into a game of chess."*

Roland held out one hand to her, and Josie raised one large forepaw and put it in his.

"You are beautiful, Princess Josie, in both your forms. You glow with magic, and your cat is one I recognize from my study of ancient texts. Will you show me your claws?" He let go of her paw, and she unsheathed her claws for his perusal.

Normally she wouldn't put on a show like this for anyone, but Roland seemed interested in solving the puzzle she presented to his agile mind. If he could discover something important that might help his kingdom, she would be happy to help in whatever small way she could. These people were her

183

people now too. Now that she was going to live in this world with her mates.

"Will you walk with me, Princess Josie?" Roland asked formally.

He didn't give her time to shift, and she supposed he wanted her to walk the halls to the ledge in cat form. Well, all right. She didn't mind, and the cat needed a good stretch before she had to be a passenger on a dragon's back for who knew how many hours.

Roland strode out of the main hall with Josie at his side. Darius and Connor followed along behind her, grinning like fools at the attention she was getting in her cat form. Everyone they passed stopped and stared at her. She felt very conspicuous by the time they'd reached the ledge from which they'd depart and saw they'd gathered a huge crowd on their parade through the hallways of the Lair.

"Thank you, Josie." Roland turned to her as they neared the edge. "I have learned a great deal, and so it appears, have our people." He stepped back, and she knew then he'd done it so the Lair folk would know what she truly was. Why he wanted that, she didn't know, but he'd definitely achieved his goal.

Josie shifted back in a cloud of white mist and smiled up at the king. Roland stepped farther away and a black mist enveloped him as he shifted to his dragon form. He had the most amazing emerald eyes as a man that held true in his dragon form. With a mighty sweep of his wings, he took to the air.

Darius and Connor gave her sweet kisses and tight hugs, then she was bundled up in a warm fur coat and given a small bag of provisions to carry. She said goodbye to Candis while the twins shifted shape, then climbed on Connor's back and away they went.

They stopped only once during the long flight for the dragons to get a sip of water from a crystal-clear lake. The countryside was dotted with farms and forestland. It was hilly in places, and she could see mountains in the distance. All in all, it was a beautiful, fertile land, free of the smog of urban life. It was lovely.

Josie took a moment to stretch and felt the urge to do a little *t'ai chi* while she was in such beautiful surroundings. She hadn't felt this much at peace in a place in a long time. Her mountain home in Oregon had some of this feeling, of course, but she was always cautious about hikers and day-trippers who came onto her land at least a few times a year. She never knew when or how she would be disturbed in her sanctuary, only that she would be.

She had none of that subtle stress here. No, these people were shifters of an even more magical kind. From all accounts the townspeople were used to magic and though her cat form might garner attention, she wasn't likely to become the target of an insane news media if she was spotted running across the hills. For the first time since leaving her grandfather's home, she felt truly free to be who she was.

"What was that you were doing?" Riki came up behind Josie after she'd finished her *t'ai chi* form and was reaching for an apple from the sack she'd carried. The men were still mostly in dragon form, some guarding while others refreshed themselves with food, drink or simply a moment of peaceful motionlessness.

"It's a form of moving meditation called *t'ai chi ch'uan*."

"It's beautiful."

"It has a practical side too. Each of the movements is either a defense or attack posture."

"Really?" Riki looked truly interested. Josie explained a bit

185

more as Riki sat beside her, taking another apple from the sack on the ground.

"It's actually a martial art." Josie stood and moved into one of the postures. "See? This is actually a block while this hand is in a strike position." She flowed into the next move. "Watch my hands and imagine someone standing behind me. See the way my fingers are curled? Aiming for my opponent's eyes. Gross, huh?" Josie smiled at Riki's astonished expression.

She looked up to find Roland watching her with narrowed eyes. He'd shifted to human form and walked over without her knowing. These dragons moved like the wind.

Riki passed him the sack of food, and he pulled out a sandwich for himself before settling next to Riki on the ground. Nico appeared and sat on his wife's other side, grabbing the sack out of his brother's hands. Josie looked around for the twins, realizing they were the only two left standing in dragon form, their necks craned and their stances alert.

"I left the boys on guard duty." Nico waved a hand in the twins' direction. "Punishment for making us worry."

"Nico, that's not nice. They're newly mated. They'll want to spend time with Josie," Riki protested.

"I know." Nico grinned and placed a smacking kiss on his wife's lips. "They're young. They'll survive. And they'll think twice about worrying us again."

"It really wasn't their fault," Josie protested, sitting again with the group. "They didn't call the storm. At least not on purpose. I think it was meant to come for them. My grandfather said all of this was part of my destiny. Part of the prophecies of a time almost completely forgotten in my world—even by those touched by magic."

"Your grandfather is some kind of mystic, Darius said." Nico's question was a leading one but she didn't mind answering.

"All snowcats are revered by other supernaturals—particularly other kinds of shifters. Snowcat holds a position of spiritual power because, of all the shifter clans, we have the most magic. Or so my grandfather would have everyone believe."

"Why is that? And in what ways are you more magical than others?" Nico continued his not-too-subtle interrogation. She decided to fill them in on her background. It was better if she told them without the elder brothers needing to pry it out of her. She figured they'd learn the story sooner or later anyway.

"The snowcat clan lives high in the mountains of Tibet. It's a remote country with a long mystical tradition. Many kinds of holy men seek enlightenment in the Himalayas—a snow-covered mountain range that has some of the highest peaks on the planet. It was the playground of ancient wizards, including the founder of my line, the one known as Marpa. My full name is Josephine Marpa. My mother was human, my father was the heir to the snowcat legacy. When he died, my mother took me to her land, which is where I grew up for the most part, among humans. She died when I was a teenager, and my grandfather came to get me. He didn't have high hopes for me. He didn't even think I'd be able to shift, but I surprised him, and myself. My snowcat is strong, even though I'm only half snowcat by birth."

She fished another apple out of the sack and leaned back against a convenient rock, continuing her explanation. "My grandfather is a holy man. A warrior monk. And he likes to keep up the tradition of snowcats being more spiritually connected and magical than all other shifters. It's not something I enjoy. I wasn't raised on his mountain. I grew up in the real world. But there's no arguing that snowcats have more magic than most shifters in my world. For one thing, like you dragons, we take our clothes with us into the shift. Almost all other shifters need to disrobe before shifting or risk ruining their wardrobe."

"That's inconvenient." Nico made a face.

"Very," Josie agreed. "It's also inconvenient to be a snowcat among other shifters. They all tend to want to make me into some sort of holy person, which I'm not. It's even worse when they're Buddhists, and they know I'm a descendant of Marpa."

"He was a wizard, right?" Roland asked.

"So the legends say. Unfortunately, one of the world's major religions also credits him with being one of its founders. Human Buddhists would never associate my last name with my lineage. It's the shifters who are Buddhists who know I really am one of his descendants. They expect me to be wise and all-knowing. I hate to disappoint them when they find out I'm just as confused as everyone else is most of the time." She chuckled, and the others followed suit.

"It's not always easy to bear the burden of lineage. I do think it's significant that we're all descended from wizards, however." Roland shot her a sideways look full of speculation. "In our case, the common ancestor is Draneth the Wise—he who joined with dragonkind. I wonder why the Mother of All put you in our brothers' path."

She liked that. The Mother of All. It was one of the names her grandfather's people called the Mother Goddess. She didn't know much about her mates' religion yet, but she had an open mind where spirituality was concerned. Considering the way she'd been raised, straddling two cultures and belief systems, she knew firsthand that there was no one true way.

Her mother's religion had looked to a male deity. Her father's beliefs had taught ways to seek harmony with the Earth, guided by the Mother of All. As a shifter, Josie had always felt a little more comfortable with her father's beliefs about the Earth spirit and the female flavor of creation than the stuffy church her mother had taken her to. Besides, the incense they burned in that place had made her sneeze.

Whatever deity anyone followed, Josie believed some higher power had been instrumental in bringing her in contact with her mates. Too many amazing things had to happen to bring them together to believe it had all been coincidence. Josie had never believed in coincidence. In fact, she was more likely to believe in things like destiny and fate—especially where true matings were concerned.

"All I know is that Darius and Connor are my true mates. My cat recognized them the minute she met them. Actually, she recognized them one at a time, but both were her mates. It's like that for most shifters. A scent, a flavor, a feeling. We know our mates when we meet them. Of course, it's rare to have two mates. I never did take the easy road in life. It's illegal in most countries in my world to marry more than one person at a time. And it's usually a man trying to marry more than one woman. The opposite is practically unheard of." She quirked a smile at her own expense.

"Dragons are like that when they recognize their mate, as are the knights who partner them." Roland finished his repast and tossed the organic refuse. "As you no doubt saw in the Lair, three-partnered marriages are the norm among knights, so you'll have no problems here."

"That's one small advantage to coming here, I guess." She stood and brushed off her pants.

"I hope you will find other compensations to living in this world, Josie." Roland was as serious as she'd ever seen him. "I don't think I could survive if any more of my family were taken from me."

Whoa. That was a warning if she'd ever heard one. Josie decided to play it cool. He was the king here, after all. Still, he needed to know the truth.

"My grandfather said I had the power to call the storm that would take us between worlds. He also intimated that I would go back to my world at some point in the future, but I got the feeling my true destiny lay here. What that destiny is, we will discover together—Connor, Darius and I."

Roland eyed her for a long moment, then he nodded. "Fair enough. We should continue our journey if we want to reach the castle by midday."

Josie decided not to say anything to her mates about the conversation with his elder brothers. She figured they already had a pretty good idea what their brothers had been up to. The looks she'd seen pass between them when she'd mounted up on Darius's back said as much.

The castle was like something out of a fairy tale. They flew over the top of a mountain and there it was, in the distance, built into the side of an even-more-dominant peak. A castle carved into the spire of rock with a rainbow of dragons flying around. When the closest dragons caught sight of their party, the loud trumpeting began, to be echoed by the other dragons within earshot.

Then Josie noticed the town. A city really. Built around the base of the castle, on verdant slopes. The farthest outskirts had open farmland and a few larger homes and compounds of different types. The whole thing looked like some fantasy artist's concept of a magical medieval city. It was breathtaking.

It also was a stark reminder that this was not her world.

"'Toto, I don't think we're in Kansas anymore.'"

*"What was that, my love?"* Darius asked in her mind.

"Nothing. Just thinking aloud."

At various heights along the mountain palace, Josie saw landing platforms similar to what she'd seen at the Northern Lair. Roland led the way as other dragons joined their small formation like an honor guard on either flank.

By the time they reached the castle, they had a real crowd of dragons. Now this was some kind of welcome home. She looked down and realized people were spilling out of the houses and businesses they flew over to wave and smile.

As they whizzed past, she noticed more than one puzzled smile sent her way until she realized she was the only one riding on a black dragon. Since the black dragons were known as royal blacks, she guessed that was a rare-enough occurrence to merit a second look.

Roland took them in an almost acrobatic arc upward that left her dizzy. It also landed them atop one of the lower landing platforms. One by one, the black dragons sought purchase on the thick rock slab. The smallest of the blacks was female, and Riki had a rough go of it when she tried to emulate her husband's smooth landing. Still, she made it in one piece.

Josie was glad of her mates' skill at setting down smoothly. She hopped down from Darius's back and followed the parade of dragons into a huge stone archway. One by one, the dragons shifted to human form. Connor came behind her and lifted her off her feet for a quick, hard kiss before passing her to his twin.

Josie's head was whirling when Darius let her go, finally. They had to scamper to catch up with the rest of the small group. Josie tried to get a good look at the elaborately carved rock in the hallways, but they had to hurry. When they entered through a huge archway, Josie stopped short. Riki stood waiting for her with an identical twin and behind them loomed the largest, shiniest dragon she'd ever seen in her life.

191

"Whoa." Darius and Connor stopped beside her, one on either side. "Is that Tor? Man, you told me what he looked like but... Wow."

The gleaming silver head perked up as she spoke his name, and his neck extended to hover just a few feet away.

*"I'm Tor. Who are you?"* The childlike voice boomed through her mind as the Ice Dragon's tongue peeped out as if to lick the air. *"Your magic tastes funny. It tickles."*

"This is Josie, scamp," Darius said, reaching up to stroke Tor's shiny scales.

"She's our mate," Connor added.

*"Your mate?"* Tor blinked and looked at her even more closely. *"What is she? Her magic is furry."*

The twins laughed outright, as did Josie. "That's because I am furry. Well, half of me is. I'm a snowcat."

Diamond eyes blinked widely. *"A snowcat? Truly?"* This was said in hushed tones.

"What do you know of snowcats, sweetheart?" The twin Josie hadn't yet been introduced to stepped forward. This was Lana then. Queen of Draconia.

*"When I was in the shell, back before you started taking care of me, Lana, Mama told me about snowcats. She said they were hiding."*

"What's this, son?" Roland came over, concern clear on his face.

The precocious young dragon was too focused on Josie to answer the king. He moved closer, his snout only inches from her face.

*"Will you show me the snowcat? Please?"* He sounded just like a little kid, and Josie realized that children were probably similar regardless of their species. *"Seeing a snowcat is*

*supposed to be good luck."*

Josie looked to her mates. Connor seemed wary. It was Darius who took her hand and spoke.

"If you don't mind shifting for him, knowing our nephew, he won't rest until he's chased your fluffy white tail around the audience hall once or twice."

Josie shrugged and called the cat. In a mist of white she became her alter ego. The silver dragon followed her change in height with rapt attention.

*"You're pretty. And furry!"* Tor exclaimed, delight clear in his tone as he looked at her. He reached out with one big talon, and she lifted her paw to show him her smaller set of claws as smoke issued from his mouth in a dragonish chuckle of delight. He was so entertained, she decided to show him a little more.

Josie dashed around the room, leaping up onto the small stone ledge that lined the perimeter of the ornate chamber. It was a good ten feet up in the air and required all her balance, which gave her cat a good workout. She began to show off, using her native agility and speed to practically climb the stone walls with her big paws. There were carved outcroppings that worked as balance points for her, given the speed of her ascent.

When she was as high as she could safely go, she jumped out and down, landing on all fours right in front of the delighted Ice Dragon. She twitched her tail and sat in front of him.

*"Did you see that?"* Tor looked to Lana first, then to Roland, then to the rest of the group. Josie had put on her little demonstration for the dragonet. It didn't hurt for the others to realize that while they might be fire-breathing dragons, she also had her talents. *"Mama described snowcats to me when I wasn't even hatched. She said they were acrobats, and she was right. She said she'd take me to see them after I hatched, but then Salomar's men came and then Lana took care of me after Mama*

*left.*"

Josie's heart broke a little for the poor, orphaned dragonet.

"That was the witch's doing, sweetheart," Lana spoke soothingly at the baby dragon's side, stroking her hand over his long neck. "Your mama was tricked into leaving. Otherwise, nothing could have made her leave you. We talked about this."

*"I know, Lana."* There was sadness in his tone that touched Josie deeply. She shifted back to her human form and bowed to the dragonet, drawing his attention.

"It's a pleasure to meet you, Tor. Your Uncle Darius and Uncle Connor told me a lot about you. You're just as smart and handsome as they said you were. I like the way you sparkle."

The young dragon preened as she'd hoped he would, his sad thoughts banished for the moment by her praise.

*"Thank you, Josie. And thank you for showing me the snowcat. She's pretty and so are you."*

"Thanks. You've heard of snowcats, huh? That's funny because Darius and Connor said they'd never seen my kind before."

Tor's face scrunched up as if he was thinking hard. *"Well, I haven't seen any here in Draconia and I never saw one when we lived in the mountains Salomar controlled, but Mama said there were lots of them farther north, in the coldest high places. Even higher up in the mountains than where Salomar lived."*

"That makes sense," she told him, knowing the others would hear her as well. "My family lives in the tallest mountain range on my world. The snowcat's big paws are designed for treading lightly over the deepest layers of snow and ice."

"If there are snowcats here," Connor said in a speculative tone, "then I think we have our answer as to what the Mother of All was thinking when She brought you to us, Josie."

"Part of the answer, to be sure." A new voice intruded from the doorway.

Josie turned to see a pale blonde...vision, walking toward them. The girl had an ageless beauty and the most harmonious voice she'd ever heard.

"Who is that?" she whispered to her mates.

"Shanya, as usual, you speak in riddles." Darius gave Josie her answer even as he greeted the beauty with a teasing grin. "Why don't you come straight out with it? Just this once."

"It is good to see you returned safely, Prince Darius, Prince Connor." She nodded to each of them in turn. "And it is especially good to see you here, in our world, daughter of Marpa. Your people are gathering even now."

"My people?" Josie was stymied by the girl's words.

"The snowcats. They have had a hard road since the great schism, when half of their tribe crossed through the storm from the place from whence you came. They have been reading the signs and listening to their own seers. Even now, I believe they travel in stealth to the northern border. Soon, a messenger will come seeking you, descendent of Marpa. You will bring hope to your people and in time, perhaps, strong allies in our fight against evil."

"Whoa," Josie whispered. She couldn't help it. This was all too much.

Connor took her hand and squeezed, drawing her attention. He spoke to Shanya but his words rang through the chamber, meant for all.

"Our mate will choose her own path, in the fullness of time."

After a tense moment, Shanya grinned and stepped forward, her hand outstretched to Josie. "Of course." They shook hands and Josie felt the real welcome in Shanya's touch. The girl fizzed with magical energy that almost tickled. This then, was one of the fair folk of this world. To Josie, she looked like an elf out of a fantasy movie. "It's good to meet you. I'm Shanya."

"Josie." She returned the girl's smile. They moved apart, and Shanya turned to Roland, bowing deeply.

"Please forgive the intrusion, my liege. I thought it best to prepare you all for what I have seen coming."

"When did you foresee this?" Roland asked.

"It only just came clear last night, sire. The first visions of the white spotted cat started weeks ago, but I didn't really understand what I was seeing. Then the cats multiplied. All male. A veritable army of them. They are on the move."

"An army of creatures like Josie, heading for our border?" Nico strode forward, clearly concerned.

"I believe so." Shanya's forehead wrinkled with tension. "Last night I had the clearest vision yet. In a dream I saw them traveling on foot over snowy mountains. Many mountains. A great distance, to reach your border. I believe they come to see the descendant of Marpa. Her coming was foretold in their most ancient teachings and the portents were read by their seers and their shaman. It is he, I believe, who called the initial storm that sent your brothers to Josie's world."

"Then they have a lot of explaining to do." Roland looked grim.

"Sire, they could be strong allies in defense of the Citadel. Their natural domain is ice and snow," Shanya reminded him in a gentle voice that held a core of iron.

Roland sighed. "Give me some time to get used to this, Seer. I thank you for the warning. I will think hard on all you have told us."

Shanya turned to Nico, appeal in her expression. "The Northern Lair should be warned. The snowcats likely do not realize Josie is mated to your brothers. There could be trouble before all parties understand what has happened. The shaman opened the rift expecting their kind to come through. I don't think they intended to send two dragons on such a journey, much less that the dragons in question would claim the snowcats' prize."

"I'll send a messenger at once. Thank you, Shanya." Nico turned and left the hall in a hurry.

# Chapter Eleven

After the long journey, Josie was looking forward to a little down time. She was also looking forward to seeing where and how her new mates lived. This was their home, after all. They'd been born and raised in this amazing castle. Never in a million years would she have ever believed she'd go from rustic cabin in the woods to monumental castle on the side of a mountain in just a few short days.

She was here now, though. She had to start learning her new surroundings.

The twins brought her to what they called the family wing of the massive castle. Everything was ornate and lovely. Carvings in the living rock depicted everything from dragons and knights in battle scenes to flowers and vines in innocent border designs and swirls.

"This one's ours," Connor said, stopping before a door that had two dragons carved on it. Most of the others in the family wing had just one dragon on each door.

"We tried separate suites once, but we're twins. We're used to being together. It got kind of...lonely," Darius admitted with a sheepish grin as he turned the knob and opened the door. "We asked them to connect the two suites into one double-sized suite for us both. We hope you'll like it." He led the way inside, and Josie followed with Connor.

"If you don't like anything, we'll be happy to renovate, remodel, even move elsewhere, if you like," Connor was quick to add.

Josie stepped inside and was immediately enchanted by the vast chamber that served as a sort of living room. There was a collection of richly upholstered chairs, including two long couches, off to one side near a fireplace. Gorgeous tapestries hung on the walls depicting various scenes, probably from Draconia's history. One wall was completely covered with shelving containing hundreds of books. Everything had a decidedly masculine air, which she had expected. She'd also expected the luxury—they were princes after all—but she hadn't expected the level of comfort. It all looked so inviting. Luxurious, certainly, but homey and warm at the same time.

"It's beautiful. I wouldn't change a thing. Except maybe..." She turned to them with a teasing expression.

"Anything." Darius seemed to understand her mood better than his twin. Connor just looked anxious. "You may have anything your heart desires."

"Well, I think you could use a vase of flowers on the end table. That's all." She grinned and skipped away before Darius could catch her. The relief on Connor's face was almost comical.

"We can leave this room as it is then." Darius walked purposefully toward the doors arranged along one wall. "We have our own small kitchen, bathing chamber and bedrooms. We'll probably want to remodel those into one big bedchamber for all of us." Darius's grin was devilish as he waggled his eyebrows at her.

"We also each have a den. A room just to ourselves. You should probably have one too. We can look into that tomorrow. And eventually..." Connor's expression grew wistful as she watched him search for words. "Eventually, we may need a nursery."

The thought stunned her. She hadn't thought much beyond mating, but children were the natural result. She stopped short, her mind racing. She was near enough to one of the couches to drop onto its soft cushions.

"What's wrong, sweetheart?" Darius came over and sat beside her, one arm going around her shoulders as he shot his brother a disgusted look.

"What will our children be?" To her shock and chagrin, her voice shook.

"Be?" Darius was clearly confused. Connor, though, she could see he knew what she meant. He came over and knelt before her, taking one of her hands in his.

"Our children will be loved, Josie. Be they dragon, snowcat or even if they cannot shift at all. They will be ours, and they will be loved."

A single tear ran down her face, and she reached out to hug him, feeling Darius's arms come around her from behind. They stayed that way for a long minute, her mates reassuring her with their warm presence. At length she pulled back, wiping her wet cheeks.

"I'm sorry. It just hit me. I hadn't thought about it before, and it took me by surprise." She stood, her mates standing also, one holding each of her hands.

"To be perfectly honest," Darius said, grinning sheepishly, "I hadn't given it any thought either. Con's the planner. You tell him what you want done with the place, and he'll be certain to get it done right." Darius pulled her back against his chest, his arms around her waist. "I like the idea of you round with our child, Josie. It makes me want to see it for real. As soon as possible." He growled and nipped her earlobe, making her squeak.

"Not too soon, dragon. I need a little time to get used to this place first."

Connor stole her out of his twin's arms and hugged her close. "No rush, sweetheart. We want what you want. Your happiness is our goal. We know you gave up a lot to come here and be with us. We will never forget that. Take all the time you want to get used to our world. We have many years of love ahead of us."

"Speaking of that." She tugged out of his arms and moved a short distance away where she could face them both. "I omitted to tell you something before, when your brothers asked in what ways snowcats are more magical than other shifters in my world. I hope you won't be angry. I wanted to tell you two first, before your brothers found out."

Both men looked concerned. "You can tell us anything," Darius said. "We will not be angry."

"What is it, beloved?" Connor's voice was as gentle as she'd ever heard it.

"Snowcats—full-blooded snowcats—are nearly immortal. My grandfather isn't actually *my* grandfather. He's my grandfather's grandfather. Snowcats live very long life spans unless they are killed somehow."

"But you're only half snowcat," Connor pointed out.

"I'll live a very long life, but not quite that of my grandfather."

"That's good, because dragons live very long lives too, but nothing like the fair folk, for example. They are said to be immortal as well, but they do age and can be killed. I think they are probably a lot like your grandfather's people."

Relief coursed through her veins. "I was afraid you'd be upset. Most shifters in my world live a few hundred years. Snowcats can live a few thousand. I'm probably somewhere in between."

Grins spread across the twins' handsome faces. "As are we," Darius confirmed.

Connor walked up to her and took her hand again. "The Mother of All brought us together, my love. She knows what She is doing."

"Although" Darius interjected, his expression somber, "in recent generations, we black dragons have been dying much too young. Assassins and so-called accidents almost destroyed our family in the not-too-distant past. We will do all we can to protect you from our enemies, but this is not a peaceful world we've brought you to."

Josie reached out to cup his cheek. "No place is ever truly safe, Darius. I was in constant danger of discovery in my world. If the wrong people had learned of my existence, I could have been imprisoned, hunted, used as a lab rat or tortured in many different ways. That's why I was always careful not to be seen by humans. Other shifters and some other supernatural races would've challenged me to a death match just for being what I am. No, no place is truly safe. I'd rather be here, with you, for as long as we have, than hiding in my cabin in the woods."

"I'm glad you said that." Darius swept her off her feet and walked with her toward one of the doors. "I think it's time I showed you my bedchamber. You should test out the mattress to see if it is to your liking."

"I thought you'd never ask."

After a romp that involved testing both Darius's and Connor's mattresses for comfort, a discreet knock on the outer door roused Connor enough to go answer the summons. He came back to his bedroom a short time later, his arms laden with mounds of sparkling fabric.

"What's that?" Her voice sounded rough from all the moaning and pleading her men had made her do. They'd even made her scream once or twice. Good thing these chambers had thick stone walls that didn't allow sound to travel too far.

"Our wedding finery." Connor grinned as he threw a pile of the clothing at Darius, who'd only just risen on one elbow to watch the proceedings. He took a smaller pile of fabric and presented them to her. "These are for you, milady." The teasing grin and obsequious bow made her laugh as she leapt from the bed to check out her new clothes.

She didn't understand the various strips of fabric and leather at first, but her mates soon set her straight. This was like no wedding dress she'd ever seen. Now the movements of the dances they'd taught her became clearer. This outfit consisted of a series of layers, each more risqué than the last. She'd be peeled out of them during the dance, as she peeled quite a few less layers off her mates in return.

The fabric was silk, satin and brocade, heavily embroidered and gorgeous. Everything was sensuous, including the buttery-soft leather and suede that showed up here and there. The designs embroidered into the fabric were a dragon motif, of course. As she picked up the final garment, a sort of coat-like thing that went over all the rest, her breath caught in her throat.

There was her snowcat, in all her glory, surrounded by the dragons, one on either side, their wings extended protectively over her even as she stood tall and strong.

"I love this." Connor came over to look at the garment as Darius stirred himself to roll out of bed and take a look. "How did they know?"

The twins looked at each other, both grinning. "Shanya," they said together.

"It had to be her." Connor clarified, "She is a seer. She's the one who told us we'd be going on a journey to a place she could barely describe. I have no doubt about her abilities."

Josie ran her fingers lightly over the design and was met with a magical tingle.

"I think she embroidered this herself." She looked up at her mates, a feeling of wonder running through her. "What a nice thing to do. This is one of the nicest things anyone's every done for me, and I'd never even met the woman when she probably started working on this. Wow."

"The more I learn of Shanya, the more I like her." Darius touched Josie's head, stroking her hair.

"She brought us together," Connor said quietly. "For that alone, we owe her more than we can ever repay."

The wedding feast was totally unexpected no matter how much her mates had tried to prepare her for it. All the princes were there. All were tall, strongly built men, even the youngest of them who looked to be in their late teens. They all had green eyes, most of the striking emerald variety. Lana and Riki looked beautiful in their finery, as did their younger sister and their mother, who were both married to sets of knights that had been introduced with the title of Prince-Consort. Many, many others had gathered to celebrate their wedding, including what looked to be every last dragon in the land.

When Darius and Connor took her out of the huge great hall for a breath of air, Josie realized that the party spilled over to every part of the castle and out into the town beyond. She could see the light of a hundred bonfires in every part of the city, and the sound of music and laughter floated on the air.

"Is all of that merrymaking for us?" she asked her mates.

"We sent money to every innkeeper in Castleton to pay for

drinks and food for every soul in the town," Connor said quietly, stroking her cheek and looking deep into her eyes.

Darius came up behind her, nibbling on her ear. "It's good to share our happiness with a celebration everyone will remember."

"But the expense," she protested faintly as her mates sandwiched her between them.

"You're worth everything we have," Connor answered, his lips hovering over hers.

"Everything and more," Darius agreed, biting her earlobe gently as she shivered.

*"Aren't you three getting a little ahead of yourselves?"* A booming dragon voice sounded with amusement through all their minds. Distracted, Josie looked upward to find a stunning blue green dragon looming over them from the battlement above. She was hanging at a precarious angle and smoky laughter issued from her mouth. Beside her, other dragons perched, looking down at them with interest. A gleaming golden male sat beside a marvelous female red. Next to them was a gorgeous female peach dragon and a shiny bronze male. She was looking at mated pairs, she realized. The blue green female seemed older somehow, than the others, as did the shining bronze male who sat on her other side.

"Lady Kelzy, you know what it is to be newly united with your mate," Connor said in as close to a wheedling tone as she'd ever heard from him.

"Give us some wing room, dragon mother," Darius added with a winning smile.

*"You've had enough wing room for now, younglings,"* the dragon answered in their minds. *"You have a party to attend and a dance to perform, then we will join you in a mating flight. We're all looking forward to it."*

"She knows I can't fly, right?" Josie whispered to Connor, but the dragons heard, much to her embarrassment.

*"There is no shame in what you are, earthbound child,"* the dragon named Kelzy said. *"Besides, a triple flight would be foolhardy at best. It is not the way we dragons do things, but for those of you in human form, I understand it is very pleasurable. At least our partners think so."*

The dragons chuckled again at her words, and she realized they were all part of family units made up of two knights, two dragons and one very lucky woman. This land was certainly strange, but the people and dragons she'd met so far had been wonderful and accepting of her differences.

"Thank you, Lady Kelzy, is it?" She tried to be polite and wasn't quite sure of the name. Connor came to her rescue.

"You heard right, my love. Forgive me. This is Lady Kelzy and her mate, Sir Sandor. Next to her is Sir Arlis and his mate, Lady Lilla. Next to them is their daughter, Lady Jenet and her mate, Sir Nelin. They are newly mated."

"It's nice to meet you all. Thank you for helping us celebrate our mating." Josie tried to meet every dragon's gaze with her smile.

*"My lady is right,"* Sir Sandor spoke in their minds in a booming voice different from his mate's. It was rougher and deeper, but still an exceedingly pleasant rumble in her mind. *"We all look forward to the mating flight. You'd best get back in there and perform the dances, younglings. Then the real fun can begin."*

His suggestion was followed by a pointed wingbeat that stirred a wind, almost pushing them toward the door that led inside. Josie laughed outright at being blown around by the bronze's huge wings.

*"Welcome to Draconia, Princess Josie,"* Kelzy said, echoed by

the other dragons.

"Ah, there they are." A cultured voice projected over the background noise, drawing her attention from the dragons. She looked over to find a gorgeous blond man walking toward them from the direction of the great hall.

"Drake." Darius reached out to greet the other man with a hand-to-elbow arm clasp, a back pounding half-hug and a big smile. When he stepped back, Connor did the same as Darius turned to another knight who had come up behind the flashy blond.

Connor turned to her, bringing the handsome man forward. Connor's expression was filled with welcome, and she knew without them saying anything more that these two men were very close friends.

"Josie, this is Drake, partner to Jenet. And this is Mace, partner to Nelin." He gestured toward the dragons as he introduced their knights. The magnificent metallic peach dragon was paired with an equally handsome man, and both her bronze mate and his fighting partner looked to be solid, less flashy but still formidable beings.

Josie unconsciously held out her hand, expecting a shake. The blond Adonis surprised her by placing a courtly kiss on her knuckles as he swept her a theatrical bow. She chuckled at his antics.

"Drake of the Five Lands, at your service."

She looked at her mates for explanation. The trained speaking voice, theatricality and handsome visage all made her think this guy was some kind of actor or something.

"Drake worked for our brother Nico secretly for the many years he spent in an exile of his own making," Connor explained. She already knew Nico was called the Prince of Spies. This guy had to be one of his agents.

"He is a gifted bard," Darius added. "Will you play for us tonight, my friend?"

"But of course," Drake answered with a sparkling grin.

Josie tried not to be too starstruck by his charm, turning to the other knight. Mace took her hand and gave her a much less showy greeting.

"It's a pleasure to meet you," she said to the more somber knight.

"Thank you for bringing the twins home safely." Mace seemed truly thankful, which made her feel really good. No one had thanked her for her part in bringing them all here, she realized, yet this quiet knight recognized her contribution and took the time to thank her for it. Still waters ran deep with this one, she surmised.

"Saves us the trouble of trying to find yet another prince of the realm," Drake joked. It was then she realized these two were the knights she'd been told about who'd gone after Prince Wil.

"You're the firedrakes." The words popped out of her mouth before she realized she'd spoken aloud.

Both men seemed surprised but recovered quickly. "You are correct, milady," Mace said in deep tones. "But that is our secret for now, until we learn how to better control the power."

"Nobody will hear it from me. I'm sorry. I didn't mean to blurt it out like that. Darius and Connor told me stories about you—about all of you—while we traveled." Her gesture included all the dragons as well as the men.

"We have heard tales of you as well, milady," Drake added with a sly grin. "As a bard, I would love to hear more about your world and your people sometime."

She looked to her mates. She didn't see anything wrong with telling him about her world, but maybe they had some objection. They looked at her encouragingly, which she took to mean they supported the idea.

"I'd be happy to."

"But not this minute," Mace broke in with an apologetic smile. "Prince Nico sent us to get you. The dancing cannot start without the guests of honor."

Drake laughed and added to Mace's words. "The younglings have been sent off to bed and all within that hall are eager to start the adult portion of the evening." An audacious wink made her blush. This one was a charmer, indeed.

"Truth be told—" Darius took her arm, "—so are we."


The dancing was even more raucous than Josie had been led to expect. The first thing to go was her ornately designed brocade robe. As the first few dances ended, she lost more and more of her outer layers of clothing. The great hall was filled with merrymakers but the newly mated trio was the center of attention.

The dances were athletic and became increasingly so as the beat sped up and the movements became more intense. Josie was tossed between her mates in the steps of the dance but after a while, she decided to add her own acrobatic flare to the moves. She began to add little twirls and flips to the moments in mid-air when she was between her two mates, and the crowd cheered as the twins beamed.

If she was going to live here, among these people, she had to distinguish herself in some way. They had to know that although they had mighty dragons, the snowcat was nothing to be trifled with. For the first time in her life, she was dealing with people fully aware of magic who had no idea of the snowcat's legendary reputation. She owed it to her clan and to herself to make them understand just how formidable the snowcat could be, but she had to do it in a friendly way.

If a few acrobatic moves began the process of their realization, so much the better. She'd prefer they came to understand her true nature in their own time. She did not, however, wish to be underestimated. She wanted to be on equal footing—or as close as she could come to it—with her mates. The people of this medieval-esque world were going to learn the prowess of the snowcat. She would do her people, and her grandfather, proud.

The throbbing pulse of the music had her giddy. It was created with a myriad of stringed instruments, whistles, flutes and drums. Simple music that made her heart pound. It was gorgeous and the handsome blond troubadour-knight was right at the center of the creation of it. After the first few tunes, he gave up his place to the delicate blonde, Shanya, who surprised Josie with how fiercely she participated in the creation of the incredible sounds the small orchestra produced that filled the room and then some.

By the time they'd gone through about three-quarters of her layers of clothing, Josie was feeling decidedly hot. To be sure, her temperature had risen along with the athleticism of the dance patterns, but she was also getting excited by the body contact between her and her now bare-chested mates. Rubbing along their muscular bodies as they tossed her back and forth between them was getting her hot and bothered. She was more than ready to take this to the next level...somewhere private.

But there were more dances to perform and a few more layers of clothing to unwind from around her body before they could go off to be alone. She put her all into the dancing, enjoying her moment in the spotlight. Josie had never been so free to be herself in public. She'd never had the opportunity to show what she could do physically in front of a crowd. Oh, she'd been tested by her snowcat teachers, but being only half snowcat and raised mostly in the Western world, she had never excelled at the martial arts skills her full-snowcat relatives took for granted.

This was a special night. She felt truly accepted by these people and welcomed. Certainly, some probably still had reservations about her. They also had open minds, and she had the freedom to be herself. Fully herself.

The freedom was unlike anything she'd ever experienced before.

And the arousal her mates inspired with these lascivious dances was even more freeing.

They twirled her between them, unrolling the last of the winding layers of cloth around her body. She was left in only a skimpy micro-miniskirt and a sort of halter band tied around her chest to support her breasts. Her men were wearing only leather pants, their gleaming muscles bared and beckoning her.

There were other trios around them, similarly involved in the dancing, including Drake, Mace and an athletic woman who must be their mate. Josie felt like part of the group in the truest sense. She sensed their acceptance, their joy in the union of her and her mates. The feeling was indescribably good. Sustenance for a soul she hadn't known was craving just such feelings of welcome and acceptance.

The final dance was even more provocative than all that had gone before. The music was a pounding beat, driving them onward, driving her arousal higher. Around them, trios were leaving the floor, seeking privacy. She wasn't surprised when Connor caught her in his arms and carried her off the dance floor. Darius followed close behind.

They made a beeline for their quarters. When they finally reached the doorway, she was surprised to see that someone had been there in their absence. A garland of flowers framed the huge doorway and when it opened, she discovered the main room had been decorated into a decadent love nest. A feast had been laid out on a side table—foods that would keep well without refrigeration and looked divine.

Darius laid her gently on the nest of furs that had been set up in the middle of the room.

"Who did this?" Her gesture encompassed the whole room and the way it had been transformed.

"Who cares?" Darius was focused on removing the rest of her minimal clothing, while Connor was removing his own trousers.

"I suspect it was some of the ladies of the Lair," Connor said as he joined her on the nest of fur and pillows. "We will thank them for their thoughtfulness...tomorrow."

"Yeah," she sighed as Darius freed her breasts and moved down to remove her skirt while Connor stalked over her prone body. One hand on each side of her head, he lowered his mouth to hers, capturing her lips with his.

Darius succeeded in removing the skirt, but didn't leave her lower body. While Connor kissed her mouth and rubbed his chest against her breasts, Darius spread her legs. Connor was on her right, Darius to her left. One mastered her upper body while the other started to do incredibly wicked things farther down.

"Now we take you together, love," Connor said in a husky voice.

"It's traditional for the wedding night, although that's usually because the dragons are spurring their knight partners on." Darius had a teasing light in his eyes. "In our case, we simply want to. Will you accommodate us?"

"When have I ever denied you two anything you wanted?" She cupped each of their rough cheeks in her palms. Sweet

Mother of All, she loved these men. They were her equals, her partners, her perfect mates. "Come to me now. I don't want to wait any longer. That so-called dancing has made me more than ready to handle you. Both of you." She purred at them, letting a little of her beast out to play.

Dragon growls were much more intimidating, and much hotter, both literally and figuratively, she found out a second later. Connor's body radiated the heat of his dragon as he came over her. He entered her in one long, powerful thrust as she cried out. Damn, that felt good.

"You're mine, Josie. Say it." He was like a man possessed, but she understood the biological imperative of the act of claiming. Her snowcat loved the heat of him, the power and the dominance. "Now and forever."

"Now and forever, Connor. I am yours." Total surrender. That's what he wanted and what she and her snowcat longed to give.

"Good." He grinned suddenly and flipped them. She was sprawled over him, her ass in the air and his cock still crammed high up in her pussy. It was a delicious feeling.

She felt something slick drizzle between her butt cheeks. It made her jump, but the liquid was warm—as warm as the hands that followed, stroking the oil into her skin and between her cheeks, down into the dark crevice that held a secret desire.

Darius slid one finger into her back entrance as Connor held her, splayed out for his brother's pleasure. The two were working together to drive her crazy with need, and she loved them for it. Like a well-orchestrated play, they prepared her to take them both at the same time. They played her body, stroking her to within an inch of bliss time after time, but they wouldn't let her come.

By the time they judged her ready, she was ready to climb

the walls. She hungered for them. They had driven her to a state where nothing existed but her desire, her need for them. She was beyond ready. She was desperate.

"Please, Darius. Please, now!" She cried out her need, hoping this time they would answer her pleas.

Darius climbed into position and replaced his fingers with something much larger and much more desirable. Pushing steadily, he claimed her, filling her beyond full with the two of them at once.

All through this, Connor had remained still beneath her. The moment Darius was seated fully they both began to move. A steady pace soon became frenetic, pulsating thrusts that drove her out of her mind.

As she became more incoherent, they sped their pace. Eventually, she couldn't even form words any longer. She screeched her pleasure, her desire, her need to the heavens as her men grunted and rumbled along with her.

They were close. Closer than they ever had been to explosion at the exact same moment.

Then there was no Darius, no Connor, no Josie. They existed only together as parts of a whole. They came together, roaring their release in unison. It was the most magical, majestic and draining release of her life.

It made them one. Now and forever.

# Chapter Twelve

When they finally left their chamber the next day, it was well after noon. The twins were grinning like fools, even as they asked around to discover who had taken the time to decorate their suite the night before. Josie took special care to thank the group of ladies, who were mates to knights living in the Castle Lair.

One of them was Krysta, the athletic woman Josie had seen with Drake and Mace the night before. Krysta was their wife and a warrior in her own right. In fact, she taught hand-to-hand combat techniques to the Guard and was a high-ranking member of that elite group.

They had taken the morning to tour the castle and thank the other ladies, then had run into Krysta near the castle gates. She'd been on her way into Castleton, so they walked together into the town.

"I'm glad we ran into each other," Krysta said as they walked. The two women were side by side, while the men walked behind, giving the girls a chance to talk. "I have heard that you are a snowcat. We Jinn have had dealings with your tribe in the past."

Josie's heart sped at the implications of her words. There really might be more of her kind in this world somewhere. "I'm sorry, I don't know what Jinn is. My mates have told me a lot, but the more I see, the more I know there are big gaps in my knowledge. And I got the impression that there were no other snowcats here, or if there were, they were just a legend. Sort of like the legends of dragons in my world."

"Oh, there are snowcats. At least, there were as of a hundred years ago. That is the last I have heard of their mention in our histories anyway." Kyrsta shrugged. "The Jinn are—or were, I should say—a nomadic people. We have different clans that roam in different parts of this world. We are led by the Dragon Clan, and they recently sent out the invitation, through the new queen, for all Jinn to come and make their home here in Draconia."

"Queen Lana invited them all to live here?" Josie was trying to piece together the facts in her mind.

"Not Queen Lana. Her sister, Queen Arikia. You know her as Riki. She is Queen of the Jinn as well as Princess of Draconia, just like her mate Nico is Prince of Draconia and King-Consort of the Jinn Brotherhood. It's complicated. Suffice to say, we Jinn would follow her anywhere and protect her to our last breath. Nico too."

"Wow." Josie didn't know what to say to that. The passion behind Krysta's words was palpable. "The Jinn are like Gypsies, I guess," she thought out loud. "There are stories about a nomadic group of people in my world. We call them Gypsies. They are known for being fortune tellers, entertainers, musicians and the like."

"That is a very apt description of the Jinn. We are also a network of spies." Krysta gave her a theatrical wink that made them both chuckle.

"Then I'm not surprised Prince Nico is their king."

Krysta patted her shoulder. "Now you're getting the gist of it. He's not known as the Prince of Spies for nothing."

"Do the Jinn also wear colorful clothing and gold hoops in their ears?"

Krysta gave her a sharp look. "I think your Gypsies and our people have much in common. But you can see for yourself, readily enough. There are many Jinn living in Castleton. Actually, we've taken over a section of adjacent land to build our own section of town that will, in time, be as populated as Castleton itself. Much planning has been done to ensure we will have room for everyone, if they decide to come. We expect many will come to see the queen and king-consort, at least to visit. Many others will wish to live here permanently, though giving up the roaming life will be hard for some. Still, we do need our agents in other lands, so not all Jinn will settle here permanently."

"This is fascinating."

"And all top secret," Darius whispered in her ear, making her shiver.

"Much of what I tell you, I say because you are now a member of the royal family. I would not be so open with others. I also tell you this—" Krysta turned to her as they paused on the road, "—because you are snowcat. My people once knew your people, and we believe you will have a key role to play in the snowcats' return."

Connor stepped forward, a frown on his handsome face. "Do you have time to join us for lunch, Lady Krysta?"

Krysta smiled cunningly. "My mates await us in the best tavern in Jinntown."

Darius and Connor burst out laughing. "Nico warned us about you, spymaster," Darius said with lingering laughter.

At that point Josie realized their accidental meeting by the gates hadn't been an accident at all. Krysta had set this entire meeting up.

They walked together from the old section of Castleton, over a wooden bridge, into the newer settlement they called Jinntown. The signs of new construction were everywhere, and the colorful pennants and tents all around were a dizzying sight. It had a carnival atmosphere with the big tents and smell of sawdust in the air. The horses were amazing-looking creatures. Working alongside them were dark men, some with golden hoops in their ears.

Josie was enchanted. She even saw a few dragons helping with the heavy lifting while men secured the giant tree logs the dragons held in place for them. Everyone, it seemed, was pitching in to help the Jinn build permanent shelters here in their new homeland.

Krysta led them past a bustling marketplace, and Josie's eyes strayed to the multitude of wares the vendors were showing for sale.

"We'll stop in the market on the way back," Darius whispered in her ear.

"We don't have to," she said quickly, well aware of the fact that she didn't have any money these people would recognize.

"Yet, we will," Connor assured her, his hand warm on her shoulder. "There are many delights the Jinn traders bring from all parts of our world. We never had a mate to shower them on before. Let us enjoy spoiling you, just this little bit."

She turned to her men, stopping in the road. "You spoil me already" she whispered, "with your love."

She hugged them both, then turned to resume walking. Krysta grinned at her, but the moment was too tender to laugh about. Josie nodded and moved silently forward, toward the tavern Krysta had pointed out earlier.

The doorway was big enough for a dragon, which shouldn't have surprised her, really. In fact, there were two dragons sitting within the tavern, munching on what looked like watermelons. She recognized them from the night before. It was Jenet and Nelin, their necks rubbing against each other as they sat close together in the bustling tavern.

Mace and Drake stood when they entered and motioned the group to the table beside the dragons. It had been set for six.

They stopped to say hello to the dragons before joining the men. Darius greeted the knights while Connor seated Josie and Mace saw to Krysta's comfort. Each woman sat between their men, and the care Josie felt from her own mates was reflected in the obvious love between Krysta and her knights.

They shared a delicious meal of roast chicken with beans and potatoes, followed by some kind of sticky desert that reminded Josie of baklava. They talked more of the Jinn and their customs, but nothing that seemed as sensitive as the things Krysta had said on their way here. That made sense if they were in a tavern surrounded by people who were mostly spies, Josie thought with amusement.

As they lingered over their lunch, the tavern began to empty out. People who passed their table had a smile and nod for them, and Josie felt glad to be included in the welcome. It was clear the royal family and the knights were well respected. And even those who gave the dragons a cautiously wide berth, spared a chance to look at them with the same awe Josie still felt.

"Now that we have a little more room to breathe—" Krysta gave a pointed look to the now-unoccupied tables around them, "—we can talk more about what little I know of your people, Josie. The clans that roam farthest northward had dealings with snowcats last, over a hundred years ago. At that time, it is said, they had few women. In fact, the snowcats were interested in trade for information about others of their kind or any other from which they could find suitable mates. The situation was dire."

"Do you know what happened?" Josie asked, fearing for her snowcat brethren even though she didn't know them.

"The Jinn spread word through the clans looking for any news of other such creatures, but there were none to be found. In all the years since, no other clan has ever happened upon another group of snowcats. That one encounter was unique and never repeated."

"The far north, you say?" Connor asked. "Do any of your people know exactly where they encountered the snowcats?"

"Unfortunately, not much is known about that initial meeting. The snowcats just arrived one night in the Jinn camp. They'd walked right past all the security measures both mundane and magical. The Jinn were understandably upset by this until they realized who they were dealing with. The snowcats were said to be holy men. Men of peace who were also strong defenders of the innocent. There were rumors of them in the north, but no Jinn before or since have ever seen them. Just that one time, when the snowcat stalked the Jinn in their own camps. They were seeking information about their own kind. The Jinn promised to help and sent out word, but were never able to learn anything to help the snowcats."

"That is so sad," Josie whispered.

"And more than a hundred years ago," Darius added, at her side. "If they still survive, they could be anywhere."

"Don't forget, if Shanya is to be believed, they will soon find us," Connor reminded his twin.

They spent a few more minutes lingering over dessert and talking of many different subjects. When Krysta mentioned her responsibilities for the Guard, Josie was interested to learn that both women and men served in the peacekeeping force within the city and elsewhere throughout the land. There was some equality in this medievalish world, and women weren't held back simply by reason of their sex.

Score one for the dragon princes, Josie thought. They were strong men who seemed to enjoy the same of their partners. At least her men did.

What she'd seen of the knights who partnered dragons was just as good. Drake, for all his roguish ways, was devoted to his new wife and the dragon he'd grown up with. Josie had heard the story of Drake's checkered past over lunch, including the way he'd been raised alongside the dragoness, Jenet, and the way he'd denied her by leaving his family, his potential dragon partner and his country, to seek his fortune among the Jinn when he was just a teen.

He was back now, older, wiser, famous and much more magical than when he'd left. He was one of the king's top advisors, alongside his fathers, who were also knights, and his fighting partner, Mace. While they'd been on their journey to rescue the stolen prince, they'd discovered a hidden magic and learned how to use it. From what Josie could grasp, they could actually call magical flames and hold them in their hands.

The dragons could flame and breathe fire, of course, but Drake and Mace could hold fire in the palms of their hands. They could also throw it at their enemies and control it. Now that was something she'd like to see in person, even though the thought of such power was more than a little frightening.

Luckily, both Drake and Mace impressed her as steadfast, good-hearted men who would use their powers wisely. They balanced each other out, from what she could see. Mace was thoughtful and quiet while his fighting partner was flamboyant and talkative. Both were quick-witted, and both were devoted to their mate and their dragon partners. They were a family to be admired, in her opinion, and she was glad to have begun a friendship with them.

They parted on friendly terms, and Josie hoped they could build on this initial acquaintance. She needed some friends in this world, and Krysta seemed like the kind of woman she could both learn from and share with. In fact, they'd already made a date for the next day to work out. Krysta had invited Josie to the self-defense class she taught in the Castle Lair for the women and youngsters who wanted to learn the basics of hand-to-hand fighting. From what she'd said, there were all levels of skill in the class, and Josie thought that a good place to start in learning the kinds of fighting forms they used in this world.

She suspected Krysta might also be interested in learning some of the *kung fu* and other skills used in Josie's world. While she'd never be as skilled as her grandfather, the grand master, Josie wasn't a bad martial artist. Among non-snowcats, in fact, she was considered an expert. It was only among snowcats that she felt her skills were lacking. Of course, these people weren't snowcats. They didn't expect anything of Josie. She'd be able to join their number without any expectations placed upon her shoulders, weighing her down.

She was really looking forward to it. The twins hadn't forgotten about their promised stop at the marketplace either. On their way back to the castle, her mates took her from one stall to the next, into well-lit shops full of lovely wares and brightly colored fabrics. The girly, feminine part of her that loved pretty things was in heaven.

The part of her that had secretly craved someone to shower her with love just once in her life, was drunk on the attention her mates lavished on her. They bought all kinds of things—clothing, jewelry, trinkets and more—paying extra for them to be delivered to the castle.

They were on their way out of the shopping area when Darius and Connor took her by the arm, one on each side, and escorted her into a jeweler's shop that had been built recently and well. The walls were sturdy, the door brightly painted as most of the Jinn buildings were. The sign out front proclaimed the jeweler within as a Master Craftsman approved by the Jeweler's Guild.

As they walked in, they were greeted by a young girl who wore a pretty pink gown. She looked to be about twelve years old and had been reading a heavy book until she saw them. She smiled as she hopped down from the high bench on which she'd been sitting.

"Welcome, Prince Connor and Prince Darius." She gave them a polite curtsey, nodding at each of the twins in turn, getting their identities correct, which seemed to surprise both men. "And you are especially welcome, Princess Josie. My Mistress is expecting you."

"Expecting us, poppet?" Darius asked in a curious but friendly tone.

"Mistress foresaw your coming about a month ago. She's been working on something just for you." The twins looked at each other with raised eyebrows but said nothing. Josie felt tingles run down her spine. There was magic here. Lots of it. And it was coming toward them.

"Welcome, your highnesses," a cultured female voice came to them from the doorway to the back room. The pale-haired beauty who emerged could have been Shanya's mother, or maybe her older sister.

"You're not Jinn," Darius said, surprise in his voice.

"I was born in the northland enclave of my people, but left to ply my trade and was adopted among the Jinn. I am an elder of the snowbear clan." She turned to the girl, who came to her side. "My apprentice, Emma, is from Wayfarer. She has the true gift. The stones sing to her." The lovely woman smiled at the girl and touched her shoulder with obvious pride and love for the child. "Emma, please fetch the ring tray from my workroom."

"We did come in looking for a set of rings," Darius said, scratching his head as the woman slid behind the counter.

"You are a seer, are you not, madam?" Connor asked as they stepped up to the counter, Josie between them. The pale beauty nodded.

"I am Liliana, Mistress of the Jeweler's Guild, Elder of Snowbear, and now with the Lady's blessing, jeweler to the Royal House of Draconia." She seemed amused with herself at the bold pronouncement. "If I did not get too ahead of myself on that last. I believe you will be pleased with the work I have done expressly for you."

The girl emerged from the back room with a tray in her hands. She gave it to her mistress with almost reverent movements.

Liliana put the cloth-covered tray on the counter in front of her. With great ceremony, she removed the embroidered cloth to reveal a set of three rings. Josie's breath caught in her throat at the face of her snowcat in the center of each design, embraced by dragon wings.

"I worked the design in platinum," Liliana said as she lifted the smallest of the rings in her hand and held it up to the light before handing it to Josie. "The eyes of the snowcat are diamond."

"They're exquisite." Josie examined the smallest version of the ring, then lifted each of the larger rings that were meant for her mates. Josie had no doubt about the woman's skill though it was hard to believe she'd foreseen so much about them.

"We'll take them," Darius said impulsively.

"I have been cautious of late concerning gifts of jewelry." Connor gave Liliana a sideways glance that lightened his suspicious tone.

"But my prince, you came to my shop. I did not seek you out to press these items on you." Her smile was understanding and cunning at the same time. "I cannot help what I am and what I foresaw. As a businesswoman trying to make her way up in the world, I could do no less than prepare for the gift fate would bring me when you walked into my shop."

"Well said, Mistress," Connor allowed with a grin. "I have learned that sometimes impulsiveness is a good thing." He turned to Josie, taking the smallest of the rings in his hand. "There is a custom among the Jinn of exchanging rings as a token of love and commitment to each other."

"We noticed in your world, mated pairs seemed to wear rings as well and thought you'd like to do the same," Darius added.

Tears gathered behind her eyes. "How did I get so lucky as to find you?"

"Luck had little to do with it, princess," Liliana said softly. "The Mother of All had a strong hand in your mating. More so than with others who serve Her. She smiles on you."

Darius took her left hand while Connor slid the ring on her finger. The moment stretched while she looked up at both of them, seeing the love in their eyes. The shop faded, and it felt as if they were the only people in the world.

Josie took each of the larger rings and placed one on Darius's finger, giving him a lingering kiss to seal the promises the ring stood for. Then she did the same for Connor. Time stood still for a breath of a moment.

Background sounds of the marketplace drew her out of the world where only the three of them existed. She put more space between herself and her mates, turning once more to the jeweler.

"They're beautiful. Thank you for making these for us."

"The design is perfect, Mistress." Connor's voice was rough as he, too, turned to the jeweler.

"Our beautiful snowcat enfolded in our wings, forever in our care," Darius whispered reverently.

"You protect her as she protects you. Yours is a truly powerful union, highnesses." Liliana bowed her head slightly in respect. "I was privileged to foresee such strength coming to our world again. To know that you will at last answer the questions the snowcats put to my clan over a century ago."

"How can I? I'm only one woman and mated to two dragons," Josie thought out loud.

"You are but the instrument, Princess. Have faith in the Lady. She guides your path as she always has. You have found your happiness. Now you will be the conduit through which your brethren in this world may also find theirs."

"Mistress, I would like to extend a dinner invitation to you. If you are free, I would like you to speak with us about this further. I would also like you to talk with Shanya, one of your folk from Gryphon Isle. She, too, is a seer."

"I have heard of her," Liliana admitted. "I would welcome the opportunity to meet her and compare notes on what we have seen."

They left the mysterious jeweler with the rings on their fingers and a spring in their steps. Liliana had promised to come to the castle for dinner that night, and Connor had sent word ahead to expect her and to request Shanya's presence as well.

Thoughts of the meeting to come later that night were pushed from Josie's mind as she watched the way people responded to her mates and to herself. They were uniformly welcoming, and some stopped Connor and Darius as they walked back toward the castle to wish them well and to be introduced to Josie. She met so many people she couldn't keep them all straight. It was clear her mates were well liked among the common people, and she sensed no fear from any of them.

Suddenly becoming royalty was strange, to be sure. Having lived much of her life in a country that had a president, not a king, Josie watched carefully for reactions to the royal presence. From all indications, the royal family of Draconia was well loved and respected, thank goodness. Josie wasn't comfortable with the whole royalty thing in general and had never been pleased to be put on a pedestal because of her snowcat nature. This was different though. The way the dragon princes were received indicated a confidence in them from the people and a genuine affection.

The town itself was a magical mix of stone, wood, color and light. They walked a meandering path. While Josie was sure that like any city, it probably had some not-so-nice areas, the parts she saw seemed to be of mixed prosperity, but all seemed comfortable. When they reached the castle, the sun was beginning its ride downward toward the horizon and shadows had begun to fall.

"Dinner is in two hours," Darius said as they walked into the castle past the Guards. "Whatever shall we do until then?"

The facetious tone told her he had some definite ideas. Wicked ideas, most likely. She was all for it.

"I believe a tour of the baths is in order," Connor volunteered a little too smoothly.

"We did promise to show you the hot springs." Darius

waggled his eyebrows as he grinned. "They are much like that big bathtub in the cougar house, only a lot larger and a lot more...public. Are you up for it, my love?"

Josie wasn't sure what she was getting herself into but she'd learned one thing—her mates always seemed to know what she would like in the bedroom. Or the bath chamber, as the case may be. She was willing at least to give it a try.

Steam wafted over the water. It was nowhere near thick enough to hide the people bathing all around the huge cavern. Josie didn't know what she'd expected. It certainly hadn't been this vast subterranean chamber containing ornately carved rock formations separating multiple pools of varying sizes.

"The hotter springs are toward the rear of the chamber." Connor acted as tour guide as they entered the cavern.

They'd made a short stop in a changing area where the twins had casually stripped down to nothing and threw on soft robes that had been lying in a pile near the door. Darius gave her one in a small size from a shorter stack of clean robes and waited, smirking at her while she quickly changed into it.

There had been nothing like a private changing room. The arched entryway had no door. Neither did the opening leading to the cavern beyond. She had heard people's voices from either side as she hastily stripped and threw on the robe, belting it quickly.

The twins had said nothing, merely waiting for her with half-lidded eyes as they ogled her. She liked that look on their faces, but she was at heart, a modest woman. Being a snowcat meant she'd never had to get used to public nudity like the majority of other shifters. As a result, she wasn't used to disrobing in a public place where anyone could happen along and see her.

There was something forbidden and incredibly naughty about the whole situation. Her eyes about popped out of her head when she entered the cavern behind Darius and Connor. They flanked her quickly, each taking one of her hands as they led her around, showing her the place.

"This is the Castle Lair's bathing chamber, reserved for knights and their mates alone. All Lairs have something like this. Ours is by far the oldest, and therefore, grandest. It started with a natural hot spring that has been improved upon both by magic and by craftsmen over the centuries. Some of the pools were expanded and tiled along the sides with seating ledges added for comfort. Some of the more volatile pools still have their natural rock formations, though they've smoothed out over the years of use. Some were sculpted by master rock carvers and others have been left completely untouched. There is a wide variety to choose from," Connor told her, continuing to walk toward a beautifully carved section of rock that made a sort of barrier in the center of the chamber.

There were pillars of rock spaced all around the place, no doubt to support the roof and the castle above. But nothing was left unadorned. The rock had been carved into figures and scenes from nature. Fantastical animals and other things she didn't recognize were also represented. Many of the statues had precious metals and gemstones embedded in them. Eyes twinkled with the light of emeralds, and she realized there were massive dragon statues standing guardian around the chamber.

"Wow. That's a lot of dragons," she whispered.

Darius chuckled. "Some of our ancestors," he supplied easily. "Members of the royal line who made improvements down here over the centuries were usually carved in thanks by the artisans they employed." They maneuvered around some of the statuary that stood in the center of the room. "Ah, the royal

229

pool."

She marveled at the bubbly water in the ornate pool. It had white tile accented with what looked like pure gold. At one end was a massive carving of a dragon in flight, its wings outstretched to shelter one end of the pool. The dragon's mate rose from the other end. Put together, the two large statues looked ready to take to flight and meet in the middle. On either side of the rectangular pool were other carvings. It didn't provide a complete enclosure, but it was more private than any of the other areas she'd seen in the giant cavern.

"This one pool is set aside for the royal family's use. As our mate, you can use this one and be assured nobody but another member of the family will ever disturb you here." Connor swept his hand around the partially enclosed area. "The carvings block most eyes. There are also hanging curtains that can be lowered if you desire complete privacy."

"We hardly ever use the curtains." Darius looked amused. "I mean, what's the point of coming here if you want complete privacy? We have private bathing pools in our chambers, and as dragons we can heat them to any temperature we like."

Which meant they came here when they wanted to see and be seen. Hoo boy. The implications of that idea made her unaccountably hot—both physically and sexually. The moist air clung to her skin making her want to fan herself, but she dared not. She was sure she'd be the center of all their jokes for the next hour if she let on how the place was affecting her so easily. Better to play coy a little longer.

Ultimately, she trusted them. She wasn't totally sure about the exhibitionist tendencies they'd told her about, but she was willing to give it a try. Still, she wanted to take it slow. If they knew how turned on she was getting just seeing this place and imagining what might go on here, she'd be flat on her back with her legs spread before she could say boo.

"The water temperature here is moderate." Connor continued the tour, taking her around the statues guarding the royal pool to see the smaller pools near the back of the giant cave. "You might have noticed the bigger pools are the cooler ones. They're more for general use, bathing and even swimming. The smaller, more private ones back here are hotter, with the hottest in that far corner."

She followed where he pointed and saw several bubbling pools near the back. Each held one or two large men either talking amiably or sitting with their heads thrown back, resting along the rim.

"As you can see, those pools are good for muscle therapy and are often used by knights and others with injuries. The mineral content of those waters is slightly higher than the rest of the complex." Connor, as usual, was a font of information. "Sometimes you'll see a healer or two there as well, shepherding their charges as they help them heal."

"On the other side is where the fun really happens," Darius whispered, bending low to speak near her ear. His arm drew along her side until she followed the line of where he pointed to a section segregated by a number of smaller statues. "Those private pools graduate in temperature. The closest ones are about the same temperature as the royal pool, then get progressively hotter as you head toward the corner. They are also bigger than the therapeutic pools. Made for two...or more."

Even from this distance, Josie could see a few mated trios in various stages of lovemaking or frolicking in the bubbling waters. For every pool with a trio in it, there were two pools on either side that held single knights. Those single men invariably had their attention riveted on one of the trios. Some even blatantly had their hands on their cocks, pumping as they watched the mates in the nearby pool pleasuring each other.

"For unmated knights, watching the joy of others is often the only thing giving them hope that someday they will find the one woman meant to share their life. Sadly, since there are few women able or willing to live with dragons and their knights, some of these men will never find their true mate." Connor squeezed her hand. "Dar and I despaired of ever finding you."

Darius raised her hand to his lips for a tender kiss. "You are a miracle to us, Josie. Our miracle."

Connor kissed her other hand and for a moment they just stood there, basking in each other's presence. Darius broke the spell as one of his eyebrows rose in question.

"The choice today is yours, my love. Where would you like to bathe? The royal pool—" he looked from the grotto sheltered by hulking statues to the more open play area already populated by a dozen people or so, "—or one of the others?"

She considered the open area and the people there. No way was she ready for something like that. Perhaps in time, as she got used to the ways of this world, she might be ready to try something more. For now, it was a lot just to be naked in a relatively public place.

"The royal pool, please."

The twins only smiled.

"As you wish, my love." Connor turned her back toward the partially enclosed area framed by giant dragons.

They entered the tiled area around the pool, and the twins immediately stripped off their robes. She could see there were little hook-like protrusions on some of the statues that were made for hanging the robes. She smiled as she took a closer look at some of the incredibly detailed carvings.

She was so engrossed in admiring the artwork, she didn't

hear Darius sneak up behind her. To her credit, she didn't jump when his arms encircled her from behind. He dropped a kiss on her neck as his hands went to the belt of her robe, untying it and pushing the soft fabric off her shoulders, allowing it to pool on the floor around their feet. He swung her up, into his arms and descended the submerged, tiled stairway leading down into the water on the side of the pool.

It was Connor who picked up her robe and absently stuck it on one of the hooks before joining them in the water. His gaze seemed glued to her bare body, and she luxuriated in the rapt attention of her two mates.

How did a woman get so lucky? Josie had no idea, but she thanked the Mother of All every single day for Her blessings.

As her body hit the water, she purred in enjoyment of the warm, bubbly feeling against her bare skin. It was the perfect temperature and the effervescence of the natural spring was something she hadn't anticipated.

"This is nice," she commented, running her hands through the water as Darius let her stand, facing him in the chest-deep water.

Connor came up behind her. "The other end is a little deeper. The floor of this pool slants from the shallowest part by the stairs to the deeper part down at the far end."

"How deep does it get?" She eyed the far end with distrust.

Cats generally disliked large bodies of water, though some of the big cats, like tigers, loved it. Josie was in between. Snowcats didn't generally bathe or swim in large bodies of water, though in the summer they did enjoy frequent picnicking near a cold mountain lake down farther on the slopes, toward the town below her grandfather's village. The water was too cold to enjoy long periods of swimming, but Josie had enjoyed her infrequent visits to the spot when she was a teen.

"The deepest it goes is about eight feet," Connor told her. "And there are places along the sides at different levels for sitting or reclining." He pointed to small depressions along the rim of the pool that she imagined were for resting one's head if they wanted to stretch out. The designers of this place hadn't forgotten anything it seemed.

She could hear the other people in the vast cavern talking and splashing, but the sounds were muted. Still, she knew they weren't alone. There were people nearby who could hear if they got loud enough. The thought should have shocked her. It didn't. It had quite a different effect altogether.

She slipped between her two men, diving shallowly to get away. Playfully, she swam down to the deep end of the pool, turning to find her two dragons were gone. Only the rippling water told her where they had gone. They'd dived underneath the water and were no doubt stalking her even now.

Josie struck out for the shallow end, swimming strong. Within three strokes, she felt the warm presence of one of her mates. He was swimming below her, mirroring her movements.

Just how long could a dragon hold his breath? Josie sucked in air, knowing he would drag her beneath the surface at any moment.

She was right. Strong arms wound around her waist, stopping her forward movement and dragging her downward. She opened her eyes in the hazy netherworld beneath the water, recognizing the glint of Darius's teasing expression. He wrapped her in his arms, kicking for the surface.

He wasn't even breathing hard when they broke into the dim light of the cavern. He didn't give her time to say anything, clamping down on her lips with his own in a passionate kiss as soon as they'd surfaced. Josie didn't mind. And when Connor teased the back of her legs beneath the water, she could only bask in the feel of his lips and teeth against her skin.

She yelped a little when Connor bit the fleshy cheek of her butt. Darius broke the kiss and smiled at her.

"Is Con being naughty?" His voice carried in the stone chamber, and she realized others in nearby pools could no doubt hear them, even if their view was blocked by the statues.

"He bit me," she whispered. Darius responded with a laugh.

She felt Connor rise out of the water behind her. His hands stole around her waist, dragging her backward as his chin settled on her shoulder, his lips nibbling at her throat. Darius let go as Connor moved backward with her, settling on one of the convenient ledges at the side of the pool.

Darius prowled through the water like some kind of devastatingly handsome sea serpent. His gaze held her mesmerized, the soft light of the cavern making the peridot of his eyes sparkle and shine with an almost incandescent shimmer.

He spoke not a word as he slid his palms over her feet, then over her ankles to her calves. Exerting light pressure, he parted her legs to stand between. The water wasn't too deep here. He could stand on the bottom, the water lapping just above his waist. The way Connor had her positioned on his lap, Darius was in perfect alignment with her core.

She felt Connor's hard cock sliding over the cheeks of her ass, the fingers of one of his hands delving between to spread and prepare her. Darius's hands continued their upward climb over her knees and onto her thighs. He moved closer, and she could see his cock, hard and wanting, straining toward the place it wanted to go—the place that slicked with heat that rivaled even the bubbling waters of this subterranean oasis.

"Are you ready for us?" Darius asked, his seductive smile reaching into her soul. She could deny him nothing and he damned well knew it.

"Almost there," Connor answered for her, sliding his fingers into her rear hole, preparing her for his possession.

"Get inside her, Con." Darius sounded the teeniest bit impatient as his fingers tangled in the curls at the apex of her thighs. She sighed as he sank two long digits inside her.

She could hear voices just beyond the statues. A time or two, she thought she saw people moving through gaps in the carved surfaces. Rather than fear, she met the realization with startling hunger. Maybe her mates' exhibitionist natures were rubbing off on her after all.

Josie knew she wasn't quite ready for a public exhibition, but she was quickly discovering the allure her mates had hinted at.

All thought fled as Darius deepened his possession, adding another finger as Connor did the same. Her body cried out for their possession, widening to accommodate their every wish. She was theirs to command, theirs to dominate, though she had never let anyone—man or woman—dominate her sexually ever before. She'd never seen the appeal in it. But now that the snowcat who shared Josie's soul had found the perfect mates for both sides of her nature, she reveled in submitting to their superior strength.

"The water will soothe you as I take possession of your luscious body, my mate. It is one of the reasons knights like to bring their ladies down here. The salinity of the water, along with other components makes it deliciously slippery where it counts most, don't you agree?" Connor nipped her earlobe as he removed his fingers and quickly replaced them with his cock.

"*Mmm.* Now that you mention it..." And she did notice the way the water eased his possession.

It was as if the mineral content had been designed to make

this kind of thing easier. Who knew? Perhaps it was. This culture seemed to thrive on triple marriages. Maybe this healing, helping water was one of the things that made such a thing both easy and possible.

Darius's fingers abandoned her pussy as Connor slid home. She missed the double penetration but didn't have to wait long to feel an even deeper connection as Darius stepped closer between her thighs. With his twin fully sheathed in her rear, Darius thumbed her nipples as he positioned himself for frontal entry.

"This is going to be so good," he whispered as he began a gentle pressure that would join them fully. "Do you like the feel of Con up your ass, sweetheart?"

He waited for her answer, unmoving until she spoke shyly. "You know I do."

"Tell us, Josie," he insisted. "How does it feel to have us both at the same time? Is it as good for you as it is for us?"

"I doubt it could be any better," she gasped as he advanced farther into her aching body. It was a good ache. The very best kind. She bit her lip to keep from moaning and Darius stopped his forward motion. Bending, he sucked her lower lip into his mouth, nibbling lightly before releasing her and pulling away.

"If anyone's going to bite your luscious body here, it's going to be me. Got that?"

Fighting the impulse to writhe, she nodded. Her body was on fire with their dominant possession. She wanted to moan but knew there were people all around their secluded little grotto that might hear. Some might even be peering in through the cracks in the statues right now. The thought sent a spasm of heat right to her core as Darius shoved all the way home. At last.

"My love." Connor's breath whispered past her ear, gaining

237

her attention. "Look up."

She did, shocked to find three green-eyed men watching her. Watching them. She gasped and would have struggled, but her mates had her firmly pinned between them. She wasn't going anywhere until they released her.

"Only the royal family is allowed to enter this enclosure," Connor rumbled near her ear.

Sweet Mother of All. That could only mean these three behemoths were family. Brothers, perhaps? She took another quick glance and realized all three were slightly older than her mates and two were identical. Another set of twins. Holy Mother, they were all handsome as sin too. She could see the resemblance to her mates. Definitely brothers.

What a way to meet the family! This world had some strange—exciting—customs. She saw the appreciation in three sets of emerald eyes...and the fire. Her mates' brothers were getting turned on by watching their brothers fuck her.

Even in the dim light, the thin layer of crystal-clear water was no shield. There was no doubt they could see everything. The three doffed their robes and hung them on the statue hooks, treating Josie to a glimpse of three very firm, muscular male backsides. When they turned around, the vision of three equally impressive and hard cocks made her blush to the roots of her hair.

She squeezed her eyes shut, feeling the rumble of Darius's and Connor's chuckles through their bodies and into hers. The vibration even reached their cocks, buried for a timeless moment deep inside her.

She heard splashing and felt the ripple of water as the three men entered the pool. She didn't dare look to see where they were. She was mortified enough. Although she had to admit, knowing they were watching her, impaled on their

238

Dragon Storm

brothers' cocks, sent a secret thrill through her that was as undeniable as it was unbelievable.

"Ignore them, my love." Darius placed a kiss on her brow as he crowded close to her. His cock pulsed in her pussy, making her aware of every last inch of him...and his twin.

"Unless their presence turns you on," Connor whispered from behind, a suspicious humor in his voice. "Which I believe it does."

"Does not," she protested weakly.

"Really?" Darius asked. "Then why did your pussy clench in eagerness when you caught sight of them? And why is it weeping with slick welcome knowing they are here, watching us?"

She didn't know what to say to that. It was true. All too true. The twins saved her from answering by taking her on a wild ride as they pistoned in and out of her trembling body. Before long, she was caught up in the motion, whimpering against Darius's chest each time the twins picked up their pace.

Once, when she opened her eyes just a fraction, she saw the other men arranged around the pool, watching her. Watching her get fucked by Darius and Connor. The other set of twins were on one side of them. Both men had their hands on their cocks, stroking in time with Darius's and Connor's rhythm. She opened her mouth, unable to hold back a pulse of arousal that stole through her like a lightning bolt as she realized the men were jerking off right along with them.

The other brother was on the other side, in slightly deeper water. She couldn't see him as well, but she was sure he was touching himself beneath the warm waters, tugging on his dick like the others.

All of a sudden, she felt all-powerful, like some sort of female fertility goddess. She had the very real possibility of

239

making five men come with her when she climaxed. Simultaneously. How many women could claim that kind of feat? Aside from porn stars, of course. Even then, five at once had to be some kind of special category.

Josie grinned as the odd thoughts flickered through her mind. Darius saw her smile and answered with one of his own.

"Our mate likes being watched by our brothers, Con."

"No doubt she just realized she holds us in the palm of her hand." Connor gasped as their pace increased yet again. Josie fought to hold on, to keep up with them. This moment was too incredible to let end so soon.

"Her hand is not where she has us," Darius joked even as he strained against her, his cock slamming hard and fast into her core.

Connor didn't answer—couldn't answer—because with only a few more intense pumps of their cocks, Josie came. She cried out, growling and screeching as an intense climax hit her full force. She pulled Darius and Connor over with her. She heard them groan and felt their come shoot into her body. It was warm and comforting, hot and incredibly erotic.

She heard three more masculine groans and knew the others had come as well. Yes, siree. Five at once. A new record. For her at least.

She was feeling a bit smug as she clung to Darius's shoulders, riding out the storm wrapped in the security of her mates' arms. The only thing she had yet to figure out was how she would ever face the twins' brothers after what had just transpired.

# Chapter Thirteen

Connor and Darius pulled out of her body with an obvious regret that made her giggle. Connor spun her around in the water, capturing her in his arms for a tender kiss that melted all her inhibitions away once more.

When he carried her up the tile steps and out of the water, her sole focus was on him. Only later did she realize his brothers watched as Connor kept her captivated, and Darius slid the robe on her shoulders. When she was covered, the belt of the robe tied tight around her middle, the twins stepped back and she became aware again of her surroundings.

Three robed men stood a few feet away, waiting. Moment-of-truth time. It looked like they were waiting to be introduced, and Josie could feel a blush stealing over her face once more.

"Sweetheart, we want you to meet our brothers," Connor said in a soft, understanding tone.

"I'm Collin," one of the twins said in a firm voice, making the first move. It was clear all the men could sense her discomfort. Collin seemed to be a no-nonsense sort of man who took the bull by the horns, so to speak. Josie was grateful for his matter-of-fact demeanor.

"And I'm Trey." Collin's twin stepped forward. "The ugly one over there is Trent."

All the brothers chuckled at Trey's little joke.

"And you're Josie." Trent eyed her with masculine appreciation, but it didn't make her feel self-conscious in the least. No, all three of these men—so obviously related to her mates—made her feel welcome. Their words were both friendly and respectful, and she could read nothing in their eyes to alarm her. On the contrary, she felt even more protected under the family mantle of strength than she had before. She felt accepted.

That wasn't a feeling she had experienced much in her life. The wonder of it brought tears to her eyes.

"What is it, love?" Connor placed a gentle hand on her shoulder.

Josie shook off the feeling. She didn't want to appear weak in front of these powerful men. They were her mates' family. Her family now too. The wonder of that hit her again. She was part of this big, loving, strong family and they seemed to accept her—just for *her*—without putting expectations on her. She didn't have to prove herself. She was accepted simply because she was mated to their brothers.

That easy acceptance was something rare and precious to her.

"How many sets of twins are in your family?" she asked Connor, declining to answer the concern in his gaze.

"Just two sets. Collin and Trey are a few years older than us, and Trent came right between," Darius answered with a smile.

"Thank you for sharing with us," Trent said formally. "We all have hope that someday we will find our perfect mate, but it is a distant hope. Four of our brothers have already found their partners. The rest of us live in hope and fear that we will never find our other halves."

Suddenly she understood. Shifters had similar problems.

242

When there was only one perfect mate for a person, it seemed a miracle to find them. She well knew that many never did, and they lived alone and heartsick for the rest of their lives, knowing their mate suffered the same...somewhere...if they still lived.

"I know," she said softly, moving to stand in front of Trent. "I never thought I'd find my mate—much less that there'd be two. Meeting your brothers was a miracle to me."

Two strong arms came around her. Darius claimed her waist while Connor cupped her shoulder.

"You are our miracle, Josie," Connor whispered near her ear.

"Would that we could be as fortunate," Collin said in a raw voice. "Your love is incandescent. Trey and I have never been sure whether we will find one mate or two separate women. The odds of finding anyone who could be either of our matches seems astronomical."

"Seeing you three together gives us hope," Trey put in. "Whether we find one mate for each of us or one mate to share, seeing the way you three are together..." he trailed off, seeming to get choked up. The idea that such a strong, mountain of a man would get so emotional touched her deeply.

Collin slapped his twin on the back with affection. "What he's trying to say is thank you, Josie." The way his voice dropped, husky with emotion made her feel special. She'd given something to these men. Hope was a rare commodity and she understood how much it could mean to someone who had been in despair.

"You're welcome." Suddenly the entire experiment took on profound significance. This wasn't just about kinky sex. This was about sharing a glimpse of what the three of them had found together.

It would be all right now. She began to understand this

culture a little better. It would take time for her to learn their ways, but it wasn't the orgy of decadence she'd feared. There were reasons for everything they did. She just had to be patient while she learned what made this world spin.

Dinner with the entire family plus Shanya and Liliana was organized chaos. All those hunky princes were overwhelming enough on their own. Add in two absolutely stunning, ethereal fair folk beauties, plus the twin women who'd married the eldest of the dragon brothers and Josie was feeling a little outclassed. Oh, the others didn't try to make her feel that way. They were gracious and kind. Josie sat back in wonder at the company she was keeping since she'd come to this world.

Whether the drastic move here would turn out well for her in the long run, she didn't know. While it lasted though, this heady company had the capacity to make her head whirl with the magic of her surroundings. It was like every little girl's dream come true. She was sitting in a fairy-tale castle perched on the side of a mountain, surrounded by immensely magical beings, accepted as one of them, welcome among them. One was more magnificent than the next, and they all seemed to think that she was something special.

Josie was more or less certain that every being in this hall had more magic at their command than she did. As a snowcat, she was used to being the most magical shifter in any group except on her grandfather's mountain. Here, her power was accepted as normal and outclassed to a significant degree, unless she was much mistaken.

The feeling wasn't comfortable, but it didn't intimidate her. No, it was actually kind of nice to not be the one with the most magic in the room. It was nice not to have others looking at her as some kind of demi-deity for a change. They looked at her strangely, but more in the way of strangers wanting to get to know the newcomer in their midst. That she could handle. The other part—the part about being the newest princess of the land—well, that would take a little more getting used to.

With her mates by her side, she figured she could cope with almost anything.

She'd had a momentary lapse into blushing embarrassment when she'd come face-to-face with the older set of twins. Trent's greeting set off another round of blushes, much to her mates' amusement. The moment passed and as the night progressed she became more comfortable in their presence.

Liliana and her rings were duly admired when she was introduced. She hadn't come empty-handed. The Master Jeweler had brought gifts of intricately carved, entwined dragons. Done in gold, they had been made into broaches for Queen Lana and her sister, Riki, to symbolize their unions with Roland and Nico.

"These are not copies of each other," Riki said with awe. "They are Nico and me..." she held up one of the broaches, "...and Lana and Roland." She held up the other, a look of wonder on her face. "They actually look like us."

"I rarely make the same piece twice," Liliana said modestly. "I wanted my gifts to be special for each of you. I hope you like them."

"Like them?" Lana picked the image of herself and her husband out of her sister's hand. "I love this. Thank you for your gift, Mistress Liliana. I have no words to describe how happy this makes me."

"It is a lovely gift," Roland added, his voice surprisingly rough as he stood behind Lana, holding her shoulder, looking at the gift over her head. "We thank you."

They sat for dinner around a huge table. The princes sat in

age order, so Josie found herself near the middle of the long table. Shanya was opposite her, and Liliana was seated next to Shanya. This dinner was an opportunity for them to meet as well as for Liliana to become acquainted with the royal family. Josie tried to be unobtrusive but knew she wasn't the only one listening in as the two fair women met for the first time.

"You are the Master Jeweler," Shanya said politely. "Your work is lovely."

"Thank you. I have heard much of you since you arrived in Draconia. They say you came with two gryphons," Liliana replied as she put her napkin on her lap. She had very dainty manners in addition to looking like she stepped out of the pages of a fairytale.

"The gryphons brought me here," Shanya answered. "If not for them, I could not have made the journey, but it was necessary."

Liliana stilled. "Yes, it was."

"You also have the Sight, then." It wasn't a question, but Liliana nodded.

"I saw you here, among the dragons and in snow, among the others. You have a role to play, my dear. It could be a dangerous one. It could also be one that brings great joy to many hopeless people. When the time comes, you must be ready."

Shanya swallowed hard and nodded. She appeared frightened by the other woman's words. She also seemed determined. What it was that stirred so many conflicting feelings in the young woman was beyond Josie's knowledge.

"Did you hear that?" Josie asked her mates.

Connor turned to her. "Hear what?"

She turned to Darius. He also wore a blank look. They

hadn't heard the exchange.

Liliana captured her attention from across the table. "The snowcat is said to have the most acute hearing of any shapeshifter in this world."

She knew. Liliana knew Josie had heard her words to the other girl. Fighting a blush of embarrassment, Josie smiled weakly at the woman and shrugged.

"Sorry."

"No apologies are necessary, princess. You are what you are. As we all are. My words were not secret, or I would not have spoken them in company."

The woman was so calm and collected, Josie had to admire her. Liliana was a cool customer and probably much more than she seemed on the surface. There was wisdom behind those timeless blue eyes.

"How old are you, Liliana?" The words popped out before Josie could censor herself. She realized how rude she must have sounded. Thankfully nobody else at the table seemed to be looking their way as the first course was served. "Forgive me. That was incredibly rude."

"Not at all." Liliana smiled serenely, putting Josie at ease. "I am just over eight hundred winters."

"Then fair folk...your people...are..."

"Immortal?" Liliana laughed and the sound was musical and enchanting. "Not quite, but we come close. I suspect you are familiar with the phenomenon." The knowing look she sent nearly made Josie gasp. This woman knew about snowcats. She knew the way they aged. Full-blooded snowcats, at least.

Josie nodded and was stopped from saying more by the server.

Dinner proceeded from there and conversation flowed.

Josie waited patiently for a chance to talk directly to either of the fair folk seated across from her, but the effort was doomed.

Halfway through the meal, a messenger came running in. He dropped to one knee in front of Roland to deliver his message. It was a boy she had seen in the hall at the Northern Lair a few days before. No doubt he'd come on a dragon's back to deliver his message.

"My liege. News from the Northern Lair." The young man panted as he tried to catch his breath. "An army is massing just over the border. They sent a demand for us to return their envoy. They claim we misdirected their magic and stole her. They have beasts with them, sire, like the one we saw with Prince Darius and Prince Connor a few days past. They roar challenge in the night."

All eyes turned to Josie. She stood, placing her napkin on the table as her mates stood at her sides.

"I'll go. I suspect it's me they want to talk to." She tried not to show the fear that crept into her heart. Those snowcats might try to separate her from her mates. Well, they could try. They would succeed only over her dead body. And she'd take a few of them with her on her way out. That much was certain.

"We'll leave at once," Connor said, backing her up. She reached for his hand and squeezed it for reassurance. Darius took her other hand as they left the table.

Nico also stood. "I'm coming with you."

"I also need to go." The voice from the middle of the table drew all attention. It was Shanya. "If you please, sire," she directed her request toward Roland, "I must go."

"Something you have foreseen?" Roland asked in a deceptively gentle voice.

"Only recently and not clearly." She shrugged as if embarrassed by her lack of accuracy. "I only know I must meet

248

the snowcats."

Liliana reached for Shanya's shaking hand. "She is right, sire. She must be present when your new sister-in-law meets her brethren. That part is clear. The rest will unfold in good time."

"We will take you, Shanya," Darius volunteered impulsively. All eyes turned to Roland. He took a moment to consider, then nodded in agreement and stood.

"I'm going too." Roland's voice was granite in its surety, and his expression was grim. "If there is to be war on the border yet again, I need to be there."

Lana clutched his hand, and the two shared a moment of silent communication. Josie wondered what passed between them, but could guess easily enough. She knew how she'd feel if either of her mates went off to war without her.

The big silver dragonet who had lounged near the fireplace behind Roland and Lana's seats lifted his head. Roland scratched his scales with deep affection.

"Take care of your mother, Tor," Roland instructed the dragon.

*"I will, Papa. If you need us, we can fly north real quick to help like we did last time."* Everyone at the table heard the baby dragon's unguarded words. Josie had heard the tale of how the dragonet and Lana had flown in beyond all expectations to save Roland's life once before during a battle on the northern border.

"Thank you, son," Roland said, clearly fighting a grin. "But I want you to stay here and keep watch over our people with Lana. They need her, and they need you. Can you do that for me?"

*"Yes, Papa."* The young dragon bowed his head for another loving scratch.

Josie was touched by the obvious love between the king and his adopted dragon child. It was clear Tor could not be more loved if he were a child of their bodies. Tor was an Ice Dragon and would always remain in dragon form. He was not a shifter. Josie had been fascinated to learn that the children of knights and their dragons were raised together as if part of one big, extended family. As a result, there were many Lair-born dragons who considered particular sets of humans as members of their family and several dragons who had a hand in raising the children of their human partners as well.

Once the decision was made, they wasted little time heading for the ledge from which they would take flight. Josie wore the lovely formal gown her mates had surprised her with right before dinner. It was warm enough for the heights at which they'd be flying and, if she wanted to make an impression on the waiting snowcats, perhaps this lovely and no-doubt expensive dress would help.

Shanya trailed behind Josie and her mates, a worried look on her lovely face. The king and his spymaster were nowhere to be seen at the moment. Josie understood where they'd gone when she reached the ledge. The older brothers had stopped off to don armor and each carried a set for one of her mates.

Not caring who might be looking, her mates stripped right there on the landing ledge and put on the layers their older brothers had brought for them. Men, it seemed, had no shame in either world. Josie stood with Shanya while the twins prepared themselves.

"Don't worry," she told the blonde girl who was chewing her lower lip in anxiety, "my mates won't drop you."

That did the trick. Shanya started, and her gaze rose to meet Josie's. She smiled, hoping to put the young woman at ease.

"I'm not worried about that, princess. I'm uncertain about my future, which is a unique experience for me."

"I never thought about it before. I guess it must be hard to always know what's coming down the road."

"I don't see everything," she admitted with a helpless gesture. "But usually I see some sort of culmination to my actions. This time, there is a nexus of sorts. A point beyond which I cannot see because the possibilities are too many and too confusing. I don't know how this will turn out and it worries me."

"We have an expression in my world. Welcome to the human race."

"I'm not human." The girl seemed perplexed though she was thinking about Josie's words.

"Well, neither am I—at least not completely—but the sentiment means that none of us knows how everything will turn out. To err is human. That's another pearl of wisdom from my world. We learn from our mistakes and most of us can't see the future. The fact that you usually know what fate has in store has left you unprepared for feelings the rest of us deal with all the time because we *don't* know. We usually don't see the consequences of our actions until they are upon us. It means welcome to the feelings all of us without foresight have every day."

"How do you survive?" Shanya looked aghast. It was enough to make Josie laugh out loud.

"Don't worry, Shanya. It will turn out as it was meant to be. Just remember one thing." She grew serious. "I am determined that nothing and no one will come between me and my mates. Ever. Once the snowcats get that straight, we'll move on from there."

Shanya looked alarmed, but the twins were finished

dressing and the sight of them in battle-scarred black leather armor made Josie's mouth water. She'd thought they were hot before, but these guys were smokin' in armor. They had that road-warrior look down. Hell, they'd probably invented it. And they were all hers. How did she get so lucky?

Connor smiled at her and she went to him, sliding into his arms and giving him a big kiss.

"Darius gets to carry you first, but we'll stop halfway and then switch for the final leg. I get you then." His eyes glowed with promises she knew they wouldn't have time to fulfill until they reached the Northern Lair. Of course, they would have an army of snowcats on their doorstep at that point, so the wicked intent in his gaze would have to hold until that was dealt with.

"I love you, Connor." She reached up and kissed him once more.

Darius came up behind her. She felt his heat at her back as his arms came around her waist.

"We have to go, love," he whispered in her ear as she broke the kiss with his twin.

She turned in Darius's arms. "I love you, Darius." She gave him a deep, hard, fast kiss, breaking off before anyone else could object. Around her, she saw Roland and Nico had already shifted and were taking to the air.

Darius stood back and shifted, as did Connor. Josie helped Shanya step up onto Connor's back and then turned to seat herself on Darius's back. The two dragons leapt off the ledge, synchronizing their wing beats as they followed after their older brothers.

The journey was long, with the promised stop halfway for a quick drink of water and a few minutes for the dragons to rest. The women mounted again, and they were off for the final, frantic leg of the journey. It got colder the farther north they traveled and Josie was glad of the living furnace beneath her that kept her warm.

When they reached the Northern Lair, dawn was nearly upon them. They'd flown all night. Josie could just make out dark shapes across the river. The snowcat encampment, no doubt. There were more of them than she ever would have expected. Her breath caught at the implications.

She knew the damage snowcats could do. They were fierce fighters with giant, nearly indestructible claws. An army of them would be much more dangerous than an army of humans, which is what they'd been up against in the last battles here, according to what the twins had told her. Sure, those humans had had magical augmentation and weapons designed to harm dragons, but these were snowcats. They had all kinds of advantages over humans when it came to fighting.

The knights had dragons at their sides, but the knights themselves were human. And there weren't enough black dragons who could fight the cats in either human or shifted form. This was a bad situation. Really bad.

They landed and were greeted by the leaders of the Northern Lair.

"You've arrived just in time, majesty," Hal reported to Roland as they walked through the corridors of the Northern Lair to a chamber Josie hadn't seen before. It was a war room of sorts, with the top people from the Lair gathered there. It contained a giant, hand-drawn map of the area with markers on it denoting the strength of the snowcat army.

"What are their numbers?" Nico asked as they gathered around the map table.

"There are hundreds of them that we can see. There may be more. We suspect many hide in beast form where we cannot observe them from the air." Jures looked grave. "They are very good at stealth."

Josie believed it. Snowcats were better at stealth than ninjas in her world. She didn't see any reason for it to be different here.

"Any more communications from them?" Roland asked, his gaze narrowed in concentration on the map.

"Yes. They are to send a negotiator across the river at first light. They demand the unconditional return of their envoy. I suspect they mean you, princess." Hal looked at her with regret in his eyes.

"I'll talk to them, but there's no way I'm going with them. I've had enough of snowcats bossing me around and trying to make me into something I'm not."

She'd definitely had it. Up to here. Anger rose in her to crowd out the fear. Darius and Connor stood on either side, lending her their strength.

"The three of us will talk to the negotiator," Connor said in dark tones. "They cannot have our mate, but we'll be glad to speak with them."

"We will *all* talk with the negotiator," Roland decreed with a stern look at his younger brothers.

Darius and Connor bristled, but Josie touched their shoulders. "Your brother is right. Snowcats respect strength. If they're anything like my grandfather's clan, they'll expect a certain amount of respect in return. Who better to show that their claims are being taken seriously than the King of Draconia and three of his brothers? They'll be able to sense the magic in you. They'll recognize both the respect you show them by coming in person and the strength of your presence."

"Sire." A new voice called from the doorway. "A delegation crosses the river in cat form."

"Showtime," Josie whispered to her mates, squeezing their hands as the group headed out of the war room and down the hall.

They went to another ledge and shifted form again. Josie mounted Darius's back and saw Shanya still with them, making her way on to Connor's back. The party swooped down to the ground in front of the mountain that housed the Lair, to the bank of the wide river. Josie could easily see a group of about ten snowcats swimming through the current, heading straight for them.

She got off Darius's back and stood with Shanya. The men chose to remain in dragon form for the moment. Josie debated whether or not to shift to snowcat form, but decided against it. The cats would no doubt be able to tell who and what she was with just one sniff.

"Here they come," Josie said, knowing her mates had her back.

She had to admit, the snowcats made an impressive sight as they leapt from the river, shook their coats dry and stalked toward them. These cats seemed larger than those in her grandfather's village. Larger and even more magical.

The snowcats ranged themselves in front of the dragons, two lines of strength focused on Josie. The lead snowcat shifted form as he stood about ten feet from her. It was an easy leap for one of them in either cat or human form, but she wasn't worried. The dragons were larger and had even longer reach. If the snowcats tried anything, they'd have a real battle on their hands.

"I am Raith of the Snowcat Clan," said the leader. He was handsome and had the muscles of a fighter. He wore robes with a high mandarin collar that looked faintly Asian in style to Josie. He gazed at her with hard eyes. "You are the envoy from the world of our forefathers."

"I'm Josephine Marpa."

"Marpa?" He looked surprised. "A descendant of the wizard line." He seemed to be thinking out loud, watching her with a measuring gaze. "You are not fully snowcat."

"I'm surprised you could sense that. My mother was human. I wasn't raised in the snowcat village. I went there only after my mother died when I was already a teen."

"But you learned the snowcat ways, surely?" His brows drew together in a frown.

Josie shrugged. "Some. I'm afraid I wasn't well accepted among the full-blood snowcats. Which brings me to question whether or not your people will accept me as I am."

"Lady, we are so desperate to see females of our kind, we cannot be choosy. You are the first female snowcat we have seen in centuries."

Not exactly a compliment, but she'd take it. If she was the only female snowcat they'd seen in that long, chances were, they wouldn't hurt her.

"You called the storm that brought my mates to my world."

Confusion etched his handsome features. "We called the storm, but it was to bring you forth. Did that not happen?"

"No. It sent two dragons—these two dragons—to my world. I brought them to my grandfather, and he took us to Marpa's secret cave to gain the magic that could bring us back here. These two dragons are my mates. The snowcat knew them the moment she scented them."

Now the man looked really upset, but she had to give him the bad news upfront. It wouldn't do to lead him, or his men, on.

"How? How can you mate with dragons?"

The air beside her stirred, and she knew Darius and Connor were shifting form.

"We are more than dragons," Darius said in an arch tone.

"We are descendants of Draneth the Wise," Connor added. "Like you, we carry both human and beast nature in our souls."

"Shifters," Raith growled. "We did not know Draconia had shifters."

"Then we're even. We didn't know snowcats existed in our world." Darius raised one eyebrow. "We were thrown into Josie's world where magic is nearly non-existent. We knew her as our mate the moment we met her and she agreed."

Connor spoke up, trying to tone down the challenge in his twin's voice. "Josie was able to call the storm to bring us back. More than one seer has told us these events were foreseen and necessary for the battle we may yet face against those who would free the evil locked away in the Citadel."

"The Citadel?" Raith looked truly concerned. "That is grave news, indeed. But who are your seers? Don't tell me dragon shifters have foresight too?"

"I am one." Shanya had apparently found her backbone and stepped forward, very close to the snowcat spokesman. "I foresaw the dangerous journey Prince Darius and Prince Connor would make and their return."

"And you are?"

"I am Shanya of Gryphon Isle. One of the fair folk."

"We have heard of your people, but we have never seen any." Raith couldn't seem to stop looking at her, now that she'd drawn his eye. Of course, Shanya was gorgeous. Josie shouldn't have been surprised.

"That's familiar," Darius observed. "Since we've never seen any of your people either."

"Until recently, the fair folk stayed in their enclaves, venturing out only in secret," Connor clarified. "Since the return of the threat to our lands, the wizard Gryffid has revealed himself to be living on Gryphon Isle with a large enclave of Lady Shanya's people."

Raith couldn't tear his gaze from Shanya, even as she swayed toward him. She seemed to be weakening in some way, her body trembling.

When she crumpled, it was Raith's strong arms that caught her. Josie stepped forward, her mates at her side.

"Is she all right?"

Raith looked up into Josie's eyes. His hands had tightened on the fair girl's shoulders, shock written all over his features. He sniffed the air as the snowcats around him moved on their paws, uncertain.

"To me, brothers." Raith's voice was a mere whisper, but Josie heard him clear as day, as did his comrades.

One by one, they shifted form to stand around him and the fallen woman. She shook in his arms. Her eyes rolled back in her head as something powerful overcame her.

"It is a vision," Connor said, concern in his voice. "Dar and I witnessed something like this right before we were transported to your world, Josie. It wasn't as bad as this, but it looks similar."

When all the cats had shifted, the black dragons did the same. Roland and Nico stood watching, concern in every line of their bodies.

"Will she come out of it on her own?" Roland asked. "Perhaps we should fetch a healer."

One of the snowcats stepped forward. "No need. I am a healer."

The man tried to touch the girl in his leader's arms but Raith pulled her away, snarling at the other man. Shanya was held tight in his arms, and he didn't appear to want to let anyone close to her.

"Raith?" Josie edged closer, calling his name tentatively. His focus was on Shanya, his hands clutching her shoulders as dismay filled his features. "Raith? Will you let me look at her? Will you let me see if Shanya is all right?"

Pained eyes met hers as the man finally looked up. He seemed utterly devastated.

"Help my mate." The desperation in his plea touched a chord deep in her heart.

"Mate?" Nico sounded the surprise everyone felt.

"She is my mate." Raith's voice was strong, filled with certainty, even as a lone tear rolled down his cheek.

"Sweet Mother of All," Darius whispered in both shock and benediction.

Shanya stilled in the snowcat leader's arms, blinking rapidly as she came out of the vision. She looked up at the man who had just claimed her as his mate and smiled the most heartbreakingly beautiful smile Josie had ever seen.

"I understand now," she whispered. Shanya seemed to gain strength from Raith's embrace. He helped her sit up, but she made no move to leave his arms. "There are mates for your brothers among my people, Raith."

Her words were met with a mix of hope and disbelief from the other snowcats. Josie watched them carefully, gauging their reactions.

"Are you certain?" Raith's voice was both hopeful and tense.

"I have seen it."

Silence met the certainty in her voice.

"Perhaps we should move this discussion indoors" Roland suggested, "where we can sit comfortably." He gave Shanya a pointed look. She was obviously weak. "We don't want war with the snowcats. In fact, we'd like to help you as best we can, seeing as our new sister-in-law is one of your people."

Raith seemed to consider his words. "We cannot fly up to your Lair."

Nico and Roland grinned. "Not to worry," said the Prince of Spies. "We have rooms nearby for just such occasions, built into the base of the cliff. A few dragons can shuttle refreshments down for us, if you like."

"That would be agreeable," Raith said. He stood, Shanya in his arms, her slight form not even straining his bulging muscles.

Nico led the way to a chamber hidden in the base of the cliff. It was spacious and contained some furnishings, including a large table and chairs. The room didn't look like it had been used recently, but it was kept in good shape. It was certainly good enough for their purposes at the moment.

Raith kept Shanya with him, settling her at his side while everyone else arranged themselves around the large table. Nico sat next to Roland, opposite Raith and Shanya. Connor and Darius were on Roland's other side, with Josie between them. The snowcats took up the rest of the chairs, each with varying expressions on their faces.

"Now," Nico began the dialogue, "we should probably introduce ourselves. I am Nico and this is my brother, King Roland."

"We are honored that you would come to us yourself, your majesty," Raith said after a moment. He seemed preoccupied with Shanya, whatever anger he'd nursed dissolved by her mere presence. "I am Raith, leader of the snowcats. This is my brother, our shaman, Teuren."

The man who'd identified himself as a healer bowed his head in acknowledgement. Raith introduced the rest of the men, one by one.

Shanya regained her strength as she sat close to Raith's side. The leader looked as if he couldn't bear to take his gaze from her. His hand held hers, and his expression was a testament to his confusion.

"There has never been a mixed mating among my people" he said with calm finality, "but I will not give you up, Shanya. Even if I must go into exile. You are my mate. Can you not feel it?"

Shanya smiled at the big man. "I foresaw it. I knew you even before I met you, Raith. The Mother of All brought us together."

Josie felt like she was intruding on a private moment. She also understood the way the leader seemed blindsided by the amazing feeling of finding his mate. She'd been through it.

"Raith, if it's any help, I'm only half snowcat. My mother was human. Totally non-magical." Josie only now caught the horrified looks on some of the other snowcats' faces.

"Josie, you should show them your snowcat," Shanya prompted. "They need to see her strength. They need to understand that the snowcat spirit thrives even though your mother had no magic of her own."

"If you think it'll help." Josie moved uncomfortably in her seat. This felt too much like when she'd been younger and subjected to the tests of her grandfather's clan. She'd passed every one of those with flying colors. She shouldn't be nervous. It was anger more than nerves that prompted her to shift rapidly, sitting on her haunches in the elaborate chair.

Josie looked around at the gathered company, trying to remember she was a princess. These people could only intimidate her if she let them.

"Did you feel her spark?" Shanya whispered. "Did you feel the surge of magic? She is potent. Josie is stronger than her forefathers. The mixing of blood benefited her snowcat. It did not harm it in any way. She is stronger for the addition of other blood."

Josie decided to show these cats a little of what she could do. As a female, she was smaller and lighter than these big males. There were carved protrusions on the walls of this chamber much like the ones in the throne room she had climbed for Tor's amusement. These were spaced farther apart and were smaller. Scaling these walls would be a real test of her agility and skill. Perfect.

Josie bounded out of her chair and leapt onto the table, using it as a springboard for her initial leap onto the wall. She circled the room, gaining speed and height as the group below watched.

For her big finish, she used the central chandelier that hung high over the center of the huge table. Padding off that, she launched into a twisting, spinning leap that landed her on all fours on the table. She landed with a flourish, doing her best to look bored as she flicked her tail toward the snowcat leader.

As nonchalantly as she could, she hopped off the table, back into her chair between Darius and Connor. In a shimmer of magic, she shifted to her human form, glad to see she hadn't even broken a sweat.

She looked at the faces of the snowcat men. A few tough customers looked guardedly impressed while some of the others seemed truly blown away by what she'd just showed them. Good. Let that be a lesson about what a half-breed girl snowcat could do.

"Impressive," was Raith's comment. "You give me hope for our offspring, daughter of Marpa."

"Oh, I think you'll be even more impressed with the kits you and Shanya produce. I'm half human. No magic from that side of my family at all, I'm afraid. Shanya is one of the fair folk. In many ways, she is a much better match for you than any other being I know. Her people live as long as you do."

"Is this true?" Raith looked deep into Shanya's eyes.

"It is. The Mother of All sees everything. She knows what is best."

# Epilogue

The snowcats were amazed to learn that Shanya's people had the same longevity as theirs. They were also impressed by her magic and her Sight. Raith couldn't take his eyes off her, which was a condition the mated dragon brothers understood all too well.

"You are welcome in Draconia." Roland smiled kindly at the newly mated pair.

"Thank you for the welcome. We came prepared for war only to find we have made a grievous error. Forgive us." It was Teuren who answered, an indulgent smile on his face as well.

"There is nothing to forgive," Darius said impulsively, taking one of Josie's hands. "We understand what it is to seek a mate. After traveling through the magical storm twice, we also surmise it took a great deal of effort to create the rift between our world and Josie's without the amulets."

"You know of the amulets of power?" Teuren seemed astonished. His eyes only widened further when all three mates pulled their amulets from around their necks.

"It shows as an armor breastplate when we are in dragon form," Connor commented. "Josie's becomes an elaborate collar, as you saw when she shifted for you."

"How did you come by such sacred objects?" Teuren looked in awe at the gleaming necklaces.

"I foresaw the twin princes must have them," Shanya spoke up, surprising the snowcats. "Gryffid had them. He gave them to me to bring to Darius and Connor, though I wasn't sure which set of twins they were destined for until I saw them for the first time."

"And my grandfather took us to Marpa's cave." Josie picked up her part of the story. "This amulet revealed itself to me, and Grandfather said it was meant for me." She wouldn't mention the gifts her mates had walked away with just yet. She wanted to see how the snowcats dealt with this first. "The three together allowed me to call the storm to bring us here. To bring my mates home." She spared a loving glance for both of them before continuing her speech. There were things the snowcats of this world had to know. "There is little magic left in my world. After the wizards battled, they dispersed all magic. It only survives in a few isolated populations of shifters. There are no dragons at all—shifter or otherwise. There is only one village of snowcats, and they keep to themselves. Shifters live in secret among humans, who dominate the planet with their ingenuity based on science and technology."

"We saw some amazing things while we were there," Darius confirmed. "We flew across an ocean in a metal machine with a hundred other people seated inside. We saw images beamed to a small box from miles up in the heavens. None of it was magic, our mate assures us. It is amazing what the human race has accomplished on her world, all without magic."

"But the other shifters we met..." Connor broke in, speaking in a subdued voice. "They had to disrobe before they could shift. Their magic was potent, but very limited in scope. It was kind of sad. None of them had ever seen a dragon."

Silence filled the chamber as the words sank in. Finally, Nico drew everyone's attention by clearing his throat. It was a calculated move by the man known as the Prince of Spies. He was no doubt, up to something.

"As my brother stated, you are welcome in Draconia. We have recently begun to interact with the fair folk on Gryphon Isle, which is located over the water to the south of our land. Perhaps some of you would like to discuss a possible visit with Shanya and the gryphons who nest near our castle? And there are other enclaves of fair folk. I could help you there. I have contacts among several of them."

All the dragon brothers looked at Nico in surprise. He only grinned. The Spymaster of Draconia always had a few tricks up his sleeve, it seemed.

Raith looked from Shanya to his brother, Teuren, and back to Nico but he addressed his words to Roland, as was only proper. One leader to another.

"I must go back to my people and hold Council. They need to know what we have learned. Then I would very much like to bring a delegation into Draconia with the idea of contacting the enclaves of which you speak on behalf of my brethren." He looked back at the girl in his arms. "Does that sound about right?"

Shanya smiled beautifully at him. "It is perfect. Oh, if only you could see what I see. The future for the mated snowcats is filled with happiness." She sat up straight, and her face turned solemn. "But there are enemies who would cause trouble for all people of good will. It is my hope you will consider working with the Draconians to battle the evil in the North. The Citadel is at serious risk."

Raith's expression hardened. "Then we will take the risk seriously, my lady. Our village is hidden in the mountains near the Citadel. In return for your help connecting with the fair folk, we will pledge our support and assistance in fighting evil in the northlands."

A satisfied grin broke over Nico's face. Roland was more circumspect, but he also looked pleased.

"To that end," Raith continued speaking, "we have news that might be of help in your dealings with the northern tribes. Salomar is no more, but his pet warlock seeks to bring the tattered remains of his army back together. To my surprise, he is succeeding. He also has the help of the North Witch."

"Loralie?" Roland asked sharply.

"The very same." Raith looked disgusted. "She is more powerful than you know. With her help, Gebel will no doubt be able to step in where Salomar left off."

"Gebel," Nico mused. "We have heard that name before. He is a warlock, you say?"

"So he claims." Teuren picked up the story. "He does have some magic, but it is weak. His use of the North Witch though, that makes him inordinately powerful."

"Why does she follow him if she's so strong?" Josie wanted to know.

Teuren turned sad eyes on her. "Gebel holds Loralie's daughter hostage. If the mother does not do his bidding, he tortures the girl."

The snowcats went back across the river, and Shanya went with them. Dragons monitored what went on in the army camp from afar. News traveled quickly when a shout of joy went up from the gathering attended by most of the snowcats. No doubt, they had just learned of their leader's mating and that there was hope for them as well.

Josie could feel the joy vibrating in the air as she rode on Darius's back the next day. They'd been invited to the snowcat encampment where a party was in progress. The rest of the snowcats wanted to meet the half-snowcat woman from the world of their ancestors and her new mates.

Darius and Connor were hesitant at first but when the snowcat men welcomed them with joyous hearts, they began to relax. For her part, Josie had never felt more welcome in her life—except maybe among her new family of dragon shifters. Nobody in this world looked at her with expectations she couldn't meet. They accepted her for what she was and even loved her for it.

This, then, was her home. The place she was meant to be. With respect, love, wholehearted acceptance of who she was...and her mates at her side.

# About the Author

A life-long martial arts enthusiast, Bianca enjoys a number of hobbies and interests that keep her busy and entertained such as playing the guitar, shopping, painting, shopping, skiing, shopping, road trips, and did we say...um...shopping? A bargain hunter through and through, Bianca loves the thrill of the hunt for that excellent price on quality items, though she's hardly a fashionista. She likes nothing better than curling up by the fire with a good book, or better yet, by the computer, writing a good book.

To learn more about Bianca D'Arc, please visit www.biancadarc.com. Send an email to Bianca at BiancaDArc@gmail.com.

*A forbidden union forged in love—and tempered in hellfire.*

# Inferno
## © 2009 Bianca D'Arc
*A Tales of the Were Story.*

One last task and Megan will be free of the debt of honor owed by her family. Spying on Dante, a powerful vampire with questionable friends, sounds simple enough. But her mission is complicated by the fact she's got something every vampire wants—tangy, powerful, werewolf blood.

It's easy to capture his attention. The hard part will be getting out with her heart—and soul—intact. Not to mention her life, thanks to a crazed bomber.

Dante isn't the kind to forgive or forget easily, especially the grudge he holds against werewolves. Still, he is instantly drawn to the injured lone wolf in his care. When he and his friend Duncan treat her wounds, they discover something that marks her as much more than she seems.

That mark is a neon sign warning to be careful, but Dante can't help himself. He wants her and nothing will stand in his way. Not her species. Not his. Not the strange woman who keeps trying to kill him.

Not even the magical poison in Megan's blood...

*Warning: This book contains sexual healing,* ménage a trois *and* quatre, *hot sexy vampires, an irresistible fey warrior and a lone wolf bitch on the prowl.*

*Available now in ebook and print from Samhain Publishing.*

# GREAT cheap fun

## Discover eBooks!
THE FASTEST WAY TO GET THE HOTTEST NAMES

Get your favorite authors on your favorite reader, long before they're out in print! Ebooks from Samhain go wherever you go, and work with whatever you carry—Palm, PDF, Mobi, and more.

Samhain publishing Ltd

LaVergne, TN USA
29 August 2010
195058LV00005B/2/P